T0161453

women. period.

Edited by
Julia Watts, Parneshia Jones,
Jo Ruby and Elizabeth Slade

Spinsters Ink
2008

Spinsters Ink
P.O. Box 242
Midway, Florida 32343

Printed in the United States of America on acid-free paper
First Edition

Editors: Parneshia Jones, Michele Ruby, Elizabeth G. Slade, Julia Watts
Cover designer: LA Callaghan

ISBN-10: 1-883523-94-X
ISBN-13: 978-1-883523-94-7

Contents

Foreword

Menstruation, the natural process our body goes through on the moon's cycle, is intended to signal that the body is not making a nest. The lining for the inner cradle is not needed because there's no call for a nest this round. On the other hand, if a baby nests there, a birth story often follows. Here at the front of *Women.Period* is our birth story. It was fall in Louisville, Kentucky, and the trees on Fourth Street were still leafed out in their beautiful skirts. The lunch rush was picking up at Ermin's, and we carried our trays up to the balcony, hunting out an empty table for four. Soup smells wafted up as we laid our food out and began our post-workshop talk about the morning's happenings; two poets and two fiction writers all in the local MFA program— four women of a range of ages and stages, ethnicities and races, sexual and literary orientations. Somehow the conversation turned to one thing we had in common: menstruation, its hidden, unspoken existence through the ages, and in fact, right up into the present sandwich-eating moment.

"Don't we all have one?"

"A period?"

"That too. But I meant a story, a poem, a memory, a history of that experience."

"Every woman, everywhere!"

"All those stories to tell . . . and nowhere to tell them."

"All different points of view . . ."

"So many voices . . ."

"Are we talking about an anthology?" There is one distinct moment of silence filled with the sounds from below—clink of a spoon scraping a dish, the cash register beep, the door swinging open, before we all begin talking at once. Our attitudes toward menstruation, like our cycles themselves, ebb and flow, depending on our ages, our desires and our situations. Regardless of how we feel about our period, one thing is certain: it is an experience that unites us as women. Anyone who doubts this fact need only observe a woman giving a stranger or near-stranger a tampon from her own purse when the other woman is desperate for one. Helping each other perform damage control when

"Aunt Flo" arrives unexpectedly is one of the few true female covenants. Despite the universality of menstruation, remarkably little work has been published on the subject. As girls, some of us may have been handed a booklet which managed to explain the basics of female plumbing while also hawking a feminine hygiene company's wares. Others of us may have passed around dog-eared copies of Judy Blume's *Are You There, God? It's Me, Margaret*. But much like we waited for our first periods, many of us have been waiting for a work that explores the universal and yet strangely taboo subject of menstruation, not from a feminine hygiene company's perspective and not just from a young girl's perspective, but from a whole range of perspectives—from women of different ages, ethnicities, religions, sexual orientations and cultural backgrounds. The wait is over. It has arrived. If reading diverse literature expands our understanding of what it means to be a human being, then reading diverse literature on the subject of menstruation must expand our understanding of what it means to be women. With many women shouting about a subject which in the past has only been considered suitable for whispers, *Women.Period* celebrates both the diversity and the universality of the female experience. We are many; we are one.

Section I:

Crescent

The First Time

Jane Yolen

It starts like a dot,
A blot on a white page,
A single letter curling
On a notebook, new bought,
And before you know it,
You have written a thousand-page
Doorstop of a novel
In blood
When all you meant to do
Was send a sympathy note
To your uterus.

A View of the Moon from the Bathroom Floor

Cathryn Cofell

I am thirteen and a woman for the first time. I have power
to stuff my body with cotton and gauze, to pierce my navel.
To have moods like the phases of the moon.
To paint my toenails the color of Jupiter.
To yes or no and mean either,
to fumble in the dark against a grinding boy
like a coin in a deep pocket.
To give or take life like a mother.

> *The moon is a yellow razor blade*
> *dull and edgy,*
> *sharp tongued,*
> *turning in inconsistent phases.*

I am thirteen and hold the moon in my hand. I have power
to tilt her to the dark side, to bury her in wrist up to the bone.
Two Siamese sisters, rubbing our backs against
the blue tile of the night sky, rubbing
our joined horizons, cringing and bleating,
one heart beating like a fallen crow in the grass.
Pushed out of the nest by her mother.

> *The moon sharpens her dull edges*
> *turning to the dark,*
> *before and after*
> *the sun dazzles*
> *in ever dizzying phases.*

I am thirteen and bleeding from both ends. I have control
of the moon but not the flow of red words from my body,

from my mother's mouth. Cannot set the moon
on her tongue and crawl down her throat,
into the womb, back into the lunar womb,
back before galaxies and Galileo.
Before she became a woman.

The new woman is a yellow mother
dull and edgy,
sharp tongued,
turning against her own
inconsistent daughter.

The Blue Box

Nancy Pinard

My body chose a bloody decade to bear witness to my womanhood. The violence of Vietnam, the Bay of Pigs, the assassinations of President John Kennedy, his brother Robert and Martin Luther King ran on the nightly news through the '60s. The American flag periodically flew at half staff while, at the sound of the air-raid signal, we kids crouched under desks and awaited our own deaths. In that morbid context, it should have been welcome news that blood could mean not just death, but life.

Just as the nation chose to memorialize Kennedy's bloody death with a charming photo of John-John saluting his father's casket, the wealthy Ohio suburb where I grew up chose to present the details of life blood by showing elementary school girls a cartoon movie. Our mothers joined us for a Girl Scout meeting in the school auditorium. Like the other mothers, mine was girdled and stocking-clad, perspiring through her perfume. I sat fidgeting on a metal folding chair, careful to keep my knees together in my green uniform dress. I was a serious child, obedient, and what would later be called *intuitive*. Something odd was coming, I could feel it—something big. It wasn't just that the other mothers had turned up. They were golfers, many of them, and bridge players, women who frequently left their daughters to the care of housekeepers. My mother played neither golf nor bridge. Having lost one daughter to pneumonia, she hovered over my days, present at every acceptable opportunity. Usually, I felt loved and lucky. That day, I felt something different: mother still hovering, but newly brittle and nervously withholding, creating a distinction between us that, to my child mind, felt fraught with peril.

After an unrevealing introduction from our leader, what followed on film was a talking rabbit—female, of course. She showed us diagrams of our insides, flower-like shapes labeled with velvet words like "fallopian" and "vulva," "labia" and "vagina." The words sounded elegant, mythical somehow, yet also disconnected from anything that might happen to me, like pricking my finger on a spindle and sleeping for a hundred years.

As it happened, I had six years to wait. At fifteen, I was a long-legged colt of a girl who had grown five inches the previous summer. That fall, when the telltale spot appeared—at the ballet studio, no less—the organic odor that rose from the stain was too like the orange flux our female terrier leaked intermittently. I stared out the bathroom window at the sooty brick wall of the adjacent building, brooding on how I'd shunned the dog during those days, pushing her away when she wanted to sneak into my bed at night. Mother called the fluid her "discharge," harnessed her in a black plastic girdle, barred her from rooms with carpet, and fretted if she ran outside unattended.

I lined the crotch of my tights with a folded sheaf of toilet paper, re-dressed, and ran off to ballet class.

Not ten minutes later, folded nose-to-knees in a *grand port a bras*, I saw my folly. The tights were pink, and I had only seen that much blood once—at recess in second grade when Betsy Billings fell on her head from the top rung of the jungle gym. I waited for the ballet teacher to turn his back before I fled, legs clamped together. I took the bus home. In the privacy of my bedroom that night, I pulled my tights and leotard up over the thick pads that waited in the blue box Mother had six years before hidden in my bottom drawer. A diaper would have been less obvious.

My dancer friends wore tampons. I bought some the next day. The instructions in the tampon box came folded so many times I expected them to contain news of who loved whom, passed to me under the desk while the teacher was writing on the chalkboard. Instead, it showed the outline of a naked woman, one foot propped up on the toilet seat. An arrow showed the proper direction for insertion. "Toward the small of the back," the directions said. I fumbled for the correct opening and shoved one little white tube up inside the other. Invisible. Almost like I wasn't bleeding, except—maybe it was my imagination—the cramping seemed worse. This was going to last three-to-seven days every month for thirty years? I doubled over and breathed deeply. The talking rabbit hadn't mentioned cramps.

With the cramps came the flooding. I hid a bowl of cold water mixed with enzyme pre-soak on the floor of my closet, bleaching the inevitable stains and hanging the tights and underpants to dry before tucking them in among the laundry. I bled heavily, but never once did I wear the Modess belt or pads, resorting instead to inserting several tampons at once, so I could flush them from sight down the john after removal. When I flooded the bed the first night of each cycle, I retreated to the bathroom farthest from my parents' bedroom to rinse the sheets in darkness. For the first two days each month, the flow was nearly unmanageable, necessitating a trip to the bathroom between each forty-five minute high school class. Still, I told no one. Likewise, I endured the cramps without a word, let alone a Midol.

Years passed. I married a pastor and we had two sons. Still, my ritual continued—hiding the blood, rinsing the stain in cold water, then bleaching it back to whiteness. The night after I first gave birth, a nurse caught me tottering around my hospital room in the dark, rinsing my lochia-flooded sheets in the vanity sink. She confiscated the sheets, re-made the bed, settled me back in, and, certain some drug was responsible, marked the front of my chart in red: NO MEDS. For the first time, I realized my ritual was unique.

I still didn't know its meaning.

I wasn't to understand until several years later when clinical depression drove me to therapy. Week after week I trudged to my appointment, reporting whatever image crossed my darkened mind. "I've been wondering how Eve felt when Seth was born,"I heard myself say one day. We hadn't been talking about the Biblical account of the first family, and it seemed a passing fancy, oddly unconnected to other concerns, until a day six months later when my therapist *again* asked about my sister's death. I didn't know what more to say. I knew Ann had died at seventeen months, but very little else. I had once seen her picture, though quite by accident, a fact that my therapist pointed to often. The poking and prodding annoyed me. My family's ways made total sense to me. Why *would* I know? I wasn't there. Ann had died one year before I was born.

What I did know I had collected from whispered snippets: the undertaker's angst when Mother lifted Ann's dead body from the casket to hold and rock; the jar of peaches found tucked into the pink satin lining, a parting gift from a neighbor who knew Ann loved them; Mother's guilt on rainy nights when we were safe and dry inside, while Ann was outside in the ground by herself. But then, as I described the stricken look in my mother's eyes the day I'd unwittingly pulled an unlabeled blue box off a closet shelf, I was hardly able to gag words past my tightening throat. It didn't contain Modess pads. Inside the box was a tiny pink chenille robe wrapped around my sister's worn Raggedy Ann.

My therapist held her emptied-out lunch sack over my mouth and told me to blow out. I watched the bag growing and collapsing with the breath of my wailing. "You're grieving like Ann was your daughter,"she observed. With that suggestion, pent-up pain erupted in a tidal wave, and I was drowning. Deep beneath the water, I felt I was being turned inside out.

Then came the miracle. In the week that followed, the depression lifted, suddenly and more dramatically than I had known possible. In that week I started to laugh, and, for awhile it seemed that the stored-up laughter of a lifetime was bursting out the seams. It was summer, my little boys were beautiful, and everything that happened seemed new, sky blue and hilarious.

Later, with my therapist, when I could both laugh *and* look back at the shadow, we began to deconstruct the release. I had trouble crediting what we uncovered. It was the '80s, a decade when *nurture* eclipsed *nature*, when science assigned a mother's ability to impact her fetus to the realm of "old wives tales." But the shift in my mood was undeniable. One week I was depressed. The next I was free. The pivot came at the moment of digging up Ann.

The calendar suggested an explanation. During the terrible year of Mother's grieving, I was in the womb, connected by an umbilical cord. For that nine months, her life was my life. Her blood, my blood. Her daughter, my daughter. Her grief, my grief. Because she was carrying me, she both had, and hadn't, lost her baby. I had become the substitute, like Eve's Seth. (Even my name, Nancy, is a variant of Ann.) And there was the rub: If Ann hadn't grown up, how could I? It seemed a breach of loyalty to Ann, to my mother, to myself. I was here to comfort Mother. To be Ann for the family. How could I grow up without betraying my mission? If I couldn't stop bleeding, at least I could choose not to tell. I could flush it down the john. I could bleach it all away.

Twenty years have passed since the revelation. My sons are grown. My mother has died. Still, I wish for a different history. I struggle to feel loved for who I truly am and wonder who I might be if I'd only had to be myself. I picture myself a young teen, confiding my womanhood and rejoicing with my mother in a happy bond. But I don't know the women in that dream. My bond with mother was forged in nine months of shared blood. If maturity is the ability to embrace the miracle of life and the reality of death, I became a woman in the womb.

Cursing the Moon

Amalia B. Bueno

Don't eat sweet, don't eat sour.
Don't drink hot, don't drink cold.
And don't wash your hair!

But go! Go and wash your face.
Put some of the blood on the washcloth
just a little bit. Mix in the soap and water.
Rub on your cheeks like that.
Scrub your forehead good
and your chin, too. That's enough.

Clean yourself now. Clean your face good.
Skin so nice and smooth.
Do this every month when
your moontime comes
because you are dirty, dirty, dirty.

That's what my best friend Perla told me
that her mother told her when she got her period.
Because you have to wash away your sins.
Cleanse and purify yourself, dirty girl.
Dirty, dirty, dirty girl she learned
from reading Saint Augustine.

Her sister Virgie said don't eat sweet, don't eat sour.
Her auntie Gloria said don't drink hot, don't drink cold.
Her cousin Mercedes said don't ever go into the kitchen
when they are cooking a meal, but snack is okay.
Her grandma Lola said don't make the rice or else
it won't turn out good. And for God's sake,
they all said, don't wash your hair!

I remember all of this, alone
when my moontime comes
quick, like a sudden inhale
of cold sharp pain
my insides turning and twisting,
between my thighs hot and wet.
I want to see my mother who will soon
be dead, my tita Maria keeps saying any day now
because of the cancer eating and turning
inside my mother's stomach.

Come, hurry up. No! No more time to go
to the bathroom. Yes, tita I am coming.
Dear sister, your daughter is here.
Come, come by the bed.
Your mother wants to tell you
something important
so be quiet and listen.

I don't hear anything because
my mother's tired eyes
are looking right through my body.
I want to tell her I promise
not to eat any sweet or any sour.
I want to tell her I will try
not to drink anything hot or cold.
And that I will never wash my hair.
But I just blink while she says
I am not as pretty as the others
so I have to study hard instead
and make something of my brains
because my face and body will not
carry me high and well enough.
Her eyes burn into my face
when she says because I am the eldest
I have to be the mother for them
and to always listen
to my father.

My stomach hurts so bad

I have no voice so I talk inside my head.
Nanay, I got my moontime,
my bulan, my monthly.
What should I do at twelve years old
now that I am a woman like you?
What shall I do with the blood?
Why and where are you going?
I will take care of the children.
But who will take care of me?

I pray to Saint Augustine, make me clean.
I pray to Mother Mary, don't leave me.
I pray to Saint Theresa, make me well.
I pray to Ave Maria, napno ka ti gracia.
I pray to my Nanay in the coffin laid out
on the bamboo floor put on display since
yesterday, mourning so much noisy grief
and clans of relatives and townmates.

The underhouse beckons quiet safety
so I bury the panty, stained dark blood
scary smelling like moss and mushrooms.
Brown slash line smeared, squeezed on white cotton
I roll and wrap in my mother's embroidered handkerchief.
Bury the blood deep, cover it with dirt handfuls.
Bury my mother, too, through dripping blurry tears.

I curse you, moon, fat round pearl
for taking my mother away, demanding blood price
for bringing my moontime like a hostage.
Every time I bleed I will see you, my moon, my mother,
your roundness like her face, a monthly imprint.

On the first day I washed and cooked the rice.
On the second day I drank sour fish soup.
I stayed in bed and waited, and bled and bled.
On the third day I couldn't stand it anymore.
I got up and washed my hair.

Blood Brother

Lynn Raye Campbell

Not every woman thinks of Fred Astaire when she gets her period, but I do. I first "fell off the roof," as my mother called it, during the summer of 1970, at age eleven. It didn't scare me even though I was the first of my friends to "fall." We all saw the film they showed the fifth-grade girls. You know, the one where they pull all the girls out of class and afterward all the boys laugh and point. No one ever actually told the boys the subject of the film, but somehow they knew the secret.

When it happened to me, I shared the secret with my mother in a whisper. She smiled and said, "I thought so. I started at your age." Then she gave me a blue box and asked if I needed any help. I did, but I didn't ask. I read the directions and struggled into the strange "belt" contraption, proud to manage it without sticking myself with the little gold pins.

"Life's full of changes," Mom said. She kissed me goodnight and went upstairs to bed, after agreeing to let me stay up for a while. "Everything will be fine," she said, and I wanted to believe her, but things didn't feel fine with all the changes going on in my life. My older sister had recently married and now lived in Maryland. My brother would soon leave for the air force. Now even my body was changing.

My brother, Chip, came home from a summer league baseball game just after Mom went upstairs. He was nice enough as a brother, but at seven years older, we hadn't been close. In fact, before that summer, I had rather vague memories of him. I remember watching flickering pictures of a small boy dancing like Elvis in white bucks in the home movies we rarely got to see and cheering for him when he won MVP honors for the high school baseball team. In years past, we played a game where I tried to get past him to score by touching the windowsill behind the low-slung brown couch. We called it living room football although Mom refused to let us use a real football in the house. I never won, and once Chip got his driver's license, I rarely saw him. He didn't have time for living room football.

The night I started menstruating, I didn't want Chip to know my secret. Brothers don't have to bleed. I worried he could tell just by looking and thought he might make fun of me like the boys in the fifth grade. But, when I got up to go to bed, Chip stopped me and asked, "Do you want to stay up and watch a movie?" Too young to understand then, I now think he knew things would never be the same once he left home. No one in the house ever mentioned Vietnam, but every night my parents sat glued to the nightly news and worried about Chip's assignment. Our small Pennsylvania town seemed safe, but on TV, I watched young men jump into rice paddies flattened by the downdraft from the rotors of the helicopters. Except for the uniforms, they looked a lot like my brother. Every night Walter Cronkite announced the daily body count and in view of these chilling facts, I laugh now at my attempts to hide my little bit of blood from Chip.

I ignored the new contraption I had strapped around my waist and agreed to stay up for a while. Chip went upstairs to change out of his baseball uniform telling me to flip through the channels to find a movie. This surprised me. As the little sister, I rarely got to choose the TV show.

We stumbled on a Fred Astaire film festival and that night set the pattern for the rest of the week. Chip came home early every night to watch the thirty-year-old, black-and-white movies with me, instead of staying out late with his friends. My favorite was *Holiday Inn*. Fred Astaire danced with firecrackers and Bing Crosby sang "White Christmas." Who could ask for more?

At first, the movies provided an excuse to stay up late, but as the week progressed, I looked forward to spending time with Chip. Mom gave her stamp of approval for the late-night visits by making onion dip and buying us Pepsi. Treats usually only enjoyed on paydays. By the end of the week, I finished my first period and Chip left for the air force without knowing he'd helped me through a trying time.

Since then, my periods have continued to be a trial. For an entire year, I fell off the roof regularly. After that I didn't have another period until I turned sixteen and then only about once per year. I felt spared a big hassle, but my mother worried and kept dragging me off to doctors. I spent many years taking my temperature before getting out of bed to check if I was ovulating. The tiny graphs where I recorded the daily reading dipped and peaked in the right places and satisfied the doctors, but not my mother. "Don't you want to have babies?" she asked, making yet another doctor's appointment for me.

Her logic troubled me. Did she want me to be like Diana Webber, a girl in my class who got pregnant, married and divorced all before we graduated high school? No thank you. Month after month, I watched my best friend, Annie, suffer with her period. She always turned completely white and I learned to get her to the nurse's office before she passed out. I felt lucky not to suffer this curse. To tell the truth I didn't want to know of any problems. I thought more about grades and graduation.

I felt that way through college, but at twenty-three I began to worry. I found a woman OB-GYN who understood my fears and problems better than all the male doctors I'd seen. She assured me I had nothing to worry about and the Pill gave me regular periods again, even though I didn't fulfill my mother's wishes when she made all those doctor's appointments. I do have regular periods, but never had the babies she'd hoped for. Mom's prayers for Chip fell on more fertile ground. He never went to Vietnam and spent most of his military career playing baseball in Germany.

Now, thirty years after my first period, I was right to believe my mother all those years ago. Life is full of changes. Thankfully, though, some things remain constant. My mother usually knows best, I still share a strong bond with my brother forged during a week of movies, and I still love Fred Astaire.

Relay

Susan Richardson
for C.

You've picked up the red baton,
eleven-year-old, no one
to compete against here. Soon
breasts will sprout like
burial mounds, hips jut out
like the weathered shoulders of cliffs.

Not only that:
When rounding the curve,
baton held high, lungs grabbing
for air, legs athrob,
you pass it to me,
resetting my errant clock.

Sprint on, Little One, Kootie,
Squeegie, Scooter-Butt, Squid,
your thirty, forty years.
Up ahead, too small to make out,
the next runner—your build,
face forward, legs on a spring,

right hand open
to the world—

1888–1988

Marianne Worthington

I wash my hands with the soft cake
of Ivory soap in my sister's bathroom
and for the rest of the morning, smell
the way our grandmother smelled.

The girl I was dances in her red formica
kitchen, the white soap fragrant as it drips
into the rust of the metal drainboard.
Even on Christmas Eve when her table
is heaped with peanut butter candy and winter
oranges, coffee and cashews, the clean
scent of soap sings loudest of all.

My daughter's baby clothes smelled
like this too. Her little cuffed gowns
and undershirts with snaps perfumed
the house as they clicked against the dryer
drawing circles around our lives.

One hundred years pass between their births.
Riding the cusp of a crescent moon they roll
over one morning to a new century
and blood-stained bedclothes. Plasma
and platelets flow forward like time,
their girlhoods left in an old world, their stains
rubbed clean with a bar of soap.

Libby

Tsaurah Litzky

My family and I are sitting around the kitchen table having supper. As usual it is not very good because my mother is a terrible cook. She thinks you can get sick from food unless the germs are burned off of it. My father and I are grimly grinding our way through charred hamburger. My mother takes a few grains at a time like a bird. When my mother is not looking, I sneak some of the hamburger into the pocket of my skirt because I am not allowed to leave any food on my plate. Later I will flush it down the toilet. My little brother, strapped to his high chair, is trying to eat mashed carrots out of a bowl. More often than not, his spoon misses his mouth and the carrots drip down the terry cloth bib my mother has tied around his neck. It looks like he has a furry orange chest. The TV is playing in the living room because my mother likes background talk during supper. Since it is 1956, I hear Groucho Marx encouraging a practical nurse from Nebraska to bet her life.

There is matzo on the table instead of the bread that usually accompanies the dinner meal because it is the second night of Passover. Last night we went to first-night Passover dinner at my grandma and grandpa's. My grandpa read from the Hagaddah about the plagues and the miracles, the hail, the locusts, the manna in the desert, the parting of the Red Sea, that let the Jews escape Egypt. I take a half piece of matzo from the plate and under its cover shovel some more hamburger into my hand so I can stow it in my pocket. My mother is staring into space as usual and my father is reading his newspaper. My brother has picked up his bowl and is eating out of it, scooping the carrots up with his tongue. I want a miracle to set me free from my family. I want to wander in the desert at the head of a revolutionary tribe. I vow that when I grow up I will write such miraculous books that people will follow me like the Jews followed Moses.

"You haven't finished yet," my mother says. "Daddy and I are finished. Hurry up, I want to clear the table." I take another bite of the ashy meat. Suddenly I feel as sick as if the charred meat had coagulated into a big stone in my stomach. The stone is growing, trying to push its way out between my legs! It hurts! I get up from the table and rush toward the bathroom.

"What's the matter with you?" my mother calls out, "You didn't ask to be excused."

I shut the bathroom door behind me and pull down my bloomers. The crotch of my bloomers is filled with a thick, dark, wine-colored liquid that I realize is blood. I think it is the Red Sea, the Red Sea pouring out of me. This is not the kind of miracle I had imagined. I'm going to bleed to death. I hear myself call out, "Ma, ma, ma," just like I was a little baby. My mother comes running, bursts through the door.

"What's the matter, do you have diarrhea?" she asks.

"No!" I yell at her. "I'm dying! I'm bleeding to death!"

She looks down at my sopping bloomers, the blood smeared inside the tops of my thighs. She smiles. I want to spring up and hit her but I do not.

She says, "You're not dying, daughter. That's your period, your very first period, your monthlies. This means you're a woman now." My mother takes a washcloth from the cabinet beneath the sink, runs water on it and washes between my legs.

"You have to be very careful to keep yourself clean when you have your period," she says, "or people will smell you. We'll get you your own sanitary belts tomorrow, but tonight you can use one of mine." She takes one of her belts and a Kotex pad out of the vanity and shows me how to pin the pad to the belt. She makes me stand up and step into the clumsy contraption, then brings in a clean pair of my panties and has me slip them on. It feels like I have a great big load between my legs.

"Come in and finish your dinner," my mother says.

"Please, Ma," I tell her. "I want to lie down." For once she grants me a request. The pad is so thick between my little legs, it makes me toe out. I walk into my room, waddling like a duck. I can already smell the blood seeping into the pad. I throw myself on my bed. I hear the sound of my parents' voices from the kitchen.

"She actually thought she was dying," my mother says. My father laughs. I push my head into the pillow so they won't hear me cry.

II

I have a new friend. Her name is Stella Cohen and she sits next to me in seventh-grade homeroom. We are the smartest girls in the grade. She lives only one building over from us in the projects. We walk to and from school together and we both wear our hair in ponytails. My mother lets me go to Stella's to do homework after school because Stella has good manners and always says please and thank you; also Stella's father is a biology teacher at Boys High. This impresses my mother, she considers teachers only a little less holy than doctors. The Cohens have a four-room apartment like ours but Stella doesn't have any brothers or sisters so she doesn't have to share her bedroom like I do. At the Cohen's the record player is on all the time. Libby, Stella's mother, loves music. She used to be a dance teacher. She has already taught Stella and me the waltz, rumba and lindy-hop. She also lets us play with her makeup.

When Alvin, Stella's father, comes home from Boys High at four o'clock, Libby greets him with a big kiss. Sometimes she makes them both cocktails, whiskey sours, which she serves in glasses that have golden flowers on them. If she has a little extra left after making their cocktails, she lets Stella and me have a sip. Usually, Libby and Alvin go into their bedroom and shut their door to enjoy their drinks. Stella and I do our homework in her room. Libby has painted the walls pink with gray trim. Stella even has her own dressing table. With a big oval mirror and a skirt that Libby made from two crinolines.

Stella and I like to take off our blouses and bras and compare our boobies. I am still a double A, but she is already a B cup. Her nipples have turned a light brown color while mine are still pink as a baby's. Stella hasn't gotten her monthlies yet, though. She says she can hardly wait because Libby told her that when she got her monthlies her beauty would flower. Her skin will become silky and soft and her cheeks will fill with roses. I point out that nothing like that seems to be happening with me. I still have the pale complexion of a bookworm. During my monthlies I carry spare pads to school in my book bag. That way I can change them so the blood won't leak onto my bloomers and smell.

III

Stella and I are doing our geometry homework in her room. It is the first day of my period. The whole bottom part of my body is in a knot and the clumsy pad between my legs is very wet. I get a fresh pad out of my book bag. "I got to change my pad," I tell Stella. She nods, her head bent over her workbook. As I go up to the hallway to the bathroom, Libby comes out of her bedroom door and steps in front of me. She is holding an empty highball glass.

"How are you two doing in there?" she asks. "Time for a Coca-Cola and Oreo break?" Then she sees the pad in my hand. "Got your period, sweetie? But you're still using Kotex?"

"Aren't you supposed to?" I ask, surprised.

"If that's what your mother showed you." Libby says.

"I hate them," I burst out. "When I have my period I have to walk around with a big stinky mess in my bloomers and I walk so funny I look like I'm crippled."

Libby shakes her head. "Into the kitchen," she says.

I follow her and watch while she pours rum into her highball glass, then adds a dash of Coca-Cola. She opens a cookie jar and gets an Oreo, which she hands to me.

"Come," she says. She leads me into the bathroom and closes the door.

"I'm going to show you something, even though your mother might be angry with me. It makes me sick to think you're being raised to believe being a woman is a chore. It's a beautiful, many-splendored thing," Libby says quoting a popular song.

She opens the medicine cabinet and takes out a small, slim blue box.

"They just invented this," she says. "It's called Tampax. You can buy it at the drugstore for seventy-nine cents." She opens the box and takes out a thin tube a little thicker than a pencil wrapped in white paper. She peels the paper off to reveal two interlocking cardboard tubes, the smaller one resting inside the larger. She puts one foot up on the toilet seat and spreads her legs wide. Her dress falls back.

Between her big, golden thighs there is a dense thicket of wiry black hair, a jungle at night. In the very center of the darkness, two plush, fat pink lips part to show two darker lips, ridged and almost purple. I can't take my eyes off what is between Libby's legs. I am transfixed, my mouth open. Libby smiles.

"You look shocked," she says. "Haven't you ever seen your mother's twat?"

"It's a lily, my mother calls it a lily," I say.

"Twat, lily, whatever," she says. "It's not what you call it but what you do with it that counts. You're too young to understand, you will later."

Libby holds the cardboard tube before me. "Look," she says. "The Tampax is made of cotton. Once you put it up in you it puffs up and soaks up all the blood."

She pushes the cardboard tube up between her twat lips, then she pulls it out and tosses it in the toilet. A slim white string hangs out of her, looking like the stamen of a flower. Now I can see why my mother calls it a lily. It looks like a big pink and purple tiger lily, a strange, soft magical bloom.

"Then," Libby continues, "when it is full, you pull it out by the string and flush it away like this." She demonstrates. "No tight elastic belts, no pads."

"But won't it break my virgin skin?" I ask. My mother had recently told me that I have virgin skin down there and that my husband is supposed to break it on the night of our marriage. She said I should never touch myself down there because I might break it accidentally. I didn't tell my mother I had been touching myself down there for years.

"No," Libby says. "That skin is called a hymen and it has a hole in it. The Tampax slides right through. Come on, try it." Patiently, lovingly she practices with me until I can put the Tampax in as easily as I can put a pencil in a pencil sharpener.

"I know it's not right for me to encourage you to have secrets from your mother," Libby says. She picks up her rum and coke, which has been sitting on the sink and finishes it with one big swallow. "It's fun being a woman though." She gives me the box of Tampax to take home.

I start to use part of the money I make babysitting to buy Tampax every month. When I get my period, I take pads out of the Kotex box my mother keeps in the bathroom and then I throw them away in the bathroom at school unused. My mother never knows I am a Tampax user. She is old-fashioned and I am a modern woman. I start to pluck my eyebrows. I buy some desert rose rouge that I put on every day on my way to school.

One Saturday afternoon Stella and I go to La Maison de Beauty on Nostrand Avenue. She gets a pixie cut and I try a short pageboy, just like the one Natalie Wood wears in *Splendor in the Grass*. When I look in the mirror, the face I see staring back at me is beautiful. I start to notice that men are looking at me on the street. I begin to dream about what it would be like to be kissed and touched by a man between my legs. I hope it will happen soon but Libby told me that the only reason to marry is for love. As a modern woman, if I don't like a man kissing me I can tell him to stop. I don't have to have a man to take care of me. As a modern woman, I can have a career and a life of my own.

Turning Thirteen

Arlene L. Mandell

You know every boy in Junior High
can see that bulky pad hooked front and back
by treacherous elastic.

You're certain blood is soaking your skirt,
whisper to your best friend:
Do you see anything? Are you sure?

For three awkward years you carry
brown paper bags that aren't your lunch
because virgins, someone said,
can't use tampons.

Finally Helene, who's been around,
demonstrates the technique. You lock
the bathroom door to practice.

Twenty years later, as you stride up
Fifth Avenue in elegant pink linen,
a woman you don't know
taps your shoulder and whispers:
There's blood on your skirt.

And the boys in homeroom are smirking.

Rags

Judy Lee Green

On a sacrificial altar
between the chicken coop
and the outhouse,
smoking, smoldering,
fiery flames
are poked, stirred,
jabbed with a battling stick
by a bewildered thirteen-year-old,
ironing board body,
pony long legs,
ginger braid-tamed hair,
tick seed freckles,
fierce mouth,
hummingbird-green eyes.
Stabbing the vide evidence
sith quiet umbrage,
she conjures
brown blood-soaked rags
to ashes
and the curse
that has pronounced her
woman
to vanish
in hoary rag smoke.

Novel Excerpt: *Rest Stops*
Kianna

Elizabeth G. Slade

The sky is leaking light now and lights are coming on. Uncle Louis asks a bum where there's another gas station and we follow along the way the guy said. It's taking a long time, but finally we find it and I climb over Edgar and run to the bathroom right as soon as Uncle Louis stops the car. The door is locked and I have to go into the greasy station for the key. My brother is still slumped in the car and Uncle Louis is doing his stretching thing when I go by. I can feel my underwear is a little wet down there when I'm walking, but I think maybe it's from being so hot all day.

Now it's dark and the lights are on inside and the man there is big and tall with a flat head and the biggest muscles on his arms, like it's a Halloween costume.

"Can I've the bathroom key?" I try to sound older.

He doesn't say anything, so I try in Spanish. He points to a long piece of wood with a key strapped on the end with a piece of wire.

"Thanks."

I go back out into the night, which seems even darker now, and around the side of the station to the locked door. The key doesn't go right in because the lock is messed up, like someone stuck a fork in there and bent it, or a knife, but I finally get it in and push the heavy door open.

The smell is worse than I was ready for and I switch to breathing through my mouth right away. I feel on the wall for the light switch and when I turn it on I almost wish I hadn't. The place is trashed. The floor is covered in junk, the seat is up on the toilet and it looks like barf in there. The mirror's missing off the wall except for one jagged corner and the sink has something spilled in it that I don't even want to guess about. I want to leave, but I have to pee so bad.

I go over to the paper towel thing but of course there're none. I look for toilet paper and I see a roll hanging on an old nail where maybe a picture hung in better days. I reach up and take it down, looking it over real careful for mess or bugs. It seems all right so I unravel some and use it like a mitten to knock down the toilet seat. It falls with a bang and even though I was the one who made it fall, I jump like I'm scared. I am a little scared. This place is spooky and nasty. I want Momi to be in here going on about how people live and cleaning it up all along.

I roll more toilet paper onto my hand, reach over, wipe off the seat and throw my paper mitten over the whole mess in there. After that I stand and try to decide if flushing it before I sit would cause more problems I don't want to deal with, because squatting over that mess is a scary thought. I have to pee so bad that I can't think on it long so I just pull down my pants and hold myself off the seat with my leg muscles. I keep my eyes up off the floor because I don't want to see anything to freak me while I'm trying to pee.

The paint is cracking off the cinder blocks and someone has written nasty in black spray paint. I'm still holding the roll so I get a wad ready. When I wipe, though, I see something I was not ready for. Blood.

I jump up away from the toilet like it's the can's fault and look again at the wad in my hand. Blood. Brownish reddish blood. I throw it in the toilet and lean over to look in my pants, and sure enough there is a big stain like the water mark on my bedroom ceiling.

I stare at it. It's not like I don't know what it is, I do. Monica got her period a couple months ago and she told us all about it and everything her big sister taught her. Rosa was so jealous she pretended she already had hers, but everybody knows what a big liar Rosa is so we all just ignored her and got Monica to tell us more details about it. Monica said her sister showed her how to put a tampon up there. First she tried to do it herself, but she couldn't get it in with her sister yelling through the door "There's only one hole you need to be worrying about." We all laughed at that part. The word *hole* seemed so funny. It all seemed real funny at the time. Now it's not too funny. It's scary and I feel dizzy and like I might throw up.

I reach out to steady myself and my hand gets in the crap poured in the sink. I pull my hand back and scream like I've been bit. My legs start shaking and I don't know what to do standing in this nasty room with my pants down and blood coming out of me.

The Lord is my Shepherd comes into my mind. It is Momi's voice I hear. Momi's voice I want to hear, Momi I want right now. I need Momi. And before I know it, I am crying. I lean back on the door not even caring anymore about all the mess. I want to go home and come out of the bathroom and see Momi sitting on the couch watching TV and go over to her real slow and say "Momi, I'm a woman now."

I can see her face exactly, how she would turn her attention from her show to me and I would say it again and she would take a minute to think what I meant and then she would light up about it. "Oh baby," she'd say reaching up and pulling me down to her. We would cuddle like that for a bit while she told me all the secrets and I smelled her strong Momi smell.

Knock, knock. "Kianna? You in there?" It is Uncle Louis's voice and I am startled out of my crying, feeling caught and scared again. I reach down and pull up my pants then look around for the roll of paper I must've dropped when I was crying.

"Kianna?" His voice sounds nervous.

After rolling off the top layer and throwing it on top of my bloody paper in the toilet, I stuff a big wad down my pants between my legs. "Yeah?"

"Oh good. Uh . . ."

"What?"

"Edgar in there with you?"

"What?"

"Edgar, is he in there with you?"

"No! Course not!" What does he mean about that? I want to wash my hands so I try the faucet. At first there's nothing and then there is a great burst and brown stuff sprays out.

"What?" Uncle Louis sounds alarmed and I realize I must have screamed.

I pull open the door so Uncle Louis will see part of what I've had to deal with, but he just says, "You seen Edgar?"

"Edgar?" I am confused. The darkness is making me blind. I feel the brown stuff dripping off me onto the floor, and the wad of paper sitting like a Subway sandwich between my legs, and Uncle Louis is asking me again about Edgar.

"Yeah, Edgar. What's wrong with you?" And if he didn't sound so impatient and a little mad, I might tell him.

Instead I shrug.

"He's gone off," he says and I begin to understand.

I push out from under the weight of the door I have been holding open, out into the night, which feels cool and refreshing after that bathroom. I walk over to the car with Uncle Louis on my tail, and lean into the passenger window.

"He's not in there," he says.

Yeah, of course he's not in there. I'm looking for his stuff, and I want to cry again when I see it's not in there. This night is so bad.

I pull my head out of the car and lean on the back door with my head back, my face up to the sky. I try to keep the tears in, but they roll out anyway. First Popi, then Momi, now Edgar has left me.

What have I done so bad? What is it they all had to get away from so bad? I want to know that. I sniff and wipe my nose on my sleeve. When I do, I feel that it is already wet. I remember the sink and feel glad it's dark out. At this point, I don't want to know what I just wiped on my face. I turn my head and wipe it again on my shoulder.

Uncle Louis is still standing there. Does he think I know what to do? I'm just the kid, not even out of fourth grade yet, just months past a decade. He's the grown-up man all educated and owning a car. He's supposed to know what to do. Suddenly I want to punch him. Make him do something even if it's to bend over and hold himself.

Tires screech and lights come around the corner fast. A couple people scatter and then holler after it when it drives away. In the streetlight, I can see their gestures and hear their cursing. Then before they're even done another car comes fast following the first. It almost hits one of the people and swerves in our direction. I hear a shot and see the man who was almost hit has a gun in his hand. I duck down behind the car then and pull Uncle Louis down, who is in some kind of shock.

"We gotta get out of here," he says in a whisper, reaching up to open the passenger door.

"Not without Edgar we're not," I say out loud.

I hear the second car backing up, then revving up and taking off. I hear shouts like the car's gone after the people, then another shot and the sound of glass breaking. Uncle Louis pulls at my arm to get in the car and I do. I pull the door closed behind me without sitting up.

Uncle Louis slouches down in the seat, sliding himself behind the wheel and putting the key in. He starts the engine.

"Hey," and I think it's me that said that, but then I hear it again and I peek up to see the man with the muscle mountains calling us from the station door.

Uncle Louis peeks up over the dash enough to see where he's going and pulls out fast.

"Hey!" The guy yells one more time and I figure it out then. Uncle Louis didn't pay.

He tears out of the gas station lot and goes down the street the two cars came out of. This doesn't seem too smart to me, but I don't say anything. This is all so messed up it's making the bathroom seem normal.

I look out the back window and see that it's partly missing. That broken glass sound was our back window and even in the dark, I can see the pieces shining as we pass under streetlights.

Uncle Louis is driving too fast, putting ground between himself and trouble. If Uncle Louis gets arrested, he's the last one I got.

"Slow down," I tell him and I hear my mother's voice.

He doesn't say anything, but he right away slows down some.

I shift in my seat trying to get comfortable on the fist of paper in my crotch and look up to the sky for some answers. It's totally cloudy up there, not one star for me to look at and I think of Edgar. I squint my eyes to make them show up, like they're there instead of all those clouds. I want to see the bunch that make a spoon that Edgar says is the Big Dipper. Just now I want it to reach down out of the black sky and scoop me up. Take me away from this lost feeling.

Late Bloomer

Amy Watkins

It was anticlimactic, something
I didn't want but had waited for,
embarrassed by its absence—blood,
deep as the ache that comes with growing.
That year my best friend, a year older,
yielded her virginity to her first boyfriend.
Again, the obvious metaphor—
the bloom of womanhood is blood.
I thought you had a right to know, she said,
but I had no right and kept my own secret.
What was my blood to this blooming?

Reign

Ellen Hagan

It was a Saturday afternoon, sun aching in the sky,
my one-piece hugged tight around me, fast
a fish below the surface, my strokes quick.
Ten years old, whipping circles in our pool,
new, backstroke and butterfly my specialties,
my blue ribbons at town swim meets.
Still played house and Barbie, rode my bike zig-zag 'round
the drive, made the hot pink hula-hoop jitter
around my un-grown, un-woman hips, still.
Still, I was shocked by the blood. No reading or
stories could prep me, stuck in my parents' bathroom,
the color of rust, soaking through my first fire-red Speedo.
A cut or wound, I searched
my thighs for the spot, threw off my suit and cried,
called my mom for rescue.
My period,
an exclamation mark, a round of soda, my feet propped,
salty chips and a story before it was time.
My mother with a box of tampons in tow.
"It's easy, Ellen, you just pop it in."
Locked in the bathroom,
the directions on the back of the toilet, my legs wide
I put the whole thing in, cardboard and all,
and declared, "I did it!" I
soaked in the tub, my body brand new to me, my mother
on the edge, telling how her sisters helped her and that since I
had none she was helping me. My confusion prompting my
mother to demonstrate the tricky tampon technique
using her own vagina. I hadn't realized.
My vagina suddenly became a new thing
A new luxury of woman,

as my mother crowned me grown-up,
crowned me daughter who could. And I could.

Strange Woman Before Me

Adrienne Anifant

At eleven years old, I began to disappear. The first gray breath of fog descended so gently, I barely noticed my own leavetaking. Drifting in thinly, at first, the fog settled around the warmest parts of me: my spirit and sex. To forestall, I tried to laugh, read and imagine as I always had. But as it became denser, my sense of reality, of life, the vectors of my ideas and feelings began to lose their form and distinction. My whole body, like an eye, strained and squinted in the ghost light to see them. But the vastness of the exterior world and my interior self began to contract quickly and, so soon, I was in danger of falling down the rabbit hole.

That wild, beating force inside me began to fade when the opacity of puberty finally caught me. It had been tracking me for awhile, because I was running, hiding, riding the cool, carefree wave of denial while coining a new concept of pre-traumatic stress disorder. In bed, I would lie on my stomach and feel my flat breasts throbbing with a dense pain. The pulsating pain became my new heartbeat. I refused to lie on my back because doing so would admit I was developing *those*. In the mirror, I'd monitor their intrusion every day and try to convince myself that they were in fact shrinking. But they continued to emerge from my body like two prosthetic noses.

My mother bought me a small bra which I pushed to the farthest corner of my drawer. Rather than suffer from the mortifying shame of being the first girl to wear a training bra in my class, I continued to ignore their annoying presence by placing Scotch tape over each pea-sized nipple. As I laughed with my friends at the outline of a training bra across Mandy Norton's back, I thanked the universe for my brilliant idea. I maneuvred the tweezers like a martial artist. Cutting the air with their tiny stainless steel teeth and bending them between my fingers, I plucked every pioneering pubic hair before it could even unpack. With each new underarm hair and ray of sunny yellow in my underwear I cried out for what I felt was the end of me.

For me, no shame could compare to the stomach-sinking humiliation elicited from the visible signs of my new womanhood; signs of my new sexiness over which I had no control. Sitting in class, I watched the teacher move back and forth, around the room, waving her hands and arms as she spoke. I'd follow the nuances of her voice. Then she'd turn and talk to the chalkboard, rolling her hands with her voice's inflection, as if she were trying to coax it to life. In my wooden chair I'd measure with my fingers how much of my expanding hips and thighs swelled over the sides of the seat. My breasts hung like two cannon balls from my chest dragging my shoulders down so they could hide in the concave of my back. When I thought of myself as an adult woman my breathing went shallow and my chest compressed. I felt clamps on my heart as I looked upon my postpubescent life with dread. Nothing would separate me from the models and actresses on TV and in advertisements, from that miasma out there of legs and nipples and stomachs. They would be my new identity, and nothing more would be expected from me.

As my body changed more and more to resemble an adult woman's, I felt more removed from my body and my own experiences of it. And if this all seemed bad, things were going to get much worse according to our school nurse, Mrs. Abrams. As she dangled a bleach-white tampon in front of our faces, Mrs. Abrams explained how our periods were going to be the most life-altering aspect of puberty. There was going to be monthly pain, rancid smell, yellow globs of discharge during ovulation, and mood swings that would turn us into sobbing, gnashing, little monsters. There was going to be missed pool parties and swim meets around "that time of the month" due to the off chance we might unleash a crimson ribbon from between our legs as we kicked and sputtered and laughed in that crackling blue. In fact, all sports were going to be impossible since searing pain would incapacitate our bodies every four weeks. And, when we did start having sex, we must politely dissuade our boyfriends "around that time" who were eager to butt like Billy goats by distracting them with an elaborate blow job (For comprehensive how-to guides, see Resources).

There was going to be—oh. Oh, yes. There was going to be blood. And to take care of that, we young girl-women were going to be plugged up. Corked. Mrs. Abrams showed us how. She rolled up her long woolen skirt to her knees and lifted one leg, resting her shoe on a desk. With the white nodule in hand she hunched down, showing us the best way to really get our backs and biceps into it; shoving that chemically treated piece of dry cotton up, down, up, down. She looked as if she were plunging an upside-down toilet. As a herd, we slouched in our chairs. Our heads began to sink lower and lower, swaying like great mammoth trunks.

But if we, my class of stained and staining comrades, only knew that a woman's evolutionary advance from the primate estrus cycle to the human menstrual cycle was critical to the development of human culture and society, then we may not have been so affected by the gravity in that small classroom and in our adolescent lives. If we knew that among all species on earth, only a woman's sexuality is divisible from reproduction; that menstrual blood was a sacred element in rituals of all Neolithic peoples; that African and Australian aboriginal people rubbed red paint on themselves and poured blood over sacred stones and shrines; that female blood once symbolized the psychic-physical union of humans through the blood of their mothers, and of the Great Mother; that a girl's first period has not always been a secret; that the menstrual blood-stained clothes of the Indian Goddess Mother, Kali, were valued as strong medicine; that today, followers of Kali still cut themselves and cover her statues with their blood; that today, initiates into the Hell's Angels prove their worth by performing cunnilingus on their girlfriends or wives during their periods; that menstrual blood is powerful; that women who live in rhythm with their cycles are powerful, then we would have felt proud to become women.

I knew none of this, so I crashed my fists against my growing breasts. They didn't seem to belong to me but to a larger nexus of images of pop stars and Playboy Bunnies with hard freakish orbs; these things brought me eerie gazes from men holding hands with their wives, lusty smiles and grunts of approval.

But when I started to bleed, I was surprised. I felt proud and held by its wonder. My blood was all mine coming from my dark inside. I knew I did this with other women; my mother and grandmother bled, and I was connected to them through it. Blood couldn't be dressed in lace lingerie or photographed on all fours. It made me human and even more—a creative, powerful, magical woman—bequeathed with a cosmic insight.

In class I would sit, my abdomen twisting and tugging with pain, in silent joy. It was as if a visceral, primeval thing was given to me. That first bright red in my underwear was weighty with the kind of honor when one is given a great responsibility that is both grand and hard to bear. My best friend Carrie would talk enviously about the boys' proverbial lucky escape and daydream about menopause as we lay on her soft, purple carpet, looking up through her skylight. I told her I hated my period too, again pronounced its unfairness, and together we'd reprove ourselves for being born female. But in the half-light of her kid room, under the hexagonal skylight, I contended with the guilt and discomfort of my lies. Because I felt, especially during the days I bled, unequivocally privileged. One day I could not make new life and the next day I could. My body could feed and take care of a life, and possibly, end it as well. The briny smell, the sinuous texture of the blood, the bright red color was inconceivable. And I loved it all. Inside I told Mrs. Abrams to chew on her tampon. I used pads. I did not want to engage in vaginal plunging, but more so I wanted see the red, to see it on my fingers and stain the bathroom tiles with ruby droplets. I rolled pieces of the tissue-thin, broken lining in between my thumb and fingers. It smelled like soil and it smelled like my big sister's room. It smelled like flesh, and life and death. And it seemed as if I had held all of those within me for centuries.

But no one said anything; there were no announcements, celebration or even a slice a cake. No blood fairies crept by starlight into my room, leaving chocolate, gifts or silver dollars beneath my pillow. Finally, when I told my mother I had my period her voice tightened, "Okay." A few days later she reported back to me that she had done what she must, "I told your father." And I could not but notice the contemptuous silence through which we all began to move in my house.

One by one "the period" happened to each girl in my class and we would secretly steal away to the bathroom, waiting for a toilet to flush so no one could hear the crinkle and tear of paper. Eventually that beautiful swollen arrogance proclaiming over and over I could make new life and Ryan Baker next to me could not dissipate into the ever-thickening fog around me. Eventually, I forgot that initial awe of my bleeding and of my body. But, it *was* grand to lie on a bed of dead leaves and soft moss at thirteen, surrounded by silent trees, to look up at the full moon shining like the open mouth of some dark goddess above me and to feel the earth so round and hot beneath me. And to know, if only for a moment, that it was for all of it—for all this life, that I bled.

Blood Diaries

Karen Howland

A
Red
drop

seeps
beneath
my knee.

Bike tire sssssssss-ings

I ask Grandma
"Why do we bleed? "

She holds me close
pink hem trembling.
Later that month she almost dies,
blood leaving her body
during the night.

In my dream, bike tires hiss
long after
the spinning stops.

Blood leaks from the tires.

• • •

Pastor Burnhardt preaches
Eve, Eve, because of Eve.

What's because of Eve,
knowledge or corruption?

• • •

Grandma reveals she conceived
Mom out of wedlock. Wedlock.
Where two people bleed freely.

• • •

December
empty and red.
My body, a bad holiday.

• • •

Church this morning.
Old gospels of blood.
Eve, Eve, because of Eve.

Later that day,
a red bag hangs by Grandma's hospital bed.

• • •

I sleep deep
red dreams.
When I wake,
the sun pulses rose-gold.
Grandma sighs yes
and pushes something
to the back of the shelf.

• • •

I run a red light.
There's too much red
against
the rain-streaked road stained
with Grandma's blood
and all that women lose,
in ways that can't be explained.

• • •

I recall the fall.
I flare

into air,
bike below.
Blood pumps fast.
I trill my entire body
is a heart, a heart!
This is the last time
I feel free
before the fall,
before I see
the anemic lining of her eye,
making payments with its lid,
eternal pale bouquets.

Going with the Flow

Elaine K. Green

It was the spring of 1965. I had just come in from shooting hoops when I heard my sister calling me from the damp, little hole that was our bathroom.

"Get in here, quick!" I heard her say, her screechy voice even more high-pitched than normal.

"What now?" I snapped, but then snapping was the only way I knew how to converse with my sister.

"I need to know if this thingie is situated on me right."

When I peeked in, I could see her back was to me, and that the "thingie" was an elastic band around her waist with an extended flap down the middle supporting a thick pad at the base. It appeared to be held in place with, of all things, a safety pin. Apparently, my sister had just started her period. My mind reeled, and a sick feeling seized my stomach. If my older sister was getting *her* period, that could only mean one thing: *mine might not be too far behind!* But that just couldn't be possible. I had already dissed that drama from my life script. I didn't want to think about having to wear that ridiculous-looking contraption, and I certainly didn't want to look at it wrapped around my sister's butt. Besides, menstrual periods were for women—and my sister was not a woman—she was an irritating twerp.

"How would I know if it's on right or not?" I hissed, before slamming the door and bolting to my room. For me, getting a period was the absolute dreaded thing—that unwritten entry permanently excluded from my to-do list. I had already survived twelve wonderful years without one, and I wasn't about to start now. I told myself that if I wished hard enough, it simply would never happen to me.

I had noticed other girls in my sixth-grade class with telltale red traces on the back of their skirts, while others opted to wear buttoned-down sweaters tied around their waists to avert any hint of detection. I laughed at them when they begged the teacher for passes to go home early. That would never happen to me I told myself. I would never suffer one day with stomach cramps like they did, endure headaches or have to sit out P.E. I liked basketball way too much for that. I wasn't ready to navigate their world of angst, unpleasant odors and BC powders. And I was becoming increasingly annoyed with Dana Street, an overdressed ninny in my science class who appointed herself the poster child for the menstrual cycle, endlessly recounting in graphic detail her mother's boring sermonettes on the subject. She even had the nerve to slip me a pamphlet about it replete with color illustrations. I slamdunked it along with her know-it-all-attitude in the trashcan behind the gym. Didn't she understand that that was not going to happen to me? Couldn't she sense that I loathed her surefooted, carefree attitude about it all? Besides, my mother had never broached the subject with me, so that alone confirmed I was exempt from that world of pain.

Then it occurred to me that my mother had never talked to me about any of the things the other girls claimed their mothers had told them—not puberty, boys, sex, my period—nothing. In fact, when my sister returned from seeing the Liz Taylor-Richard Burton movie, *The Sandpiper*, I overheard my mother instruct her to take me to see it because it was time I learned about "that." Not sure what "that" meant, but I knew it probably wouldn't be anything I'd be interested in hearing all the gory details about. And that was fine with me—the less I knew the better. Besides, how could Liz and Dick possibly quell the whirlwind that was swirling about in my head at age twelve?

Later that year Hurricane Betsy blasted through our town, pummeling everything in its path. Right after she whizzed past our house and we had breathed a sigh of relief, the unthinkable happened: the burgeoning levees swelled past their capacity and the lake burst forth bleeding profusely not only into our neighborhood, but through our front door—a tide so fervent nothing could stem it—not my tears and certainly not my refusal to accept that it was happening. The thing I remember most was my mother's incredible calm in the face of disaster. We evacuated via rescue boat to my aunt's house, our lives forever changed.

That night as I was dressing for bed, I noticed the peculiar black-brown smudges in my panties. I cried and called my mother. "Not now," I kept telling myself, "not here," my embarrassment markedly worse because I was not even in the privacy of my own home. Mother calmly explained that it was a natural thing—that things happen in their own time. As she spoke I was suddenly aware of how unflappable she had been throughout my young life. How even when Dad left, she didn't miss a beat, and valiantly held our family together. She always seemed to go with the flow, always accepted things bravely and dealt with them as they came. I'm not sure why I was crying so much, but it probably was because deep inside I knew this day would come. I just didn't want to face it. My mother and sister were there for me, affirming me, encouraging me. Calmly, they welcomed me into the new, unchartered world of womanhood. I realized I was joining an elite group—that I was not a child who had to be protected from every little thing anymore. I no longer had to be afraid or be handled with kid gloves all the time. For the first time, I talked to my sister without snapping at her. At that moment I realized I was a woman just like she was, and that meant I needed to take life as it came—to go with the flow. Whenever I think about my period, I remember my mother and sister, fearless and unswerving, and I can deal with life's storms.

Scraps

Jill Kelly Koren

You need new underwear
My friend said to me
These are really icky
I say it's icky to bleed in new ones

My friend said to me
It feels nice to have new underwear
I say it's icky to bleed in new ones
It's easy for her to say

It feels nice to have new underwear
She uses her mother's credit cards
It's easy for her to say;
She shops at Neiman-Marcus

She uses her mother's credit cards
To take me out to breakfast
She shops at Neiman-Marcus
She buys the best of panties

To take me out to breakfast
She wore her best new panties
She buys the best of panties
Does she even bleed?

She wore her best new panties
She throws away the old ones
Does she even bleed
If you scratch beneath the skin?

She throws away the old ones

Panties, rugs, and lovers
If you scratch beneath the skin
Would you find Neiman-Marcus there?

Panties, rugs, and lovers,
Bear the taint of moon-full bleeding
Would you find Neiman-Marcus there
Among the scraps of longing?

Bear the taint of moon-full bleeding
My mom now does my laundry
Among the scraps of longing
She finds the taint of blood

My mom now does my laundry
She says, These are really old,
As she pulls the spent elastic,
You need new underwear.

A Jewish Santa Claus
He Was Not

Lana Hechtman Ayers

Once a month the Kosher butcher,
wearing stained, brown coveralls,
delivered a giant bloody linen sack
next to our milk box.

Inside were brown packages tied with string,
dripping with more blood.
And in those: chicken parts, lamb chops, chopped beef,
minute steaks, liver, even an entire cow tongue.

Kosher slaughter is more humane, my mother said,
the animals' throats are slit and they bleed to death.

I watched as mother carefully unwrapped each parcel,
letting the excess blood drip
onto white paper towels that quickly turned red.
She rewrapped everything, cellophane first, then shiny foil.

After labeling all with strips of masking tape,
she hauled them down to the deep freeze.
It was my job to cart those dripping paper towels
to the trash, where they loomed like giant carnation heads.

My mother told me she was engaged to a butcher once
but broke it off because he had rough hands.

This, my mother's monthly ritual, would someday be mine:
Jewish females, unclean with blood,

made to touch blood throughout our lives, to become
Kosher parcels for Jewish men to unwrap.

There's Always a String Attached

L. Mahayla Smith

It was the summer the Beatles released *Sgt. Pepper's Lonely Hearts Club Band*. The summer that Pablo Neruda won the Viareggio prize for his poems of passion. The summer when all the hippie chicks dropped acid along with their birth control pills, and the youth of America believed that all anyone really did need was love, love, love. It was the summer of 1967, the summer of love, the summer . . .

I started my period.

I was thirteen years old and lived in Macon, Georgia, a town physically distant from the streets of London, San Francisco and any "happening" place on this globe—and as psychologically removed from free love as the recently launched Mariner probe was from Venus. Yes, Macon, Georgia, for all intents and purposes, was another planet. And my personal orbit was very small indeed.

It was a different time and place—an era when dinner table conversation was restricted to genteel topics such as Sunday sermons, or maybe, on a serious note, the Vietnam War. Mama's favorite topic, barely sufferable to my father, was the spouses, new houses, cars and the children of her eight sisters. I had exactly thirty-seven cousins spread out over two decades of births and all as colorful and rambunctious as the strawberry to auburn shades of their red hair might suggest. Certain topics, however, were verboten from discourse completely. One was Daddy's family, a hard-drinking lot of moonshine-producing rabble in the Kentucky hills who apparently did not get the news when prohibition ended. And the chief number one topic that was never, ever, no matter what not open for discussion in any public forum was human reproduction.

To say that my parents took a minimalist approach to sex education would be akin to stating that it is a bit nippy on an Arctic ice floe in mid-January. To this day, forty years later, I've received a single nanoparticle of procreation tutoring from my parents.

That item of Sex Ed I had was a short dissertation by my Montgomery, Alabama-raised, Scarlett O'Hara clone of a mother. She didn't dress up in a revealing red outfit, but there was an air of drama to her presentation about entering the world of feminine fertility. On the morning of my eleventh birthday, a frosty Saturday in February, Mama tiptoed into my bedroom just before dawn and sat down on the edge of my bed.

"Gina," she whispered, touching my forehead, then running her fingers through my carrot-orange, wooly curls.

My eyes opened slowly. In the pale breaking light of the window, I struggled to focus on my mother in her yellow chenille housecoat, pink plastic curlers and fuzzy blue house shoes. She still smelled of last night's Noxema face cream.

"What's wrong, Mama?" I croaked, rubbing the backs of my hands across my eyelids. This had to be bad news.

In a conspiratorial tone, she leaned forward and whispered, "It's time I told you about your little red-headed cousin."

This was from the outset, a very confusing talk. Was one of my thirty-odd red-headed cousins dead? Or secretly descended from Queen Elizabeth? Was he or she, God forbid, adopted? Or perhaps worse—did my cousin have a daddy that was Japanese, Vietnamese, Negro, Italian or some other non-Anglo Saxon bloodline? I sat up. Whatever the news was, it was going to be scandalous.

"What Mama?" I managed, my voice high and strained. I grabbed my teddy bear and held on tight.

"Haven't any of your friends talked to you about their red-headed cousin yet, Gina?" I know now that Mama was hoping one of my girlfriends from the grade school had spilled the beans about the menstrual cycle in the bathroom at school or on the playground during a kickball game. If so, she could walk right out of my bedroom and crawl back under the quilt that was on her and Daddy's bed, saying, "Great. She already knew, so no use to me repeating it," as the door creaked shut behind her.

But I didn't answer Mama. I just stared with sincere bewilderment.

"All right then, Gina. This is about becoming a woman."

"Okay," I said. Mama shifted on the bed causing the mattress to creak.

"Honey, when a young girl becomes a woman, her little red-headed cousin comes to visit her once a month."

"Which cousin?" I dang sure hoped it wasn't my Uncle Buddy's son. He was four years old, a hell-demon on a tricycle who dismembered my Barbies and wiped snot on my Cinderella bedspread.

Mama looked at me like I couldn't add two plus two. "Gina, this is NOT a real cousin. It's a saying. A code ladies use to talk to each other quietly in public about—well, things. One day soon, you will become a woman, and when you do, you are going to go to the bathroom or wake up in the night and you will find a spot of blood in your panties."

"Blood?" I blurted out. I was alarmed. The most blood I had ever seen was from a paper cut or a skinned knee.

"Keep your voice down," Mama whispered. "This isn't a conversation we want your father or Bishop Arnold next door to hear. And yes, blood. It could happen to you anyplace and anytime."

I spoke barely audibly, "Am I gonna bleed a lot, Mama? How will the blood get in my panties?" I was on the verge of an anxiety attack. Not only was I confused about the current conversation, there was the dirty panty issue. My mother bought me days of the week panties and if I got any stains in them at all, she would make me go to the bathroom with her and show her how I wiped my butt, screaming the whole time, "Why can't you just clean yourself right? I would expect this from your father, but not a proper young lady. We, in case you do not know, Princess Gina, are not well off financially, and every time you do this, I can't just buy you a new pair of panties." Here she always paused, readying herself to lay on the ultimate guilt trip. "I have to buy a whole week."

But this time, my mother was entirely silent. "Mama?" I said, shaking her arm. "Am I going to die?" The only regular reference to bleeding around our house was Jesus on the cross and that situation turned out mighty badly.

"Oh, no, honey," Mama said, reaching over and giving my hand a pat. "You are just going to become a woman. A lady who can have babies and become a mother. It's a normal thing. It happens to every young girl."

I was still mystified. I wasn't quite ready for motherhood yet. I wasn't even ready for junior high school.

Mama reassured me. "It isn't anything to worry about, Gina. Whenever you get a spot of blood in your panties, come see me, and we will talk more. If you are at school, go see the school nurse and she will bring you home." Mama leaned over and kissed me on the head. "Go back to sleep now, pumpkin." Mama stood up and went out the door. Then I heard Mama and Daddy distantly in their bedroom down the hall, talking and giggling.

There was no way I could go back to sleep that Saturday morning. I did stay in my bed and miss my favorite cartoons, milling about thoughts of womanhood and having babies. And blood in my panties. It was the first time Mama and I whispered where Daddy couldn't hear us. I felt very much like a spy on a secret mission. Maybe even *Mission Impossible*. I wondered if this was a mission I could choose not to accept.

• • •

When school ended on Memorial Day two years later in the summer of 1967, I spent most of it staying in our small Jim Walter pre-fab home. Or out in the yard chasing fireflies and hummingbirds. Disney World was still a concept. Going to Florida was what the rich kids did. Europe was where our fathers and grandfathers fought the Germans. Mama, Daddy, Glenn, my older brother, and I went to church Wednesday night and twice on Sunday, to the ball field on Tuesday and Friday if Glenn had a baseball game, and over to the neighbors' houses on their birthdays for homemade cake and delicious, hand-cranked vanilla ice cream. We lived in the dark ages before gelato, mint chocolate chip and before Baskin even met Robbins. We didn't mind all the vanilla of our lives. Like nearly everything else, we had no idea what we were missing. During those oppressively hot and humid days of the summer of '67, when sweat clung to your skin and clothes like a baby chimp to its mother's chest, I was developing new interests and feelings. Things that thirteen-year-old girls are aware of that twelve-year-olds are not. The women of America, young and old, lost Elvis to Priscilla back in May. My girlfriends and I were looking for diversions to help us get through the languor of late afternoon thunderstorms and the nerves that were wracked from obsessing about junior high school in the fall. Most of my pretty peer group either switched over from the King to the daily worship of Ricky Nelson or the Beatles or they found a real live boyfriend.

But not me. I chose a different path and found all the excitement I could ever want at a Baptist church camp near Valdosta, Georgia. A more remote setting was unimaginable to my thirteen-year-old mind. Youth ages twelve to fifteen from the Faith and Hope Spirit-Filled Independent Baptist Church boarded a school bus in Macon on a Monday morning and drove down state highways, stopping only for gas and buying Coke in short glass bottles for ten cents. We liked to look on the bottom of the bottle and see where it came from. I got one from Seattle, Washington, and felt a sense of being very special to have gotten one from so far away. The bus eventually turned off the main highway onto a narrow dusty trail surrounded by a forest of Georgia pine. The heated needles produced a smell that wafted in through the bus windows and made us think of cleaning floors. The hot Georgia air seemed to move slow and thick like road tar as we tried to inhale it, and we looked forward to a week of cold showers. But mostly, I daydreamed about the turquoise waters of the Bible camp swimming pool. The fact of the matter was that no thirteen-year-old went to Bible camp because they loved the Lord. We went because church camp had a swimming pool and none of us did. We got to enter that refreshing blue refuge three and sometimes even four times a day. It was the closest you could get to heaven in August in the South. Since we knew we were approaching camp, the road seemed to wind on forever, but it was only about five miles back to the rickety shacks that would be our homes for one full week. When we passed the softball field, the counselors, mostly older teenagers, were already there playing a game of slow pitch softball. On the mound stood an older man of tremendous height and girth with brown hair graying on the sides and thick, black-rimmed glasses. He was not an overly attractive sight, but we would see plenty of him. He was Preacher Skeeter, the youth evangelist that the Independent Baptist Churches of South Georgia hired to keep the children of fine, upstanding Christians out of their hair for the last dog days of summer. As we got down from the bus and marched over to the open-air, tin-roofed structure to get our cabin assignments, I saw buses arriving from other churches, expelling their dungaree- and culottes-clad contents likes wasps leaving a nest full of smoke. In a couple of hours, the camp would be buzzing madly with activities that would go unabated for seven days.

On the very first night of Bible camp, away from the comforts of home and parents, crowded into a rustic, sweltering cabin packed full of bunk beds and other girls my age, I accepted Jesus Christ as my personal savior during bedtime devotional. It wasn't that our counselor Debbie was a budding Billy Graham. It was a direct result of thinking long and hard about Preacher Skeeter's Monday night sermon while Debbie was reading Psalms 119 aloud in the cabin. Even today, Psalms 119 usually makes me sleepy, although Deuteronomy and Numbers are even more effective. On that first night of church camp, our preacher had shouted all the information a thirteen-year-old could handle about accountability and sin and then begged us all with tears streaming down his cheeks to respond to the gospel invitation during thirty-nine choruses of "Just As I Am." Based on Preacher Skeeter's lesson, I did realize that just as I was, I would be the first to climb up the stairs when Satan sounded the "All aboard on the train to hell," but I couldn't muster the nerve to walk to the altar in front of all 124 teenagers from seven different independent Baptist churches in Georgia and confess what a wretched soul I truly was. I was reviewing my personal inventory of evil—throwing popcorn over a fat lady's head and into her cleavage at the movies, putting a paper cup on my cat's head and watching it try to back out of it, pretending my pillow was Paul McCartney and giving him deep French kisses repeatedly in my bed at night. Even though Preacher said Armageddon could happen any time, any minute, and I would be lost, I prayed the Lord would give me enough time to find a slightly smaller audience for my declaration of guilt and profession of faith. So I waited a couple of hours with the fear that an airplane might fall from the sky—or worse. Maybe Mr. Nikita Khruschev, infidel and leader of the Communists in Russia, would drop the atom bomb and end it all right there in the piney woods before I could repent. But it didn't happen like that at all. When Debbie finished the Psalm, and asked if anyone wanted to say the prayer, I raised my hand and said I wanted to be saved. All the girls in my cabin were jubilant. They all hugged me and got down on their knees in fervent prayer for my everlasting soul. I must admit, I felt pretty good when that was over. I had confidence the devil would pass over my bunk and have to look for a replacement. I was considering all of the reforms I would have to make when sleep snuck up on me like a distant rainstorm inches to the edge of a front porch.

I didn't see how the second day of Bible camp could get any more eventful. But it did. Right before the pre-lunch swim, when I was changing into my bathing suit, my little red-headed cousin finally came to visit me in my panties—the ones with Tuesday written right on the front. I had several friends who had started their periods recently and I knew there were special things they had to do now, but I didn't really know exactly what they were. I did gather that having a period was neither deadly nor an immediate prelude to having a child. Of course, my mother, was nowhere in sight. I couldn't even call her. I wouldn't have tried if I could have, because all the phones in Valdosta, Georgia, were party lines. By midnight, the whole town would know that Regina Wilson started her period at Bible camp and had very little idea what to do. There was so little going on in Valdosta, it might make the front page of the paper. Nope, there would be none of that. I went to my cabin counselor, Debbie. I took off my panties and showed her the spot in my underwear. I said, "Look. My little red-headed cousin. I am supposed to tell my mama."

Debbie just looked at me and then, with perfect Christian camp counselor compassion said, "Gross!"

It wasn't exactly the answer I had expected. "He has never come to visit before." I explained.

"Foot fire," said Debbie. "They covered the plan of salvation with us in counselor training, but they didn't really talk about girls getting their period for the first time. Do you have any sanitary napkins or a sanitary belt?"

"No." I shook my head. "What am I supposed to do?" I was nervous. I started to cry. They didn't sell that sort of thing in the camp store and I didn't know how to use it anyway.

"Hey, hey, Gina," Debbie tousled my hair. "It happens to all girls. You're gonna be just fine." She gave me a hug. "Let's go see Sister Gladys. She will know what to do."

"Am I gonna miss pre-lunch swim?" I asked Debbie.

"Most assuredly." She advised me, adding, "And afternoon and midnight swim. You are pretty much landlocked for the rest of the week, kid." This revelation made torrents of tears spill. My heart was broken. I had been obedient to the Savior and this is what I get? This womanhood thing was not working very well with my summer camp plans so far.

By the time I reached Sister Gladys' cabin, I was wracked with sobs. Sister Gladys was Preacher Skeeter's wife. They stayed in a slightly more high-end cabin with a double bed and a window air-conditioning unit. Sister Gladys still came to the door sweating and waving a fan with a picture of Jesus in the Garden of Gethsemane on it. She weighed in at 300 pounds and was shaped like a misshapen marshmallow balanced on two toothpicks. The Sister had an exceptionally high voice and sounded like a five-year-old girl dispensing advice.

"My stars, ladies, what in heaven's name is wrong?" Sister Gladys asked, observing my obvious state of distress.

"Uh ... um ... " Debbie appeared to be thinking and choosing the right words to address a topic not open for discussion. Finally she suggested, "Can we talk in the bathroom, Sister Gladys? Alone?"

Sister Gladys raised an eyebrow, but conceded to do so. They went into the bathroom. I was not invited behind the unfinished wooden door. Hushed words occasionally escaped beneath the crack, and after a few minutes, Sister Gladys and Debbie emerged, both with wide smiles, as though they were going to reveal to me that somehow I'd won the Hope Diamond from collecting S&H green stamps.

Sister Gladys nodded at Debbie, and she went scampering out the front door with a short wave good-bye. "See you at afternoon preaching, Gina."

"Now, Regina," Sister Gladys began, waddling toward me with her outstretched doughy arms. "You have indeed been blessed by God. Sit down, child, and let us count your many blessings."

I sat down next to Sister Gladys on a church pew in the cabin. "Let's begin at the beginning" she said. Ordinarily this would mean, "You tell me what just happened to you."

I opened my mouth to explain that while I was getting ready to go swimming, I found blood in my Tuesday panties. The point that I failed to consider here was that this was a preacher's wife, and when she said "the beginning" what she actually meant was The Beginning. "Gina," Sister Gladys said before I could get out a single word, "What do you know about women and the curse?"

"Well," I started through intermittent gasps of breath and tears. "If women curse, they should ask for forgiveness and wash their mouths out with Lifebuoy soap. 'The same fountain cannot produce both sweet and bitter water.' James three-eleven."

She stared blankly at me, but then began to chuckle. "Oh, no, Gina, I am not talking about cursing, I am talking about The Curse that God visited upon Eve and all women after the Garden of Eden. The curse of childbearing."

I stared at my tennis shoes. My tears stopped. I didn't realize I was going to get a pop quiz on Genesis.

She squeezed my hand. "Gina, this is nothing to be ashamed of. God has visited us with a curse, but it is also a blessing."

I was more confused than ever. I had no idea what Sister Gladys's point was, but she was the preacher's wife, so I smiled and nodded. Grandma Rogers told me, "If you don't know what people are talking about, honey, just smile and nod. They don't care what you think anyway."

"Do you remember what happened in the Garden of Eden, Gina?"

"Yes, ma'am," I whimpered.

"Remember that the serpent tempted Eve with the fruit."

"The apple," I said.

"Correct. Or, at least, traditionally it was thought to be an apple, although biblically, one cannot state with certainty. Anyway, Gina, Eve ate it and then she was aware that she was naked."

This never made any sense to me. Even in my dreams, I knew when I was running around with no clothes on. But I didn't think Sister Gladys really wanted to know this opinion so I just said, "Yes, ma'am."

"The Lord cursed Eve with childbearing. And in order to bear a child, our womb must prepare a soft bed of blood to receive a tiny baby."

I didn't know much about anatomy. It might have been the first time I ever heard anyone say the word "womb" out loud.

"Yes, ma'am," I said, wiping my nose on my T-shirt.

The crack of a bat and excited voices strayed past the window from the softball field. Sister Gladys stretched her neck toward the open window for a moment, but then looked back directly at me. "If you don't make a baby within a month, the soft bed issues forth from your lower area and you see blood. It is just a normal thing. Nothing to worry about although at times I have cramps so bad I sure do wish Eve would have been more in the mood for a fig." Sister Gladys put her hands on her burgeoning lower belly and rubbed it in circles. "And the water weight gain is also a problem. I get so bloated."

I was beginning to wonder if God loved me at all. I also wondered how anyone could tell when Sister Gladys was bloated.

"But I digress, child. I understand that you don't have any sanitary napkins or belt," she said.

"No, ma'am," I confessed, head bent in contrition.

"Well, we are going to have to talk to Preacher Skeeter, honey."

My eyes grew round and I shouted at Sister Gladys, "No way! I mean, please don't, Sister Gladys. Please don't tell him about my little red-headed cousin. Please." Tears started to sneak out of the corner of my eye again as I pleaded.

"Well, honey, it's nothing to be ashamed of. Skeeter has seen my sanitary napkins and everything. Why, he's the preacher. He knows all about these things."

"Why do we have to tell him?" I asked, panicking. But even as I asked, I knew there was nothing I could do. Preacher Skeeter was gong to find out that I had been cursed.

"Well, Gina, I am not on my monthly and neither is Debbie. We don't have any supplies here. We could ask around, but chances are, no one has an extra sanitary belt. I guess we could safety pin a pad in your panties for right now. But the fact of the matter is, you are going to be here for five more days. You are going to need supplies. Preacher Skeeter is going to have to walk to the general store up on the big road and buy you some Kotex and a napkin holder."

This was more bad tidings than I could bear. I fainted.

When I woke up, I don't know if it had been two minutes or two hours, but I was lying on the double bed in Sister Gladys's cabin. I didn't fully remember what had happened yet, but I heard Preacher's voice. He was whispering, "Now, Gladys, why can't she just put toilet paper in her panties?"

"Honey, this is her first period. She needs to know what to do and be properly educated about women's things. Besides, she could bleed through the toilet paper and it would get on her clothes. These children's parents just send them here with one week's worth of clothes."

"Well, doesn't anybody have some extra Kotex around here?" Preacher

Skeeter's belly trembled beneath his softball jersey as he threw his arms up in exasperation.

"Debbie is out asking," Sister Gladys replied. "But if you don't think it's your time of month, you don't bring such things to camp. You know how the boys always go through the girls' things and leave brassieres and other embarrassing items hanging around on Friday night right before camp breaks up. These girls don't want to be victims of their pranks. And some of these girls are just like Gina. They don't need these things yet."

Preacher Skeeter was stretching his imagination to find an excuse not to walk up the road five miles in the blistering temperatures of late August to buy feminine hygiene products and then carry them five miles back down the road. "Who would do the preaching, Gladys?" His sweat plummeted toward the floor in big globs, as he prayed the Lord would let this cup pass from him.

"We can rearrange the schedule and give the kids more time at the swimming pool and playing horseshoes and have a late night preaching," Sister Gladys said.

Preacher Skeeter realized he wasn't gonna outsmart Sister Gladys. But you could still see the consternation on his face as he struggled to think of an argument that might get him out of this fix. "Well, Gladys, what did women do in the Garden of Eden? I mean, Adam didn't run out to the general store and get Eve a box of Kotex."

I sat up a little. I wanted to see what Sister Gladys would do with that one. Her eyes narrowed and she looked at Preacher with disgust. "We are not going to take bark and leaves and stuff it in Gina's panties. You know their parents always send them to camp with their good underwear in case those boys hang them out in public." Her hands were on her hips now and she turned her back to Preacher Skeeter. When she did, she was surprised to find me awake, staring at her and her husband.

"Oh, honey, we didn't know you were awake." She turned back to the preacher. "Did we, Skeeter?"

"No," said the preacher. He plastered a smile on his face so wide that the silver fittings of his bridge work were visible. Preacher Skeeter rallied amidst the adversity, "But I don't want you to worry, my young sister in the Lord. Consider the lilies of the field. They toil not, neither do they spin and yet Solomon in all his glory . . ."

Sister Gladys interrupted. "What he means Gina is that he is going to go into town and get you a Kotex."

As his smile melted like butter in frying pan, Preacher Skeeter wagged his head back and forth and said in an unenthusiastic and resigned tone, "The

Lord will provide."

Knowing the preacher not only knew I was menstruating, but that he was not happy about my condition and was being called upon to do something he wouldn't ordinarily do any more than he would smoke a doobie during holy communion gave me a charge of painful emotion.

"I just want to go swimming," I said. The faucets were back on and I started to sob. "I want my mama."

Sister Gladys rushed over and put her arms around me. "Now, now, child. This isn't the end of the world."

But I wished it was. After getting saved last night, I was fully prepared for the world to come to its fire-and-brimstone conclusion. But I was not prepared for womanhood. I moaned, "I'm not gonna get to go swimming all week."

Suddenly, Sister Gladys dropped me back on the bed like I was a burning brick. She smiled angelically. Sister Gladys had just experienced an epiphany. "The Lord is surely merciful," she said with unveiled excitement.

"What, Gladys?" asked the preacher, watching his wife flit across the room like an erratic, obese moth.

"Skeeter," She was brimming with pride now. "I brought a box of Tampax." She rushed over to her suitcase and started pawing through the side pockets. "You know, I took them to the Jekyll Island last year so I could go swimming if I started my monthly. I never did start and I just never took them out of my bag." She snatched the box out of the luggage and displayed it to us like she'd found the Holy Grail.

Preacher Skeeter put his hands over his eyes as though the deacon had opened a *Playboy* on the altar during scripture reading. "Don't go waving those things around like a flag on the Fourth of July, Gladys. Lord have mercy."

He ran over to the small kitchen and ran water from the sink into a glass. He turned it up and gulped it, water splashing down the sides of his face.

Sister Gladys winked at me, but then her face turned sour. "Oh, no. Wait a minute."

"What? What's wrong, sugarplum?" said the preacher, wiping his mouth on his jersey.

I was looking back and forth between them like they were battling each other at Wimbledon and thinking, "Plum? How about sugar dumpling?"

"Well," Sister Gladys started, and looked a bit uncertain if she should have this conversation in front of me.

The preacher tapped his foot on the wood floor impatiently. "Gladys, say what you got to say. I mean, I don't see how it could get any worse."

Famous last words indeed.

"Skeeter," Sister Gladys paused and then blurted out loudly, "It's her hymen."

"Her hymen?" he repeated.

High men? What's high men I thought? Wasn't it bad enough that one man was involved? Being a women was getting entirely too complicated.

"If we put a tampon inside her, we are going to have to bust her hymen."

"I'm not sure I see the problem," said the preacher.

Sister Gladys threw her ample butt right onto the edge of the bed and the mattress sunk several inches causing her to become off balance and nearly fall onto the floor. When she regained her balance, she said, "Skeeter, for a man of the cloth, you sure do act stupid sometimes."

Advantage out. Not graceful, but still, the point to the preacher's wife.

The preacher looked at his wife and said with obvious irritation, "Well, what would you have me do?"

"Her husband is not going to believe she is a virgin," explained Gladys. "He might ask for an annulment and deny her the opportunity to be a mother." Sister Gladys was getting all worked up. "And all because she started her period at Bible camp and didn't have any Kotex!"

I wasn't sure exactly of everything she was talking about, but it did seem to possess all the elements of a Greek tragedy. I started to cry again, but this time, just an exhausted snivel.

Preacher Skeeter scratched his head. He went and sat on the church pew. Sister Gladys sat perilously close to the edge of the bed with a frown on her face and a box of tampons grasped limply in her right hand.

After a minute, Preacher Skeeter stood up and looked as happy as if he only had to go through the regular three verses of "Just As I Am" before souls began to come to the front of the auditorium for salvation. "I got it. I got it. Hot diggety dawg."

Sister Gladys and I both said, "What?" in stereo.

"A letter," Preacher Skeeter announced.

"A letter?" inquired the Sister, rocking her ample self on the edge of the bed in an effort to generate the momentum to actually stand up.

"Yes sirree, Sweet Jesus. Just like the apostle Paul wrote not only to the people of his day and time, but he also wrote instruction to Christians in the future. I am going to write Gina's husband a letter that says what happened to her hymen."

Sister Gladys looked a little skeptical, but after several seconds of reflection, she seemed to warm up to the idea. "Well, you know, Skeeter, that might just work. I mean, if a girl has a letter from a Bible-educated evangelist that says her hymen was destroyed at a Bible camp under extenuating circumstances and that, of course, there was no sin involved, I believe a Christian man would accept that as a sign from God that all is well and that Gina is worthy of being the mother of his children."

Preacher Skeeter nodded with pride. "It would certainly be good enough for me, Gladys."

"Well, all right then," Sister Gladys said with enough gusto that it seemed to fuel her finally standing up and facing me. "Gina, let me teach you how to use a tampon. You can go swimming, Gina, if you have a tampon."

"Really, Sister?" I asked with disbelief.

"Yes, Gina. Swimming. And," she added with a glance toward the preacher, "baptized down at the river with all the other new believers on Saturday morning before the buses come back."

Preacher Skeeter was inspired. "Praise Jesus. All things work together for good to them that love the Lord."

God had wiped away my tears. I was saved. I was going to go swimming four times a day and all was right with the world. God truly loved me.

Of course, these were the feelings I had before Sister Gladys took me in the bathroom and spent the next hour trying to instruct a thirteen-year-old girl who knew nothing about love, sex or human pelvic anatomy, the proper mechanics of tampon insertion. Seems that even in a perfect world, there's always a string attached.

Eve's Curse

Louise Robertson

Eve's curse is the curse of knowledge.
When Eve's curse arrived, I was
nearly ten years old. There were
two black girls in my class: Amanda and Norma Jean.
I was friends with Amanda. My mom came to help
at the grade school fair. At one point,
when it must have started
already, I said to my mom I had to go
to the bathroom. I knew
the curse was coming. I said, "Norma Jean
can take the money." My mom said, "You
don't let one of them have the till."
The bleached yellow-green grass rose up
with the hill to the bathroom. I had known
it was coming all along. The spot
of red on my pants—that blood would
stain and coat and spread and rain
from a place—it was there when I was born, a thumb-
sized womb. Later, when the African-American
job candidate is not discussed, later when three
white men talk about the "angry black woman"
and how to "slap her around," I am
the deaf person asking,
"What did you say?" And the sun
shines on all the white children
playing while my new knowledge
seems to be something already forgotten
by those young voices
evaporating in the afternoon.
Eve's curse is the curse
of knowledge. And you can't leave it

there with the yellow-green grass
and the cool tiles in the bathroom
and the warm red spot on your
cotton underpants.

Menarche and the Maplewood Fire

Markie Babbott

The locker room stall becomes a chipped paint confessional.
Cold oval seat, a sorry latch hooks the door ajar.
Coin-etched graffiti: *Boys Suck.*
Shorts rumple around my ankles like elephant skin,
there is a maroon stain in the shape of Lake Erie.
Girls laugh at the trough of sinks.
A toilet flushes. Someone is showering with Prell.
I feel like a horse pawing sawdust across pine planks.

I awake to a foggy, sharp odor; my father sits
at the end of the bed, says he has some terrible news.
Maplewood Stable burnt to the ground in the night,
the horses are dead—
acrid air stings my eyes, and I am sleepy too—
torqued panic of horses untethered in hay filled stalls,
latched in, snorting smoke, stomping, screaming,
their people screaming, stampeding to air then reversing,
trampling the foal. Sooted frothing mouths,
maroon striped flames, firemen stern and wet.
Thirty empty horse vans litter the slope.

Think of the field mice, swallows and barn cat, Moses.
Think of my friends sneaking Marlboros in the hayloft.

Learning to be Girly: A Period Piece

Ashley Wrye

"You have *got* to go in there and tell him," my mom said.

"I'd rather die," I replied with the melodrama of a teenager.

This debate lasted five minutes and ended with my mother getting her way. I had to tell my brother that I'd had my first period. She won the argument by pointing out that we shared a bathroom and she didn't want him to see blood on the toilet seat and think his bowel movements were the cause. My brother's record-setting sit downs usually demanded the attention of whoever was closest. We were expected to come in and see the fruits of his labor; oohing and aahing like we'd just witnessed the next coming of the Christ child. Mom knew that if my temporary embarrassment could spare her a few minutes of bathroom alarm and feigned admiration, it would be well worth it.

I wasn't exactly the most educated in the workings of a woman's body. Before my mom inundated me with Judy Blume books, I thought that a menstrual cycle was the porcelain figurine of a clown in blackface riding a bike that sat on my great grandmother's coffee table. It was pretty common that my incessant reading had caused that kind of confusion. In fact, it wasn't until I asked my mom what "whores de vores" were that I realized that "hors d'oeuvres" was actually a French word.

My mother was never too shy or proper to talk about feminine wiles, but I was embarrassed at being a girl. As the only girl surrounded by a brother and male cousins, I had no problems teasing them about wet dreams and inopportune erections. Bleeding from my vagina, however, was a totally different scenario.

I have spent the majority of my life afraid of being "too girly." In fact, there were certain things that made me feel too feminine with no rational thought behind them. Earrings are near the top of the list. To this day, I can stroll around in high heels, skirts and complicated looking lingerie, but putting earrings on makes me feel like a fraud. There's no real reason that I associate earrings with overt femininity. Men wear earrings all the time and often their earrings are bigger, nicer and more garish than anything I own. But whatever the reason, I don't wear them now. When I was growing up, I used to wear earrings all the time. I would hide them in my pocket and wait for my parents to drop me off at school before running to the bathroom to put them on. I wasn't forbidden to wear earrings, but I didn't want my parents to see me being girly.

Being girly around my friends, however, was an entirely different case. While I wasn't quite ready to declare myself at home, at school I was doing all the things that girls do. Putting on makeup for the fun of it, showing off our new bras; everything we did related somehow or another to our sex. Of course, in a few years, we'd be cursing these same things: makeup, bras and the like. We were always ready to move on to the next phase of puberty. From panty liners to maxi pads to full-blown tampons; our feminine hygiene products were like badges of our progress.

Now the only progress I was thinking about were the steps to my brother's room. He was stretched out across his beds. We'd slept in the same room until the summer he sprouted to over six feet tall. Mom put his beds together and bought king-sized sheets so that he could lie across them diagonally.

"Matt, I have to tell you something. Well, I don't *have* to tell you something, but mom's making me," I said.

"If it's about me taking you to school next year, I already know. She told me I'd be driving your ass. Don't even think your little friends are getting a ride too," he said.

"No, that's not it. Um, well, I, uh, got my period this morning."

"Oh. So, *why* did mom think I needed to know this?"

"In case you had any, you know, questions or problems."

"Nope. I know all I need to know about that."

"Did Mrs. Wilson teach you too?" I asked.

"No, Mr. Ungentheim," he said. "Mrs. Wilson wouldn't know a testicle from a volleyball."

We had both been through the embarrassment of an abbreviated sex education course. Our middle school didn't have an extensive class. In fact, the majority of it consisted of a video sponsored by some tampon company. Our PE teachers were the unlucky ones who did triple duty. From dodge ball to the circulatory system to the hymen, they were the ones who had to continually prove their usefulness to the school board. For my class, it was Mrs. Wilson, a gruff but sensitive coach who wore track pants no matter what the occasion. The most memorable thing about the class was the pounding of two protruding fingers and subsequent rings against the chalkboard drawing of the female anatomy. The pounding punctuated her words: "The fallopian tubes are about as big as your pinkies."

It was sitting in the stuffy classroom with no windows behind the gym when I started to realize that being a girl wasn't really all I thought it was going be. A week later, it dawned on me that I was right. My insides felt like they were knotting themselves and everything, my front, my back and my middle, was being controlled by one giant string that someone else was pulling on. I made my mom pick me up from school instead of walking the mile home. Your first bout of cramps gets you sympathy. Your second bout of cramps gets you a heating pad and a sigh.

It was during the car ride home that mom told me I had to tell my brother. Then I had to tell my dad. I thought he'd take it like I'd seen most TV dads take it: a tearful look, a big hug, and some muttering about being a woman. However, my dad also doubled as my softball coach, so he was more concerned about how the mood swings might affect how I'd take it when he gave me the bunt sign in the seventh inning.

"We should come up with some kind of signal or code for when you're on your period," he said. "Just so I know when I need to watch what I say to you."

"How about we forget the code and you just always watch what you say to me?" I said.

"Well, if you watch a third strike, I can't be held accountable for anything, so let's just stick to the code," he said. "What about 'Code Blue'? When you get upset with me and it's that time of the month, just say 'Code Blue' and I'll know to shut up and leave you alone."

"Wouldn't Code Red be more appropriate?" I said.

"Yes, but that would be too obvious," he said.

Lucky for me, my dad didn't really keep track of my monthly cycle. This allowed me to claim "Code Blue" many more times than was physically possible.

All of this made me learn that my period would make me a raving bitch to my dad, in cramping pain and very girly. Plus there was the constant fear of staining that would end up as a funny anecdote and my obituary in the "So Embarrassed You Died" pages of a teen magazine. From clowns to codes to cramps, the beginning of my menstrual cycle made being "girly" a permanent period of my life.

Variation 7: Girl

Alice B. Fogel

I never told you because you'd make this big fuss
and do some fucking ritualistic
hang-your-panties-from-the-weeping-
cherry-tree-in-the-yard sort of thing—/—oh,
you never told me it would be like something hot liquifying
my thighs, like a hot seabed. It drags its craggy stones
down my back. / In fact no one ever mentioned this: /
intrusion from within. /—Just because your mother wouldn't
talk about it and *her* mother slapped her face
and who knows what all the mothers did before that,
cover them with earth and wine, chant hymns to the goddess.
If I ever have a daughter here's all I'm going to do:
say, That's nice honey, or You go girl, or whatever
is hip when *she's* fourteen and let her pierce anything she wants.
/ Or the stain like a tattoed rose on my clothes.
Can I please stay home?

/ I'm fine. / Well maybe unsteady on my feet
as if just coming to shore. Rocking, rocking. Mutiny.
Strange lands. I spiral that island, spinning, aswim.
/ Yeah I know I can get pregnant now, but I'm not
planning to just yet. Don't worry, Mom,
I think I can give you till my junior year at least.
Why do you need to know *that?*—I threw them away.
No, I gave them to my boyfriend, I'm making a pillow.
What do you care? Maybe I burned them—with incense
and smudge sticks and a ring of girls. /
You can put your hand over my forehead /
but stop talking. I already know what to do. /
Cross the moat to the haunted house, that ancient castle
of rooms inside rooms that just opened one more door.

Sure / whatever / we ll plant flowers where I buried
the panties. / Fucking *flowers,* Mom. / *Maybe they'll even grow.*

What Hattie Told Me

Lynn Fetterolf

Riding down the road,
she nearly ninety, me several decades younger,
reminiscing as women will, we discussed
the onset of becoming women:
that huge event separating
girl from grown-up.

She told of finding blood when visiting
the outhouse at her one-room school
and, fearing she was dying,
ran home before succumbing
to whatever illness had befallen her.

She couldn't tell her mother.
No, mother needed her
to help with housework and babies.
Yet she feared dying enough to cry
alone in her room for nights on end
after carefully washing and hiding
the towels she'd used to soak up the flow.

When suddenly the bleeding stopped
she was convinced her ardent prayers
had saved her life.
Later, when eavesdropping
on some older girls at school,
she learned the truth.
Her heart was broken that it hadn't
been her virtue or her prayers
that stopped the blood.

La Trenza

Nilda Vélez

Girls don't matter. At least, at twelve they don't. My waist-length brown hair gathered in a braid, my one dimple and my high-pitched laugh made me *tan chula* when I was younger, but paired with the new lumps growing on my chest and the sudden roundness of my hips, they were just physical reminders that I was in between. I didn't want to hold my grandmother's hand anymore, but I nuzzled in her breast to hide my tears and feel her hand stroke the back of my head. She tried to embrace me before I left for school, but I danced toward the door so Sharron wouldn't see me act like a fifth grader.

"We're gonna be late," she said, watching me look at myself in the mirrored wall of our microscopic two-bedroom apartment. I had to make sure I was looking my best for the first day of middle school, or at least that I was well scrutinized.

"One more second," I said, putting the topaz necklace I saved for special occasions around my neck.

"That's beautiful. You bought it at Gimbel's?"

"No, it's my mom's." I stared at my entire reflection and wondered if she hated her skinny legs too.

Middle school was a different universe than elementary school. The eighth graders were enormous, the change of periods were social warfare in the hallways and making new friends was like staying awake during double math periods. At least at the beginning of sixth grade, Sharron and I were allies, but even she couldn't save me from the grief I face inside MS 199.

Each school year was broken up by holidays and by the time Columbus Day rolled around, Sharron and I had managed befriending two others: Gracie, a sweet and pudgy girl, newly arrived from Puerto Rico and Ana, Sharron's neighbor from three buildings over.

Before Halloween, we had fingered the enemies: the girls who squealed when something presumably funny happened and darted their eyes when boys, specifically those deemed 'cute,' entered the room, and the ones who looked my way and made me feel disposable. Knowing your enemy was key in sixth grade because all a weakling could do was avoid them. Overcoming them by joining forces with other mature and enlightened students and confronting them directly in a sophisticated, well-articulated manner like they do in films never happened, at least not in Harlem or in MS 199.

By Thanksgiving, the four of us were actual friends with delicious secrets about Mrs. Stapleton's flirtations with our female gym teacher and the never acted upon, but heavily discussed crushes on two boys in our class. School was tolerable, made better by lunchtime chats, made worse by the scrutiny of other girls, the outsiders we called them, and their judgmental gaze.

Jessica Alvarez shot these looks at the four of us what felt like every day during lunch. Mr. Bill, the lunch aide, began each lunch period by demanding that each class sit together at one, assigned table, but that almost never happened. Ana made her way over to us and so did Jessica. She sat at the opposite end with her own friends; the kind of girls who were so prematurely alluring, even girls eyed them sexually.

One December afternoon, I sat eating the hot school lunch, telling Gracie about a dress my grandmother was sewing for me out of creamy purple fabric. Jessica glided by and tugged my single braid just hard enough to make my head jerk up and look at the cracked ceiling. We sat silent, trying to pretend that nothing had happened, but Ana, ignorant to the decorum of ignoring bullies, spoke.

"I hate her."

"Me too," Sharron agreed after a moment. "It's like she's bored."

"Forget it." I meant it. Being the youngest of five siblings, I knew a braid pull was nothing in the grand scheme of getting your head smashed in and I was more than willing to forget it completely.

"Why can't she sit at her own table?" Ana's disdain was pure, but unresearched. I knew just talking about it would somehow align the planets so that she would come over and do it again. I had to avoid that at all costs, not because I greatly feared her, but because my friends respected me and I had to maintain that.

"It doesn't matter—"

"Yes, it does," Ana said. "She thinks she can say whatever she wants and I hear her talking about *everyone*. In the bathroom, she was saying how fat Maria looks in corduroys and they're supposed to be friends. What a phony."

Before I could even begin begging Ana to keep her voice down, Jessica came sauntering over, her hemmed skirt swishing, directing her enormous gray eyes at Ana.

"If you babies have a problem with me, you should get up and tell me," she bellowed, mostly at Ana, looking over her neatly trimmed bangs. "Or at least not be dumb enough to talk about it so loudly that the whole table can hear you."

We sat there silently stunned. Even Ana looked down at her string beans.

"It's not my fault your mommy still braids your hair and you wear hand-me-down sneakers." Her voice morphed into a high-pitch mimic of baby talk. "I'm sure next year, when you grow up and get your periods, your mommies will let you pick out your own clothes—"

"I already have my period," Ana announced and girls who were at least our acquaintances burst into laughter. I just stared right through her.

"Well, excuse me." And with a few more biting comments, Jessica turned, letting her loose hair make a swirl, and went back to her side of the planet.

By Easter, Gracie had her period too. When we first found out Ana had gotten it, I resented her. Not for keeping it a secret, but just for having it. She was different from me, more mature and mature enough to not even want to talk about it. Gracie and Sharron, though, wanted every detail. It seemed like for the next month all our lunchtime chats were about how she smelled, how much they cost, how to put them on, tampon directions, what to wear, pains, getting out of gym and boys. I was so jealous I had made two scenes at the table declaring in the most dramatic fashion that the topic was boring and already discussed ad nauseam. But by the time Gracie got her period, I was hooked in too.

"Oh, my God! Why didn't you call me?" Ana was the designated point person for all matters menstrual.

"I don't know. My mom didn't really say anything about it. She just brought home the napkins and put the brown paper bag on my bed," Gracie replied.

"How do you feel?" There was genuine concern in Sharron's voice. She waited for the answer by making her bushy eyebrows into one row that plummeted above her nose.

"Like a freak show. Everyone knows." Gracie leaned toward us. Her voice was an exaggerated whisper. "I know they know."

Her paranoia made us nervous.

"And my mom said I can't wash my hair until it's done," she added.

"What?" Sharron and I exclaimed in unison.

By the end of the school year, Sharron got her period too and I was the only one left in lil'girlville. The three of them were part of this exclusive association of women who met daily, not just to talk about periods, but about worldly things like who would get a locker next to George Rivera in seventh grade and if kissing could get you pregnant. They mattered.

When it was time for me and Grandma to pack for our yearly summer vacation in July, I was resigned to the fact that I would probably be left back in sixth grade because I hadn't started my period. In apartment twenty-one, my older brother and sisters would have a summer filled with new jobs, first kisses and trade school applications. I was being carted off to Florida. I'd pretend to listen to Titi Paola tell me the same stories about Mayagüez and argue with Carmen about who will go first in Monopoly. I'd sit on stiff couches in strangers' homes, pretending to be interested in adult talk, but actually longing to lay Ken on top of Barbie. Fingering the links of my mother's topaz necklace and looking out onto West 135th Street, I imagined what fantastic stories I would make up to write on scenic Orlando postcards since I knew nothing even remotely fantastic would happen, period.

I was wrong. On the third morning of waking up next to Carmen in her twin bed with the stupid Wonder Woman sheets, I felt a pain in my abdomen that was foreign to me. I prayed to God that this would be it. I scurried to the bathroom, slamming the door closed with my bare foot. I peered into my underpants and was so delighted, I literally yelped. I woke my grandmother up to tell her the exciting news.

She yawned and spoke in the same breath. "Ah, well, now you can't hold Carla's baby when we visit them next week."

"What?" I was stunned by this seemingly unrelated response to my explosive news.

My grandmother grunted in her usual, dismissive way. "Aye, Lenita, you know you can't hold a baby when you're having your time."

"Oh." I had no idea what on earth she was talking about.

I grabbed my most mature looking outfit from my suitcase, a matching linen summer set with a print of small yellow flowers from Korvette's, and went to shower. I was careful not to wet my hair and scrubbed hard between my legs to assure that no smell would waft from there later. I dressed in a hurry, but remembered to use deodorant and splash Jean Naté behind both ears, both knees, and rub it between my wrists.

"Lenita, became a señorita today," my grandmother announced to Carmen and Titi Paola before coffee had even been poured.

Carmen squinted to understand and I pursed my lips out of embarrassment and annoyance.

"Lenita, that's wonderful! ¿Ahora es una mujer, no?" I was suspicious of my aunt's enthusiasm simply because it was coming from an adult. I just nodded.

"I suppose now we should stop calling you Lenita. Elena is such a beautiful name anyway," she said.

With my official name change declared, I plopped down at the table and helped myself to the cooling toast and farina. I was acutely aware of the mattress in my underwear and shifted my body in the orange vinyl chair to get comfortable. The dampness from my shower and the omnipresent Orlando dampness, made my thighs stick and peel to the kitchen chair.

"We'll go get you your own things after breakfast," Titi Paola said to me in a stage whisper.

"Why are you telling secrets," Carmen whined into her bowl, her pigtails covering her round cheeks.

"Oh, Carmencita, they're not secrets. Stop being so *entrometida*," her mother replied with all the dismissiveness older Latinas use when addressing nosy, younger ones.

After we ate, I was ordered to do the dishes. As soon as I stood, I felt a rush of liquid moisten the pad between my legs. I stood at the table with a dirty bowl in hand and an open mouth. The odd sensation grew up to my abdomen and the familiar ache from earlier that morning returned. I wanted to whine and complain about how womanhood was preventing me from washing dishes, but that seemed like something Carmen would do. I gritted my teeth and washed the plates, spoons, knives and glasses without speaking a single word, while everyone else prepared for our morning outing.

In the aisles of a drugstore, my grandmother weaved a cart from side to side, looking at colorful products she didn't need, but enjoyed talking about. Instead of my usual song and dance for candy and comics, I was hovering around the health and beauty aisle, mad at my mother for dying two years ago; for not doing this for me. I resented her for leaving me to buy sanitary napkins alone on a Saturday morning in a crowded Woolworth's in an alien city.

"Where do they keep the pantyhose?" my grandmother asked no one.

She was an exceptionally beautiful boricua, with long silver hair she collected in a thick hairnet held securely by a ribbon. She was wholly from an era more divine than anything I would ever know. Her complexion enhanced by light powder, her painstakingly pleated skirts, and discreet scent of talcum powder spoke to a ladylike perfection that seemed impossible to attain. She loved me with such tenderness and totality that I knew being her was being right. At twelve, though, I fell short everyday.

I sidestepped in the aisle and darted my eyes about the shelves as if I was planning to steal something and fly out of the door.

When it came to talk of emotional, private or embarrassing matters, my grandmother morphed into a distant star; still beautiful, but so far from the reach of my hand, it tiptoed around reality. I loved her so precisely, minding my manners, making decisions with her approval in the forefront of all my actions, that it was frustrating to simultaneously be so disconnected. I could not tell her I wanted to buy tampons. The words literally would not form on my lips. I could not tell her that having my period, carrying tampons in a denim purse to school in September, and applying lip gloss at my locker in front of George Rivera would instantly erase all of my shortcomings and make me unequivocally happy. She wouldn't understand how simple it was and I began to cry.

"We're standing on line," Carmen announced from the top of the aisle.

Moved by sheer panic, I took the package of tampons and held them between my arm and my hip, with the label facing inward. My aunt and grandmother were second in line and without a moment's hesitation, I dropped the package into the cart and made for the door. Leaning against the glass partition, I wiped my tears and suddenly felt proud of my brazen act, but waited for my grandmother to come pounding through the doors, with disgust dancing in her eyes. But it never happened. With three bags of purchased items, the two and a half women walked past me to the car. I sat behind Titi Paola and felt the squish of the sanitary napkin when I reached for the seatbelt. I held my breath waiting for someone to say something, anything, about me, about tampons, about death, about growth, but it never happened.

After *tostones* and leftover chicken, I went to the bathroom to read the back of the box. It hadn't occurred to me that I wouldn't know how to use a tampon and was relieved that Ana had explained that an instruction booklet was inside each box. But to my amazement, it wasn't behind the tile cleaner under the sink. I had hidden them there while everyone's attention focused on Carmen's dirty church shoes. I knew my grandmother had taken them and now I would have to articulate a case as to why I should use them.

"Where are the things?" I couldn't look directly into her eyes for fear of passing out.

"What things?" Perhaps my grandmother, even with all her tenderness, knew exactly how to torture me.

"That I bought. For my thing." I flipped the hairs at the end of my braid around my thumb and forefinger, staring at the cream tiled floor.

"Oh." She folded her newspaper and reached for her mug. She took two sips. "Use what Paola has. Those things aren't for you."

The blasted tears balanced at the corners of my eyes. "Abuela . . ." My voice was so small and the tears rolled down my face out of anger that menstruation hadn't made me stronger, more mature. It didn't move me.

"Lenita, those things are not for pure girls. You know that." And that was that. Any more pleading wouldn't have mattered.

The summer closed with me writing brief postcards with unimportant details of Floridian weather and trips to the beach. Packing my one-piece bathing suit, I hoped my tan was enough to morph me into Jessica Alvarez in September, but I knew no one would notice a change. There was no change from the tan. From the little hairs plucked from above my eyes. From my period. I felt the same.

At the end of August, I was waiting at the luggage carousel in La Guardia, *una mujer*, and getting my hair rebraided by my grandmother. I had fallen asleep on the plane and it had come undone. I let her fix it, restoring the neat braid with the white ribbon on the end.

"Your mother wore her braid just like this, but she would make such a fuss." She brushed the stray hairs away from my face with the palms of both hands. "There you are, Elena."

Tomorrow

Rebecca Lauren

When the school nurse told us the boys had to leave

we thought, Great, finally someone's told
about the bra snapping, the way they always take
the best football and won't let us play
or how every day Cody Ludwig calls Andrea *fat* or *porky*
on the playground and gets away with it

We were wrong
This was no day to celebrate our girlhood
Instead, from a video, Orphan Annie taught us menstruation
She was older now, tiny breasts poking through a neatly-pressed
blouse I missed her rags, the movie house dress,
those patent leather shoes She leaned into the camera
confiding, *I know how hard it is to grow up*
We grew scared

Annie winked at us as if we were girls
at the orphanage, hiding her dog in the laundry cart
It didn't matter that we weren't from New York
and our parents hadn't given us lockets in case of fire;
we shared something with Annie We learned
to bleed when we wanted to swim, to carry purses
filled with lipstick, Midol, and pads, to cry
in the bathroom She was there for us

Meanwhile the boys sat with Mr Lawrence
in the cafeteria They explored wet dreams
and diagrams and how they shouldn't be ashamed
of what spewed forth It was natural It meant
they were becoming men and they knew

where sex came from Boys exploded
Girls controlled with cotton

Years later, I couldn't find the clitoris

on the anatomy chart we breezed through
in health class It was all the same down there
Only penile penetration mattered—in losing
your virginity, in pregnancy, in marriage, in rape
My teacher called the rest "masturbation"
or "foreplay"—how you kept from having sex
I didn't know women had orgasms or wet dreams
I was sixteen when I had my first roller coaster moment,
pulsing before an AP exam with a pillow
between my legs—good clean cotton, like Annie said

And if I had to go back
to that fourth grade classroom where Annie bleeds
on camera with her frizzy hair—*Look what happens
when all that red gets out of control*—I'd straddle
Daddy Warbucks' knee and tell him how I bleed, even now,
how I am more than a motherless vagina, how I want to reach the top
of the Chrysler building so it shines, sparkles, explodes
like a geyser between my legs Then I'd leave the mansions
of men for the sky I would save little girls

I would tell the president how to make me smile

The Road to Womanhood

Amanda McQuade

There is nothing
like the feeling of blood
trickling down
your leg when you 're ten
and you think
that you 've just been stabbed,
then you remember
your mother, how she explained
with that medical book
that should only be used to kill giant bugs,
how nature was going to pay
you a visit. That 's how she said it too.
Nature was coming with a suitcase
full of blood, and at that moment
I hated nature for the sticky
way the blood was clotting
in my panties like congealed fat
from a Thanksgiving turkey.
Maybe that 's what this is all about
really, Thanksgiving.
Mother is dancing and thanking
God in my ovaries.
Maybe that is the cramping—
her feet pounding my uterus.

Urged

Stella Brice

The stable is unspeakably narrow. There is a smell to it: huge penises &
piss & mare juice & oiled leather. I am twelve & not yet bleeding but
this
smell will coax the reluctant menstrual out of me, eventually.

Here is an ordered sense of manualized flesh. Walk, trot, canter. Saddle.
Stable. To be stabled. I can name the hundred parts of the horse. When
we wash
them down after our riding lesson, we push at their massive shoulders.
MOVE!
we roar & they obey us skinny girls! They obey us! I am mistress of all
this

Beautiful tangy muscle. This ripple, this sensitivity, this weight is mine
to command. In my Jackie clothes, I look good on top of it with my
whip. On
top of my rich animal. Power. Power. Power.

Strapped in & led & urged.

Seeing Red

Kathleen Gerard

When her bra flew across the room and snagged atop the rabbit ears, the sound on the nine-inch, black-and-white television turned instantly to static. Snow filled the screen. I looked from the bra, hanging like a tattered flag at half mast, toward the culprit—my oldest sister, Maureen. She was standing on the other side of our bedroom, topless. Her elbows smothered each of her breasts and with her fingertips over her mouth, she stifled her amusement.

"It's not funny," I snapped, peeling my body up from the bed and making a beeline for the TV set. "I fiddled all night to tune in that channel."

"Well, I didn't do it on purpose."

"Yeah, I bet," I said, ripping her over-the-shoulder-boulder-holder down from the antenna and throwing it back across the room. "You just think you're cool, 'cos you've got big *beasts*." I pointed to the seventeen-year-old chest of amply-endowed Maureen.

When I was about five or six, I mistakenly referred to the word *breasts* as *beasts*. It was met with gales of laughter and not soon forgotten—by me or my sisters. The term stuck.

Maureen, along with Patricia—my other sister, fifteen—and I, had all inhabited the space of four walls. The Master Bedroom. My parents had taken the smaller room across the hall to better accommodate the three of us. But now that I was eleven, the room—with its peach-colored walls and matching shag carpet—seemed to be shrinking. With each passing year, our hormones and rebellions raged, making it feel as though the walls were growing narrow, closing in around us like a funnel.

It was Patricia, the middle sister—the pragmatic mathematician of our trio—who'd divided the room into thirds. She'd done her best to compensate for the space limitations. Maureen, *The Queen*, as I'd taken to calling her, was the oldest, so she got her own bed and corner of the room—complete with a bookcase. That left Tricia and me to share a daybed and dresser, but we got first dibs on the TV. Tricia got the top portion of the bed and I, being the youngest, was exiled to the pull-out trundle portion tucked below in daylight. In consolation, Tricia convinced me that I had the best view of the nine-inch, black-and-white. It sat with its rabbit ears perched high atop our dresser. When I was younger, I used to take whatever my older and wiser sisters said as gospel—along with proudly slipping into their hand-me-downs. But now that I was in middle school, I was outgrowing the whole kid sister thing.

Maureen was the one who'd started it that night. She'd been grounded for cavorting past her curfew (again!) with her beau—a bad boy who'd run with a fast crowd and had locked horns with my father on countless occasions. It was becoming a regular habit for Patricia and me to be awakened in the night with shouts like rounds of gunfire ricocheting back and forth between Maureen and my parents. I'd roll over to face Tricia, to see if she was awake. With both of our heads on our pillows and our eyes wide open, we'd stare at each other through the dark amid the orange-glimmer of the night-light and listen to the power struggle being waged downstairs.

Maureen was as relentless in justifying her actions and double-talking my parents as they were in standing their ground. And because my trundle bed was about two inches lower than Tricia's, often, in fear, I'd slip my arm beneath her mattress as if I longed to crawl beneath it—a refuge as close and tight as a womb that might shield me from the fiery, deafening madness beyond the door.

So aside from resenting all the space Maureen was privileged to in the room, I duly resented her chronic rebellions—almost as much as having her around, crowding our four walls that weekend. All day on Saturday, she sighed and moaned in true drama-queen fashion, filling the room with the potent aroma of nail polish and exotic facial masks that made her look exactly like the monster I painted her to be. I swore that the eleventh commandment for her was never stay home on a Saturday night—and I hated the fact that my parents actually forced her to break it. That's why by nine o'clock that evening, her cabin fever had become contagious. It wildly infected me.

On the night that Maureen's bra went flying across the invisible room divide—past the heap of her dirty clothes that perpetually expanded upon the floor—Tricia and I had been engrossed in *Mary Tyler Moore* on the black-and-white TV. When I couldn't tune the show back in, the brat in me reared its ugly head, relentless.

"And why don't you put on a new pair of *undies*," I barked at Maureen, glaring at her bare back and bikini briefs as she reached for her nightgown. "You look like a pauper. The elastic on those is all ripped."

"No they're not, dummy. It's a sanitary belt." She gave the white elastic band that hugged her waist above her bikini-cut panties a big twang.

I crinkled my eyes. "A what?"

"Yessiree. Someday you'll have a pair of *beasts* just like these and elastic of your very own." She gestured to her chest and the belt before she channeled her head through her nightgown.

"Oh no, I won't," I protested, the fine hair on the back of my neck rising. The very idea of what Maureen proposed was horrifying to me. *How would I play softball and basketball if I had to lug those big things around?* "I won't be like you—ever!"

"Oh, yes, you will." She was gloating, a self-righteous hand on her hip. "You just wait."

I turned to Tricia, the quiet, unassuming and grounding force in my life. I gave her a look that pleaded, *Please tell me she's not serious?*

But all Tricia did was gaze back at me, staid and unemotional. "You better go have a talk with Mom."

"What kind of talk?"

"She'll know."

"Yuck!" I blurted to my mother after she explained things to me. I felt sick. "Why is it called a period anyway?"

"Because it *is* a period. It's a period of time at the end of a monthly cycle. It lasts for a few days then it returns again the next month. It's one thing you'll be able to count on coming back—again and again—for most of your life."

"It's a curse. That's what it is."

"No, it's not a curse. Not at all." My mother, a proverbial teacher, inhaled a deep, exacerbated breath. She smoothed a manicured hand atop the grooves of her soft, chenille bedspread. "It's a beautiful reminder from God each month—a sign that one day, when you meet a wonderful man and get married, you can make a baby and give life to the world."

I listened to my mother's romanticized notions, but in truth I didn't hear a word of what she said. Meeting a wonderful man, getting married and having babies was the farthest thing from my mind. I shivered, repulsed by the whole concept of my body blooming with *beasts* of my own and having to deal with a bloody mess each month.

Once I stepped from my mother's room, I prayed for amnesia. I vowed never to think about anything that happened that night—ever again. Humbled by the discoveries, I was grateful to go back to playing sports and wrestling with the rabbit ears. I stopped giving lip to Maureen and no longer complained about how short the sleeves were becoming on my hand-me-downs. I even pulled out my trundle bed each night, prepared to expect the bickering that persisted in the middle of the night.

But the sheer will of my obedience wasn't enough to hold back the tide of all that had been prophesied to me that night.

In the end, *Mary Tyler Moore* tossed up her hat on the streets of Minneapolis for the last time. The rabbit ears broke. I was forced to retire my undershirt and slip into a training bra. And once she turned eighteen, Maureen and her *beasts* moved out. I should have been thrilled that Patricia and I now split the room fifty-fifty and finally slept, uninterrupted, through the night. But instead, when Maureen packed up her things, I was sad to find my three-dimensional world reduced to two. It was as though, in my sister's wake, no amount of tuning and fiddling could bring things into focus. Her departure seemed to strip the color from life.

It wasn't until a few months later, when I'd stepped from the bathtub and felt a hot wetness between my legs and saw red that the memory of that night vividly reemerged. That's when it hit me. All the while when it seemed that those four walls were closing in around the three of us, they were really swelling; oozing with joy and love—even amid the tumult and the angst. Like a diorama on exhibit inside my brain, the vibrancy of that not-so-distant past was suddenly framed, and it filled me with a stunning sense of nostalgia.

Willow "M"

Willow Hambrick

When girls had to wear dresses to school, I remember
buying a plaid dirndl skirt. Rust and olive green wool
squares covered gartered fishnet hose, all accented by
a matching purse just big enough for two Kotex pads,
in case, as Momma said, I were "to start" unawares.

That dirndl skirt gave scant protection during Milwaukee
winters at the bus stop. Warm and unencumbered, boys
in sock hats and boots jumped, punched, and cajoled.
The girls stared in envy, wiggled just their toes, and froze.

Every time I re-centered my weight from one leg
to the next, my purse slipped, my slip slipped,
wool squares scratched through fishnet holes,
and the thin tie under my faux-fur hood caught
my Adam's apple, persuading me to stand still.

I was in Junior High, and looked the part, as the eyeliner
I had learned to apply so carefully in Charm School
had pooled in the sticky corners of my eyes, which were
unmercifully magnified by tortoise shell, cat-eye glasses.

In gym class, I wore a blue cotton jumpsuit that snapped
over the tight, itchy curve of my new Maidenform bra.
The girls stood quietly on a line on one side of the gym.
The boys stood as boys do on the other side.

"Here," the boys yelled to Mr. Krantz as their names
were called. When Miss Jacobs called each name, the girl
would softly answer "M" if she were menstruating. If
she said "M" too furtively, she would have to say "M"

louder, so Miss Jacobs could record the days of her cycle.

I always wondered if the boys, clearly within earshot,
knew the meaning of my red face when, by decree, I sat
with other stoic "Ms" like exiled choristers off to one
side. Did my boyfriend, Martin Moster, ever ask what
Willow "M" was all about, or why she wasn't allowed
to swim or do gymnastics for a portion of each month?

And, if some boy whispered what truth he knew of periods
and pads, what then did Martin think, as he carried my books
from gym class to art, about the mystery beneath my rust
and green skirt, until such time when the roll was called,
and I became just plain Willow again, off the bleachers,
holding deep the blessing, the curse, the gathering rage.

Will the Swimming Pool Turn Red?

Cathy Warner

The permission slips came home yesterday. The girls in fifth grade are going to learn about menstruation today. The boys are going to play medicine ball in the gym. Of course our mothers had to sign the forms so we can see the movie today. I knew my mother would sign the form, but I had to wait for her to get home from work, and she worked late with her boss, Skip, and I was supposed to be asleep, but I slid out of my bunk bed when she got home, pretending that I'd been asleep, and said, "Mom can you sign this?"

She glanced at the paper, said, "Fine. Hand me a pen," and "Goodnight," when she handed it back with her neat cursive *Mrs. Carolyn Preimsberger,* even though she is divorced from my father.

I knew she wouldn't be all excited that I'm going to learn about periods. Not like my best friend Katy's mom, Cora, who came over one Saturday morning about a year ago when I was helping my mother cut back the bougainvillea on our front porch.

"Guess what?" Cora had said while she hurried up the sidewalk and stood at the edge of our porch, a pile of hot pink flowered branches between us. Cora looked up at my mother like a poodle.

"What?" my mother asked, her shears in one hand.

"Katy is a woman now." Cora paused, then looked at me and added under her breath, "She began menstruating this morning. Isn't that wonderful?"

"Oh, the curse," my mother said. "Poor thing, she's only ten. I was ten. I was miserable. How does she feel?"

"Fine, she's fine. I tucked her back in bed with a hot water bottle, ginger ale and a comic book. But I should get back, in case she needs me. I just had to tell you the good news. My baby's a woman!"

Cora glanced over her shoulder in the direction of their house across the street, and said to me, "I don't think Katy'll feel up to playing today."

"Okay," I said.

"Can I take her some flowers?" Cora asked.

"Help yourself," my mother said.

Cora picked up a few small branches of the bougainvillea. "Don't worry," she said to me before she left, "your turn will come."

"Periods," my mother had said once Cora was gone, "are a pain."

That's all she told me, and I learned little more from Katy, who's a year older than me, except that having your period means you can have a baby, although she doesn't know exactly how.

Now, here we are in Miss Coppack's classroom with the curtains closed and the screen pulled down over the chalkboard and boys off in the gym. Mrs. King, the old librarian with boobs that sag to her waist, wheels in a projector on a cart, opens a metal canister, threads the projector, then sneaks out of the room while the film flaps and the numbers count down from ten. Then a grainy film that looks like it's left over from the '50s plays. It's about a girl who wants a certain yellow dress for Easter but can't have it because there are darts in the bodice, and that means, according to her mother, that the girl has to be a woman in order to wear it. The people who made the movie obviously don't sew, and I know that if I were the girl and really wanted the dress that my mother could alter it in a flash, although I'd never buy an Easter dress because we don't go to church and I can't buy anything unless I need it and it coordinates with my wardrobe and is on sale at J.C. Penney where my mother works.

During the film we watch lines and diagrams appear on the screen. There's something like an egg timer with strange ram horn coils, drawn in what would be the belly of an outline of a girl who then grows taller and then wider at the hips and then develops outline breasts and hair, down there, gag, and then there are more diagrams and dotted lines that move through tubes and into holding tanks and out between the outline legs.

But all I hear is blood, which Katy hasn't really talked about, and even though the movie has a happy ending, because like the diagram girl, the movie girl turns into a woman just in time to buy the yellow dress and wear it on Easter Sunday, what I really want to know is—will the swimming pool turn red when we have our periods and P.E.? So, I raise my hand and feel my face turn beet red when Miss Coppack asks if I have a question.

"No," she says. "The swimming pool won't turn red," and then, "Let me demonstrate." She fishes her purse out from under her desk, rummages through it, pulls out a plastic case, opens it, and taps out a white paper cigar. Then she fills the classroom sink with water and says, "Gather 'round," and we do, shuffling reluctantly. I end up closest to the sink because I am shortest and Melissa and Georgeanne are standing behind me, and I feel their breath on the top of my head.

"This is a tampon," Miss Coppack says, and with her fat pink fingers, tears the paper wrapping off. "Now," she says and looks at us as though deciding what to do next. "Cathy," she reaches for my hand, "make a circle with your fingers, like this," and she pushes my fingers into an *O* that I hold above the sink.

"Let's say this is the vagina," she says and she holds the cardboard tube up under my *O*. "You insert the tampon into the vagina like this," she says. She pushes the white cotton missile from its cardboard sleeve up through my fingers and then it plops into the sink.

I stand there, grossed out, watching it expand like a sponge, until she pulls it from the water and holds it high so everyone can see. It looks like a dead lab mouse hanging by the tail and I feel sick to my stomach. She tugs a brown paper towel from the dispenser and wraps the tampon in it. "See? You can swim and no one will know," she says, as though that will reassure us.

She tosses the soggy bundle into the wastebasket, pulls the plug and the water slugs out of the sink while we shuffle back to our desks. There're just a few minutes left until the boys come back for lunch, so Miss Coppack picks up *From the Mixed Up Files of Mrs. Basil E. Frankweiler* and reads from where she left off yesterday.

In the book, which I usually like, some kids are living in the Metropolitan Museum of Art. I think about the girl going into the bathroom, and how now I know what's in those metal machines on the wall, and how it was okay in the movie when they showed a box of pads and belts and how these days because it's 1971, you don't have to wear belts, because the pads can stick in your underwear. That was weird but not too horrible. But the movie didn't talk about tampons or show them, or say anything about putting them inside your vagina, which although it's somewhere in a girl's body, in my body too, I guess, I don't really understand where, and I don't think Miss Coppack should've showed us that.

I'm not the only one who thinks so. When we're outside at lunch recess, Melissa, whose mother works in the school office, says, "Oh God. Can you believe it? That Miss Coppack would actually show us that. She's so weird."

She laughs and I laugh along with her.

"My mother won't let me use tampons," Georgeanne says.

"Oh," I say because that means she's a woman too, like Katy, and I don't know what else to say.

"Wait until next year's movie," says Melissa. "The boys see it too, in a different room, and we learn about S-E-X."

That night, my sister and I sprawl out on the couch watching *Love American Style* waiting for my mother to get home from work. There's this goofy part in the TV show in between the love stories, where couples are in brass beds traveling down the street and the ladies have flannel nightgowns and curlers in their hair and the men are wearing striped pajamas and it makes my sister laugh. My mother has a brass bed and I wonder if it could wheel down the street like on TV. My father never let Lisa and me in their bedroom because his gun was in the sock drawer. But, now that he lives in Long Beach, Lisa and I can go in and jump on the bed. There's a big white puffy curtain over the window that reminds me of a parachute. My mother says it's called an Austrian shade and that my father hated it, saying, "It looks like a funeral parlor in here."

"Sorry I'm late," my mother says when she finally gets home. "Skip and I were cataloguing the new samples. But, I brought you Taco Bell." She drops her bag on the floor by the couch and heads into the bathroom.

"Goody," my sister says and spills the contents of my mother's bag onto the couch between us. We pick out the paper-wrapped burritos from the pile of my mother's things—wallet, tape measure, brush, loose change, lipstick and tampons. I see the tampons, white and scary and gross, just like Miss Coppack's and now I'm not so hungry. I bet there are no pads in our house, and if I ever started my period, I'd have to go over to Katy's house and ask Cora for a pad, and she'd hug me and kiss me and tell the whole neighborhood. I have to say something to my mother.

The bathroom door is open and she's rinsing her pantyhose in the sink. I stand in the doorway.

"Mom," I say, "we saw that movie in school today."

She lifts her head and looks at me through the mirror. From her reflection I see that her mascara is smudged beneath her glasses and her hair is loose from her ponytail holder. "And," she says and holds my gaze for a second.

"They said you should keep some pads in the bathroom," I say.

She doesn't answer.

"Just in case," I add.

"Okay." She squeezes out her hose and nudges the bathroom door closed with her foot to hang the hose on the door rack.

"Thanks," I say and hope that she will buy them soon and that it will be forever before I have to use them.

Novel Excerpt: *Below the Heart*
Staining All the Way Down

Vickie Weaver

1964

RJ walks the two blocks home from school for lunch every day. Today, Mrs. Hall told her, "Do not return after lunch." She thinks RJ has the measles. She does have a rash, but it's from the sweater. Her mother's sweater. RJ's wearing it buttoned up the back because it makes her feel glamorous. The sweater is the same color as a new blue Crayola Crayon, and it's made out of banlon. When she gets sweaty, like she did today at morning recess, banlon makes her break out. Her arms and neck are embossed with little pink bumps, perfectly formed like Braille. Last month Mrs. Hall had taught the class that Helen Keller could feel bumps and read an entire book. RJ lightly touches her hand to her arm, imagining that she can read herself. There is nothing she can make sense of.

She did not try to convince Mrs. Hall that she is not contagious. RJ's mother, Lucky, says RJ has already survived every disease known to their family doctor: three-day measles, German measles, old-fashioned measles, tonsillitis, chicken pox, athlete's foot, pneumonia. She's suffered a second-degree burn on her leg. Once she stepped on a rusty nail at the Kirby's next door, and had to have a tetanus shot that gave her arm a fever. Two years ago, a yellow moth flew in one of her ears and tried to fly out the other. An attendant at the first-aid station down the block poured water in her ear and drowned the bug in her head. RJ is certain she knows when she is sick, and today she is not. Sixth grade is boring, and she's glad to be out of school. She is more than ready to move on to the seventh grade building because it looks like a red castle.

Mrs. Gregg, their next-door neighbor, is sweeping the sidewalk, so RJ skips around her with a wave. The round woman wears dark-rimmed glasses and has a moustache. Her husband died of a heart attack last year, in his office at work. RJ recalls the whispers about his death, how his secretary was with him until the end, and that when the ambulance arrived, he was hard as a rock. RJ's mother talked about rigor mortis. And then she'd say, "Well, look at his wife, wouldn't you work late?" Once RJ ventured her opinion that anyone would love Mrs. Gregg because she looked like Mrs. Santa Claus, and her mother laughed. "You don't understand, RJ."

A new station wagon with wooden sides is parked in front of the Catholics' house. Their name is Mark, and they keep to their side of the street. Lucky calls them the Catholics, as if that were their family name, but not to their faces. RJ knows what her mother will say tonight. "Look, Mr. and Mrs. Catholic bought a new car." RJ wishes she were Catholic. Catholics are rich, and have big families. RJ knows that if they do something bad, God tells them it's no big deal, they only have to say Hail Mary and kiss a necklace. RJ's Baptist belief means that she has to go to hell and burn even for something like saying "darn it."

RJ likes lunch at home because she has the house to herself. When her mother is there, she smokes it full and makes the house feel small. Lucky works at the five-and-dime on Grant Street. Otto Baab, their landlord, lives in the back room off the laundry porch. Lucky and RJ have the rest of the house, though Otto shares the kitchen and bathroom with them. RJ has been in Otto's room. She and her mother keep Otto's clothes washed and ironed. She's stacked his underwear, unlike hers because it has a slit in the front, and made rows of his black socks in the top drawer of his dresser. She's hung his shirts in his closet, dusted off the little black-and-white TV and the record player, folded the newspapers left by his reading chair.

The bathroom connects Otto's room to their part of the house. He sleeps in the day because he works the late shift. If RJ has to use the toilet just before midnight, when Otto gets off work, she holds herself down there, and does a silent barefoot dance by the bathroom door until he finishes his bath. She does not knock. The two females take care of Otto because the army doctor warned that he can fall asleep just like that, and when Lucky shares Otto's malady with someone, this is where she snaps her fingers for emphasis. "Just like that." Snap. RJ has never seen one of his narcoleptic episodes. Otto watches out for his renters, because there is no man in their family.

RJ sits on the couch beside her Barbie doll, who has been waiting there since RJ left for school. Barbie is dressed like Dorothy, from *The Wizard of Oz* movie, but with white plastic high heels. Lucky sewed the outfit just last week, though she has been trying to wean RJ away from dolls by reminding, over and over, "You will be twelve soon." The couch used to be Aunt Sissy's, and it is hard. It is covered in grass green nylon that Lucky says will last forever. RJ doesn't like to sit on it when she is wearing shorts. Aunt Sissy gives them her furniture when she tires of it. Lucky is proud to tell that Uncle Buddy makes good money at the Chrysler factory, so that her sister can afford to change her mind all the time. Aunt Sissy loves to redecorate.

Lucky decorates her own house with ashtrays. Or more exactly, dishes that she uses as ashtrays, because they add a little pizzazz. There is a milk glass candy dish with scalloped edges that has been in the family over thirty years. It is the only thing RJ's mother and aunt have fought over, besides cigarettes, but Lucky won't give it up. It makes Sissy mad when she visits and sees it full of ashes and butts. She empties it and washes it every time. It's on a maple end table, another castoff of Sissy's. At the other end of the couch on a matching table, there's a china teacup, wilted roses painted on it, perched on a gold-rimmed saucer. A clear Pyrex pie plate, chipped on the edge, daisies painted on the glass underside, is in the center of the coffee table. A footed bowl of jade green glass sits on top of the Motorola television set. Dishes all over the house are full of gray that scatters with a gentle breath and melts to dark sludge when it gets wet. RJ has seen Lucky lick her index finger, stick it in an ash pile, and then pop the finger in her mouth. Cigarette butts smashed on one end, red lip prints marking them as Lucky's, that's how the house is decorated. RJ is surrounded by the evidence of her mother's one true love, and Lucky even carries its name.

RJ goes into her bedroom to change her clothes, and Barbie's. It is cool today, but she dresses for summer. She has grown so over the winter that she is taller than her mother. She zips last year's shorts, but they don't feel right. The coordinating blouse won't button, so she chooses another outfit. It fits better, but she doesn't like it anymore. It looks like something a little girl would wear. She is excited about shopping for new clothes to celebrate her birthday next week. And every day she prays to become a woman, because her mom has promised to let RJ shave her legs, for one thing. She slips a one-piece, black-and white-striped swimsuit on Barbie, then sets her on the dresser. No swimming for Barbie today, she's on her period.

The green bowl on the TV makes RJ think of Jell-O. She runs water in an aluminum quart pan and sets it on the front burner of the kitchen stove. The spoon rest is painted like a fancy rooster with wildly colorful feathers. She and Otto bought it for her mother last Christmas. The three depressions for spoons are filled with cigarette ashes and butts. While the water boils, RJ takes the bowl from the living room, dumps its contents into the turquoise plastic trashcan, and washes the dish with hot suds. She dumps lime Jell-O crystals in the bowl and pours a cup of steaming water over them. She burned herself two years ago making Jell-O, so she is very careful with this part. Adding ice cubes, not cold water, makes the Jell-O set fast. Because Otto likes ice, she takes time to refill the aluminum tray.

She skips to the bathroom. The door is open, so it's okay to go in. There is another door on the opposite wall that opens into Otto's room. It's shut. She sits on the toilet and pushes hard, and urine shoots out. When she wipes herself with Charmin she almost misses the pink on the toilet paper. She wipes again. She got her period, so she's finally like her best friend, Annie. Her head spins when she thinks of all that Lucky promised when RJ becomes a woman. A pair of nylon hose, high heels like Barbie's, Tangee lipstick and shaving her legs. Lucky has told RJ that the boys will go crazy over her freckled legs when she's a woman.

She is so distracted by thoughts of what is to come that she almost forgets what her mother showed her with Kotex and a new sanitary belt of her own. The excitement of having a period subsides. Threading the Kotex through the sanitary belt, adjusting front and back, her panties too snug now, she walks bowlegged back into the kitchen. Will she have to walk this way one week out of every month? She cannot think that she has ever seen any woman walk bowlegged.

Sitting at the chrome-rimmed kitchen table, she takes the last bite of a bologna sandwich, then plops peanuts into a bottle of Coca-Cola. They fizz and she sips. Her nose gets wet and that makes her cry little dry sniffs. Her stomach hurts, an odd stomach hurt, and she recalls Aunt Sissy's words: "the curse." Back on the toilet, RJ can't go again, but senses a drip. The water in the toilet spreads in a pink circle. RJ has seen this before when it happened to her mother. Aunt Sissy says it happens to everyone. Do women ever bleed to death? It seems RJ has heard whispers of such.

She bangs on Otto's door, something she has never done. She cries for help.

Otto opens the door wide and swirling air rushes over her. He's wearing red pajama bottoms and his black hair is sticking up, like their Hoover sweeper has vacuumed his head. Otto never wears a pajama top, he's told her, because all the hair on his chest keeps him warm.

"RJ! Whatsa matter?" Otto takes the tearful girl by the shoulders, looking her over. Moths are not flying around her head, and she isn't crying about a burn. He holds her tight, and she cries into his fur, mumbles that she does not feel good, not knowing how to explain to a man.

But she has not flushed the toilet.

"You don't feel so good, huh? There's my girl," he says, tearing off toilet paper for RJ to dry her eyes and blow her nose. She is gasping wet hiccups, her shoulders lifting with each one. "It's okay, I know what to do. What I do for your mother," soothes dark-haired Otto. He kisses the top of her head and takes her hand. She calms because Otto has always taken care of her. He drove her mother to the hospital so that she could be born.

Back in the sunny kitchen, the Coca-Cola has stopped fizzing.

"Did you have lunch?" She nods yes.

Otto draws a glass of water from the faucet and takes the bottle of Bayer aspirin off the windowsill.

"Here. Take two."

RJ has never taken more than one adult aspirin, but she follows Otto's direction.

"Go get into your pajamas." Puzzled, she hesitates. He gives her a soft nudge.

"Go, now, put on your pj's."

She exchanges her shorts for pink-flowered pajamas and walks back into the kitchen. It is disheartening that walking is not the same. It will not be possible to run at recess anymore, and that brings to mind other things her mother has complained about and RJ has never fully understood until now: no swimming, no tub baths, no tight slacks. RJ cannot believe that shaving her legs will make up for what she gives up.

Otto is dribbling some of Lucky's Mogen David wine into a Flintstones glass with Baby Pebbles on it. The wine is an inky shade of purple and RJ anticipates her tongue will turn the same shade.

"Take a couple sips." He touches her arm. "Did you wear your mother's sweater today?"

She nods meekly and sips cautiously, the rich grape liquid spreading sensations from the back of her throat up into her nostrils, down her throat, staining all the way down.

"Okay." Otto puts the bottle back into the refrigerator. "Did you make me some Jell-O?" When she smiles, he tells her, "Thanks, sweetheart. We'll eat it later. Now let's go."

"Go?"

"To my room."

"Is this what mother does?"

"Not every time. Just the bad times."

"Every time isn't bad?"

"I don't think so."

Otto makes his bed every day, but right now it is rumpled, full of action, the covers thrown back to answer RJ's knock. It's sleepy dark in the room because the shades are down and the draperies closed, but Otto does not pull the string by the light in the ceiling.

Yawning, Otto motions RJ into his bed, and she obediently crawls in and covers up. His bed is familiar to her because she and Lucky change it every Saturday. They like Otto's smell on the sheets. Lucky calls it "Otto's Essence." She says it's Old Spice aftershave mixed with the man smell that comes from the hair on men's bodies and the mystery of their dreams. RJ watches Otto as he lifts the orange lid of the record player, takes a forty-five from the stack on the shelf, and puts it on the turntable. He leaves the arm off to the side, so that the record will play again and again. When the needle touches the forty-five, fuzzy scratching comes from the well-worn grooves. The record is not perfectly flat, and a rhythmic beat, like a heartbeat, separate from the song's beat, blends with it nonetheless. Smokey Robinson's voice whispers to them. He sings that he doesn't like some girl, but loves her anyway. It makes no sense to RJ, but the song is her mother's newest favorite. Lucky comes into Otto's room when he's at work and plays it. She never stays long because Otto does not allow smoking in here.

Otto gets into bed with RJ. It surprises her but does not alarm her. They share the pillow, and he pulls her toward him, so that they are together, her back to his chest. She inhales the security of an unspoken promise when he adjusts the sheet over them. His arms slip around her, and he fits his hands over the flat of her stomach, hot, pressed hard and close, transferring heat to where she is creating blood, the place where her mother says babies grow.

"Ssshhhh, just sleep, little girl, sleep," Otto croons, and Ritzie Jane feels herself loosen. She lies there in Otto's arms, pain dissolving under the warmth of his big, square hands.

In the Fifth-Grade Locker Room

Rebecca Lauren

We removed our sports bras through gym shirt sleeves
faced gray lockers like criminals, busied ourselves
with intricate straps and hooks, stole
glances at forbidden skin on either side.

Parts of us were rounding, sprouting
hair. We'd learned in secret to use razors,
to pack pads in our knapsacks and bleed
discreetly, posing as boys as long as we could.

Shower stalls glared at our backs with steely eyes,
dared any of us to perform a preemptive
striptease, to stand as the 3-D diagram
of how our bodies should be developing now.

Even after the long, sweaty mile on the track
no one ever volunteered, except Janet. She was slow,
shut up in a dark closet for days at a time before we were born
with no way to break the locks on her mind.

I imagine she swung from plastic hangers
until they snapped, dressed herself in coats—
layered peacoat over raincoat over windbreaker
to keep out the shadows that told her not to cry.

Now barefoot, she braved the tiled shower floor alone
and when her breasts flopped freely, we aimed to look
away but the preview of what was to come
stood before us, mouth gaping to the spray.

Ceremonies in Blood

Gwendolyn A. Mitchell

For years she tried to keep blood blue
until the day she woke up dead.
Menarche, the first blood,
her last morning.
Women fill the house with whispers.
It's time to tell her
she cannot be touched,
she must have a room away from the others,
gather her things, burn old sheets and clothing.
Tell her she is to welcome the secret
ceremonies of blood.
She rocks in the cradle of hands.
Tell her to keep away from the men
and the man-myths.
If she thought she was dying,
if she woke up dead,
a woman wouldn't tell such stories.
Man said, Keep her silent,
away from the water,
stay clear of her,
stay out of her sheets,
wait for the cleansing.
And the women said,
Tell her the power of springs,
show her you have no scars,
no open wounds.
Tell her the truth,
not to fear the blood,
not to mourn its absence.

Woman Blood

K. Coleman Foote

Long before I turned thirteen, the year the blood came, I discovered that woman hurt. I was real little, about eight or so. I had stolen a slate from school and was at home, spelling words with chalk. When I saw that "God" spelt "dog" backward, I got wild about those letters and wrote all kinds of words that could hide inside each other. I was so stunned by one that I forgot my place and ran shrieking to Mama in the kitchen, where she was washing dishes. The look she gave me should've folded me into a neat little girl package, complete with ribbon.

"Mama, 'woman' got 'man' inside!"

She almost dropped the heavy iron skillet in her hand. "What you say?"

"'Man' go inside 'wo*man*!"

I was beginning to spell out the word when my vision snapped to the kitchen sink on my right. My cheek howled with the force of her slap.

"Where you learn that?" she yelled. "I bet it was that Mary. Lele, don't you ever let that come out your trap again!"

I couldn't figure out what I done wrong. It seemed to be something I said, but I never could tell. In that three-room railroad flat that froze pipes in the winter and sweated us onto the fire escape during the summer, a slap came as quick as a "bless you," only more when it wanted to, like a sneeze. No matter what I did—get angry, not get angry, talk back, act dumb and say nothing—anything could make Mama or Daddy hit me. Especially if I happened to be nearby when they got on each others' nerves. "Why you just sitting there like that?" Whack! "How many times I gotta tell you not to listen in on grown folks' business?" Whack! "Lele, did I hear you say something?" Whack! "You think you so cute, don't you?" Whack!

For the longest time, I couldn't look at any man or boy without recalling Mama's slap that day. I made me a simple solution. When I ain't have to speak to anybody who wasn't a girl, I avoided looking at them. When I had to talk to them, I fixed my eyes just above they head. I got used to them rubbing they hair or looking over they shoulder when I was around them.

By the time 1932 rolled around, I was thirteen and thinking that maybe it was a problem. Jimmy Spitarelli, the Italian boy from upstairs, was always inviting me to a game of stickball in the street with him and his friends, 'cause they was one boy short and none of the other girls around wanted to play. I loved me some stickball, and I wanted to play, so I had to look at those boys in order to catch and throw correct. If I missed too many balls, they'd kick me off the team.

I wondered just how odd it was—this business of not being able to look at men and boys. I sought my girlfriend Mary, who lived down the hall. Girls went to her for advice since she was the closest thing to a woman they could talk to. We was the same age, but her chest and hips had popped out way before everybody else's. She was the only one of my friends who been kissed and had a boy put a hand under her skirt. That made folks call her fast, so I wasn't allowed to play with her when no grownups was around. Mama said something about nature planting greedy boys in reach of girls who flowered before they time.

Whatever that meant. Ain't matter to me. I might not follow Mary over that new George Washington Bridge like Mama was always prophesizing, but we grew up in the same building and was too close for even the threat of Mama's wrath to pull apart. Our friendship was like those cracked and missing tiles on the floor in the entryway: they made folks trip, but they was always there.

"You not peculiar, Lele. You just bashful," Mary told me, snapping on gum and dancing from foot to foot like she had to pee. We was huddled by a window in the living room, hoping Daddy couldn't hear us over the clanging of the radiator and his shuffling through his newspaper.

"Bashful" sounded worse than peculiar, but Mary told me it just meant I was a little scared by them. In that big-mama way of hers, she said that most girls our age was feeling the same. She said that life was a big schoolhouse, and that we all graduated at different times.

She giggled suddenly, tugging on my dress and motioning toward my room.

"Daddy, Mary and me gone go play in my room," I said, holding my breath for his response.

A grunt came from behind the newspaper. Me and Mary scampered into the old pantry that was my room. Daddy mumbled for us to stop running indoors. We sat on the floor so that my bed hid us from the doorway, which was kind of hard since the walls were barely wider than the bed. Digging her sharp nails into my arm and telling me she'd do worse if I went blabbing on her, Mary whispered that she liked to start fights with boys.

My eyes got wide. "You mean fist-fighting?"

"Ssh! They won't do it, stupid. Sometimes they might push me, or hit my arm when nobody looking."

"But what that gotta do with—"

"I'm getting to that." She smiled so wide I could see the two spots in the back where she said her daddy hit her hard enough to knock out her grownup teeth. "That way, I get them to touch me. Why don't you try it? No one'll ever know what you up to. Come on Lele, I know you be getting the feelings."

I felt like asking her why we'd want some boy slapping on us when we both got enough at home, but she would just tell me to be quiet again. "What feelings?" I asked.

"Oh come on! You know what I'm talking about. With boys."

My hands twitched. It was my time to shush her. I swore that Mama could see through walls, and I could already hear the floorboards creaking outside my room. I stuffed one of my rag dolls into Mary hand just as Mama stopped in the doorway.

"What y'all two doing in here in the dark?"

It wasn't all that dark, but to admit that was to call for a knock upside both our heads.

"We playing with dolls, Mama," I said, holding one up.

Mama wiped her hands on her apron and seemed to sniff the air. Sweat sprouted on my lip as her eyes slid between me and Mary for a few seconds. "Hm," was all she said before she went shuffling into the living room to talk to Daddy.

Me and Mary let out a long breath together. We glanced at each other and had to smother our snickers with the dolls. Mary bent close and whispered about the light-headedness, the goosebumps caused when boys was around. I felt a rush of excitement that I wasn't alone in this one. Mary may not have been "bashful," as she called it, but she couldn't mind how her body behaved, either. I added moist palms, a racing heart and short breath to our growing list of mysteries.

There was one that I left out. I ain't want to bring it up unless Mary did, because it happened in that don't-touch-don't-talk-about place. I wasn't womanish like Mary, so who was I to let it leave my mouth? When Mary ain't mention it, I told myself it must not be one of those things she was talking about. She'd laugh at me again if I found the nerve to say it. Just thinking about that feeling made me become silent and fiddle with my dress hem. Mary seemed to want to say something too, though. Her yellow cheeks was turning red, and her mouth kept opening like one of those penny-eating toys that went hungry following the Depression days. Anyway, it was time for her to go home and take some extra flour to her mama.

We never did talk about it, so I had to figure it out on my own. That don't-touch place was part of us, but we girls learned early on that we didn't own it. When we got old enough to bathe ourselves, our mamas warned that the devil would make us go blind if we just thought about touching there. And I *did* feel down there. Once. By accident. When it decided to bleed one day, I thought it was the devil killing me slow.

My fingers was cold and trembling as I put on clothes I felt would be proper for my setting out. I lay in bed, waiting for death mouth to suck out my last breath. By the time Mama rattled me awake, my bed sheets and the back of my dress was red. I thought I must have reached some kind of heaven, 'cause I ruined the good sheets and one of my good dresses, and Mama was quiet. She wasn't smiling as she removed the sheets, but her eyes wasn't cold and mean, either. I followed her into the kitchen, prepared to grab the pail to clean the sheets in, but she motioned for me to get the zinc washtub instead. She tossed some logs into the woodstove and lit them. Setting a large pot of water on the stove, she told me to remove my clothes.

I was so stunned I couldn't move. Her arched eyebrows spoke for her mouth: "Do I have to ask you again?"

Maybe she gone boil me alive, I thought as I removed my dress with fingers clumsy as when I put it on. She told me to toss my clothes on the floor by the kitchen window. *But before I die, first she gone make me wash the things I soiled*, I thought, watching as the water in the pot bubbled. I shivered in the chill of the morning. Folding my arms across my chest, I tried to recall the last time Mama seen me naked.

She ordered me to step into the washtub, which I'd filled halfway with cold water from the tap. I closed my eyes as she lifted the pot from the stove. I heard her slowly pouring the boiled water into the washtub and heard her sit on the kitchen stool. Something soft and wet touching my leg made me flinch. Opening an eye, I saw Mama sitting below me with a washrag in her hand. She wiped my legs. She ain't washed me since I learned to walk, so I wanted to ask her what all the fuss was for, but I kept my mouth shut. You didn't question your elders in those days unless you liked picking switches for them to skin your hide with.

"Open your legs, girl," Mama said, cutting her eyes up at me. "How'm I gone get you cleaned up?"

My legs was sore 'cause I'd been clenching them together while Mama scrubbed me. I thought she would've been proud to know that I kept them closed tight. She never told me to do it; I gathered it through my bedroom wall, when she and Daddy would stay up late talking in the living room. Whenever Mama spoke her sister Lille name, the word "loose" was close to follow. They said Lille got herself in trouble at thirteen "'cause she couldn't keep them bony legs of hers shut." Lord knows I already irked Mama enough, so I'd tried not to make my legs loose like Lille's. But Mama was sitting there waiting for me to obey, and I ain't want to chance a smack.

I separated my legs and turned my face away from her. I held my breath as the washcloth moved like moth wings over the no-touch place. She brought me a bunch of old rags and told me to put them between my legs, get dressed, and stay in bed. Something of a twitch crossed her lips. If any look she ever gave me could be called a smile, I think that was it.

"Lele, you's a woman now," she said quietly before turning away and picking up the washtub. It was full of pink water.

I died and became a woman! And Mama had touched what I was supposed hide from everybody, even myself. It made no sense. Did it mean I could touch there now? And what about the drunk feelings around men? Was it just that looseness had traveled through the blood, skipped over Mama from Lille, and somehow passed to me? Would men be able to smell me and discover I'd become a woman? What if somebody got me in trouble, like Lille? Mama would throw me out and let me fend for crumbs on the cobblestones, just like she said her mama did Lille.

Then Jimmy Spitarelli from upstairs went and kissed me outside our apartment and called me his woman. His mother found us on her way back from shopping at the market up the street and started paddling Jimmy arms and head with a big wooden spoon. Jimmy used to laugh about that spoon. It hurt so good, it tickled, he said.

Daddy poked his head out our front door, and Mrs. Spitarelli told him what happened. Daddy's slaps rained on me before I could get inside. He accused me of trying to make our business known to everybody in the building. "You tramp!" This's exactly why he ain't want a girl, he said. "Whore!" If he had found a son of his on top of some girl, he just had to pop his head. "Hussy!" But a daughter—you had to beat it into her, or she would let anything under her skirt.

After a while, he removed his belt and whipped me. I fell down and covered my face. I knew crying or screaming would make him hit me more, but when that belt tore into fresh welts, I couldn't hold back. Daddy kicked me, daring me to holler again. But I screamed when I noticed the blood dripping from my face. Everything went black.

When my eyes opened again, it was still dark. For a second, I wondered if grown folks' expression about "beating you into next year" was true. Maybe I really did die this time as punishment for touching down there. But my eyes made out the familiar orange glow crossing my legs. It was from a kerosene lamp in the window of the building next door.

I was lying on my bed but felt like I was floating somewhere near the ceiling. My skin surged like those chilly waves on the Jersey shore, but I couldn't feel no pain. I couldn't feel nothing, in fact, but that rolling of my skin. A dark, wet spot stained my pillow. At first, I wondered if it was blood, but it was too close to my eye—the one that was almost swole shut. I wondered again why that thought didn't scare me, or make me mad. I ain't intend on crying. Mama and Daddy taught me early on that my tears was the best excuse for more beating, more pain. I had gotten to where I could stop my tears easy as turning off a water tap, so I don't know what went wrong that night. I decided that if I ever figured out how to stop my tears again, I'd make sure to hold back all that woman blood too. I would miss Mama touching me soft when the blood came, and I'd pine for Jimmy's kiss, but if it was the blood that made men like Daddy wild enough to kill, I wanted to find that loose tap between my legs. I wanted to tighten all the taps so nothing inside me would leak out again.

Fishing

Caroline Malone

You have been fishing.
Down to the beaver ponds
with a dead trout bug-eyed
glaring beneath the rock
you smashed it with.
Afraid to remove the hook,
in a panic forgetting
to screw the lid on tight
stuffed a glass jar
of salmon eggs
into your front pants pocket.

In the bathroom
your grandmother cries
the time! the time!
Mother comes running
while the men watch KTVB
weather, probably grinning,
the time, the time.

Stunned seeing your twelve-
year-old face contort in the mirror
as the two women explore
your pants. *Am I bleeding
to death?* Some secret
disease.

The salmon eggs had spilled
upside down running into
your underwear. You have to
go back in the den and watch
the news with men.

Sleeping Beauty

Eileen Moeller

Like a frog out of the water,
like a big clumsy fly caught in a screen,
I entered womanhood
flailing my long legs.

Jumping Double Dutch
in sneakered feet,
pounding a Morse Code of denial
into the sidewalk,
so it echoed
throughout the neighborhood:
not me, it said, not me,
I'll play with dolls forever, I'll be a boy
if I want to, I'll go off and play by the railroad tracks.

Or spinning crazy like a top
in the grass of the backyard,
almost mowing mother's roses down with my arms,
then swooning beneath our peach tree
heavy with ripe fruit.

Dizzy, it always made me dizzy,
and sleepy too, this newly tilting
pigeon thrumming inside me.

Thought I'd never want a prince
bending over me,
his face so much like a brother's
with its teasing wheedling eyes
and mouth that kisses too hard.

Ernestine's Fifteen Minutes

Toni Powell

I live at 17 Royal Palm Way on Grebe Island in Ft. Lauderdale, Florida, with two adults and one dog. Only one of us has to bleed every month. My grandmother, Maureen McLaughlin (I call her "Granny the Gruesome") is, in addition to being the absolutely meanest person in the world, also one of the oldest, and couldn't POSSIBLY have had a period since dinosaurs roamed the earth. My grandfather, Jack McLaughlin, is definitely the kindest, sweetest man in Florida, but he's still a man so he's excused from the whole mess. Then there's me, Emily McLaughlin. I'm sixteen and I bleed copious amounts of gunk every month. Finally, there's Ernestine, my dog, who was spayed early in her life and will miss the joys of periods, pregnancy and puppies. Now Ernie probably wouldn't mind skipping the pregnancy part but she'd absolutely love to menstruate. Ernestine has a passion for tampons, especially used ones, or maybe I should say 'preowned.'

What is it about dogs? They're so sweet and wonderful and, at the same time, so absolutely funky and gross. For Ernestine, there is nothing, not even a double ice cream cone or sirloin steak, not that she gets much opportunity for sirloin, that beats a bloody tampon and I do believe that is just about the most revolting thing ever.

It's not like we just offer them to her like a gift. Oh, please. I make sure that all my tampons go into plastic bags inside a wastepaper basket and that the bags get thrown in the garbage, but you know what? Ernestine is brilliant. Every once in a while she gets ahold of a nasty tampon and drags it behind the sofa in the living room where you can hear her make horrible smacking and chewing noises. Yuck!

And when she can't get to the tampons, there's always Plan B, which involves dirty underwear. But not just anybody's dirty underwear. No, Ernie has her favorite, and when it comes to dirty drawers, Granny's are the best. Of course, I don't have a clue as to how my dog gets Granny's undies, but it has happened a couple times. Heh, heh.

Actually, Granny had never allowed me to have any pets, not even a hamster ("Oh, Emily, really. They're just furry rats.") or a bird ("Nasty little creatures!") so acquiring Ernestine was a major achievement. But when I saw this pitiful little thing hanging around my high school one afternoon, I knew I had to share my life with her. She was silly looking: part this, part that, part everything else. In fact, it was all those parts that worried me. I knew that even if Granny agreed to let me have a dog she'd have a serious problem with Ernestine's mutt-ness. You know how when you get a dog from the Humane Society you're told that it's a shepherd mix or a collie mix? Well, Ernestine's a "mixed mix" and Granny doesn't like mixes of any kind. Animals and humans should be pure. Pure white, preferably, for humans, but for dogs all Granny cares about is that they be pedigreed and the harder they are to get and the more expensive they are to buy, the better the dog.

When I knew I had to convince Granny, somehow, to let me have Ernestine, I did what I usually do. I went to PapaJack, who, except for being kind of a wimp sometimes, has to be the most wonderful grandfather in the world. "PapaJack," I said, pulling Ernestine out of my oversized "POETS ARE SEXY" sweatshirt, "my life will be seriously diminished without this dog. Help me, please?" This time I didn't even have to beg or pout because I could tell right away that he was falling for Ernestine. She's so ugly she's beautiful and, besides, PapaJack loves strays and orphans. We sat down and devised a plan.

"What did the vet say about her when she saw her?" he asked. "Did she know what Ernestine's mixed with?"

I shook my head. "She just laughed and said that Ernie's probably a little bit of everything. No particular breed."

PapaJack sat there for a few minutes staring at Ernie, who was licking his fingers and nuzzling the buttons on his shirt. I knew she was working on how to own those buttons. Suddenly, PapaJack got his big "Eureka, I've got it!" smile on his face.

"She's an Albe. A full-blooded Albe." He looked so happy that I was happy too.

"Okay! Only what's an Albe?" I desperately wanted to believe we were on to a plan that worked, but an Albe? At the vet's office, I'd spent some time looking at a book I'd found that was full of pictures and descriptions of all the pedigrees in the world. The Albe was definitely not one of them.

"An Albe is . . ." PapaJack got this smug I-bet-you-can't-top-this grin. "An Albe is A-Little-Bit-of-Everything! And we aren't really making this up, Em. We got this from the vet. Oh, and the official pronunciation is Al-bee." He sat there for a few minutes looking very official

So, from then on, Ernestine was a genuine Albe. What we didn't know then was that before we were through, our little story about a made-up breed of dog would grow to become as big as *War and Peace*.

Albe or not, Granny did not fall madly in love with Ernie at first sight.

"What on earth is that? And don't bring it in here! Honestly, Jack McLaughlin, you should know better. I don't want any dirty mutts in our house and especially not now! I'm having an important dinner reception here next month and I want this house to look—"

"She's not a mutt, Granny," I interrupted. Actually, I don't usually interrupt people but if you don't interrupt Granny, she'd never stop. Everybody including wimpy PapaJack interrupts Granny. The gardener even interrupts Granny, for God's sake.

"This dog is . . . is . . . an Albe." I stutter when I lie. It's one of my very worse defects. "A pureblooded Albe. Very rare. And hard to find, too." I was so nervous I was repeating myself. I'm a real dork sometimes.

"An Albe?" Granny's eyes squinted at Ernestine, trying to figure out how much she might cost. "That . . . that thing is pedigreed? Hmff." Granny's snort needed work. It always sounded more like a swallowed sneeze than sneer of contempt. "It doesn't even look like a dog. More like a raccoon. I don't think I've ever heard of an . . . an . . . And if it's so rare, just how did *you* get her, Emily?"

"A f . . . friend gave her to me. Her parents were given Ernestine as a g . . . gift from a very rich businessman because her dad helped him . . ." Blah, blah, blah. Damn, I wished I'd written this down. I knew this part of the story had to be good because Granny knows I only have babysitting money to spend. Any pedigreed dog would cost hundreds, maybe thousands.

". . . and Albes helped bring people fleeing from Hitler over the mountains by . . . by . . ." easy, Em, you're making Ernie sound like a Saint Bernard. Don't go there. ". . . um . . . they used to herd camels . . ." Come on, girl, you can do better than that!

"Camels? Now, really, Emily, I don't believe camels move in herds?" Oh, man, now I've really messed up, I thought. How did I get from the Swiss Alps to the Sahara? I knew I was losing Granny; she probably would've gone for some version of a smaller Saint Bernard-type dog helping people over mountains but when I jumped to camels, she really freaked. When she doesn't believe me, Granny's little black eyes get squinty, her two penciled on eyebrows join together and she looks exactly like E.T. did when he got scared. I gave PapaJack a panicked look, suddenly stumped.

"Now, Emily, don't you remember what Dr. Sanchez said? Albes were primarily responsible for assisting the French Resistance fighters during

World War II." God bless PapaJack! "They helped them find safe places to hide . . . umm . . . Jews? Yeah, that was it. French Jews. And gypsies." Sweet! My grandfather is so smooth; he'd remembered that Granny loves everything French. At that moment I fell in love with him all over again.

So Ernestine got to stay. The deal was that she was confined to my bedroom and bathroom and, sometimes, the living room as long as she stayed off the furniture. And Ernie was okay with that. Until the night of her Coming Out Party.

Granny had been trying forever to get an invitation to join a group of women that reeked of money. She'd always wanted to be among the richest and most powerful in South Florida and many of these, the female ones at least, belonged to the Florida Ladies Everglades Mission, or FLEM. Granny had connived, contrived, bullied, badgered and sweet-talked these women for years and finally got one of them to sponsor her for membership. She'd been a member for only six weeks when she volunteered to have one of their receptions at our house.

On the morning of the FLEM Party, Granny called us into her study.

"Here are the rules," she told us, glaring at me first and then at Ernestine who had plunked herself between PapaJack and me. "First, don't let that dog go anywhere near the Florida room or pool area. Keep it . . ."

"Her!" PapaJack and I both corrected her.

"Keep the dog in your room, Emily, until the guests all leave. And I mean it. This will be the most important night of my life!" She started to stomp off.

"What's the second rule?" PapaJack asked. Granny ignored him.

When the magic hour came and the first pampered old princess appeared, Kim, my best friend, and I were giving Ernie a bath. She was covered with suds and looked adorable. We were just pulling her out of the tub when Kim's cell phone rang. When she saw it was Rafael, her to-die-for boyfriend, she let go of Ernie. I grabbed at Ernie to get a better hold on her but I could feel her slipping out of my hands. What happened next reminded me of one of those Marx Brothers movies that PapaJack loves so much.

Ernie slithered out of my hands and jumped out of the tub, shaking herself all over, probably trying to get all that orange marmalade bubble bath smell off of her. The sudsy stuff flew everywhere including our eyes, which stung so much we grabbed for dry towels rather than Ernestine. Feeling free at last, she raced over to the wastepaper basket and grabbed Kim's very recently used tampon. She probably would have stopped there to drool over her new treat but when she saw us getting ready to grab her, she stuffed the tampon in her mouth and ran into my bedroom.

Just as Ernie jumped on the bed to enjoy some quality time with her tampon, the door opened and PapaJack stood there, looking panicked.

"Em, we've got to hide Ernestine. One of the women at this party is a breeder and judges dog shows for the American Kennel Club. She'll take one look at Ernie and . . . Oh, oh. Dammit!" As he reached for Ernestine, she leaped off the bed and headed for the door. PapaJack tried to grab her but she was too slippery. The dog-with-tampon raced out the door and through the house, headed, I guessed, for what must have seemed to Ernie as a piece of heaven: the living room couch.

Then we heard the screechy voice we'd all dreaded. "Oh, there's my little Albe now. You know, the dog that the French Ambassador gave to friends of Emily." Oh, shit, where did the French ambassador come from? "Here she is, the little sweetheart. Oh, isn't that cute? The girls must have given her a bath. Oh, dear, is she bleeding? Emily, dear . . . EMILY!"

Crap and triple crap. I ran into the living room hoping to scoop up Ernie before the other women saw her. As I reached the corner of the hallway Ernie galloped past me, down the hall and, oh please God no, into my grandparents' bedroom. Quadruple crap!

"Don't you go in there, you nasty little piece of shit!" Unfortunately for Granny, a whole gaggle of ladies had formed a line close behind her and had heard her unladylike description of Ernie. But "piece of shit" was preschool talk compared to what she said when Ernestine, now barking in shrill claps of joy, ran out between Granny's legs and into the living room. She was now wearing a pair of Granny's dirty drawers wrapped around her head like a turban. At first I thought she'd dropped the tampon somewhere. Then I saw it, wrapped up in the panties. Granny screamed and the ladies gawked. I knew I'd pay big time for this night eventually, but I also knew I'd remember it as one of the best moments in my life.

Ernestine and I stayed with Kim for a couple weeks after the party to wait for Granny to cool off. One evening while I was there, I read that Andy Warhol once said that everybody gets fifteen minutes of fame in their lives. I thought that was such a cool line that I quoted it to PapaJack. He laughed.

"Not Ernestine. Let's face it, Em, that dog's fame has just begun."

Dream Bloom

Marianne Worthington

I.

I dream of a garden I've been to before and maybe
it's a real garden in someone's backyard in an old
northside neighborhood or maybe it's the garden
of my grandmother's friend Lee who wears
tight wool skirts with cardigans and pearls
and tells dirty jokes while showing her flowers
and my grandmother laughs and laughs until
she goes in to make more strong, black coffee
on the stove, or maybe it's the garden of my
Sunday School teacher who always made a lawn
party for Easter with sugared grapes and bunny
cakes and lime punch with vanilla ice cream
floating like clouds on a patio table full of yellow
daffodils, or maybe it's the garden I wandered
into while playing in my aunt's piney woods
at the edge of her yard, a secret earth crowded
with purple iris and clover, honeysuckle
and three stone steps that lead to an empty
greenhouse, or maybe it's just a place I know
in my dreams, that hidden spot only reached
through sleeping memory, a patch of sickly
smells and sunflowers and river rocks where
shadows appear as the sun filters
through the canopy of the sugar maples.

II.

In my dream I am showing this garden
to my daughter. I have brought her to this little
shady spot have led her here through the backyards

and garden parties and sandy woods paths so
she can taste the sunlight and the syrup
from the honeysuckle blossoms and can hear my
grandmother's laughter peal through the leaves,
and she can choose a spot to plant more purple
flowers but when she pricks her fingers
on an heirloom rose and the blood flows
and streams like ribbons from her fingers
and my womb tightens like a fist when I see
the blood, crimson, staining our party dresses,
the sun dims and the birds still to her passage,
and I feel like crying when I wake up.

When I Heard Her Whisper

Andrea Potos

That summer day Mother sunned with our neighbor Jeanette,
in our backyard closed off by a new chain-link fence,
I lingered in the driveway, riding my Schwinn in slow circles
so I could look through the fence and watch her,
a towel draped over her belly
as she lay there burning;
wearing the black bathing suit
with the straps pulled down, her body molded
like a statue of Juno I'd seen in a school book; her skin
slicked with the baby oil she used to soften
my own chapped cheeks in winter,

and when I heard her whisper
how it was that time of the month—
the aches and cramps, the bloating
that made her feel pregnant again—
how *it's just as bad now you know* I peddled
like a blast of wind down our driveway
away from my mother.
I was only ten and excused
from so much truth—
I had years yet
before the blood of her destiny
became mine.

Wolf Woman

Karen Howland

Be careful
if you
invite a wolf over.

Your mother will be livid
as this visitor refinishes
the woodwork.

You'll grin as lamps
shine wolf hair over fringe
room whitening beside your mother's face.

Familiar markings will disappear,
you'll lose your way. Unrecognizable
in the bathroom mirror, bravery arises

you are part of her pack.
A howl shatters the mirror. Yours.
Sharing disregard

you mark territory you
didn't know was yours.
Your mother vanishes

in the kitchen, as always.
Walls fall away.
The moon comes for you.

Legs throb with new beauty.
You leap. Fur and bones eclipse
house. Your home is the roaming

of your soul. Deep and reaching,
no longer crouched beside dad's black boots
and mom's matted slippers, you lunge

into a cambria of breathing trees.
Luminous animal, capable paws,
instincts intact, you blaze North,

bristle with coarse stories of stars.
Track ecstasy. Smell the moon
let it smell you. Smiling wild

feral female free.

Section II:

Full

The Menstrual Hut

Annie Finch

How can I listen to the moon?
Your blood will listen, like a charm.

I knew a way to feel the sun
as if a statue felt warm eyes.
Even with ruins on the moon,
your blood will listen, every time.

Now I am the one with eyes.
Your blood can listen, every time.

Red Benediction

Anastacia (Stacey) Tolbert

She.
Waltzes slowly. Knocks on vulva's door.
We.
Do a strawberry dance of preparation.
She leads/make her home/in the cradle of my flesh
Left/right/left/right
There. Period.
Detoxify deliberations.
Covenant truth. Testify.
We.
Celebrate our mothers. Sing *bloody hallelujah*.
Hands lifted in the shape of a maxi pad.
I will stay free
Insert grace
Breathe in what I know to be true
Until it is complete.

Places to Leave Your Blood

Pamela Grossman

On your white sheets, as a target mark
On the seat of Brian's boyfriend's outgrown jeans—
they belong to you now, and you are bleeding
On the white lace nightgown with blue ribbons,
a gift from your cousin Jane
You'll bleach and scrub it, but the stains won't fade
On a five-dollar bill, because you reached between your legs
to see if the blood had traveled through your black wool slacks
and so your fingers had blood on them
as you took the bill from your wallet
to buy a newspaper, on your way home
On the newspaper, on a headline about Somalia
On a lover's mouth and hands
On a friend's friend's pale yellow couch
Just a faint shade on the fabric—maybe they won't notice
All over your pale blue leggings
on your second day of a new job,
and indelible on the steel gray cushion of your new office chair
Yes, you are a working woman
On the 6 train, on the I train, on the L,
small but evident pools of your blood lying still in your wake
You were embarrassed the first time
You've come to feel resigned
On a lover's sheets, in bold relief
You have mixed feelings about this
You think that perhaps it is just, as he treats your blood like a toxin
But he looks so wounded, so forlorn, you wonder
Maybe you should pay him if they don't become clean
Dream of leaving your blood
on your old lover's new lover's doorsteps and windowsills
Anyone entering or leaving her

home will think, will have to think, of you
On the pink tile floor of your bathroom
(When you were a child, you loved to mix pink and red)
On a wooden crate you found
You're planning to use it in a sculpture
Remember reaching inside yourself, to get the blood,
to brush the blood onto the wood, and laughing,
laughing at your life—In oceans,
on towels, on pillows, and on your own tongue
because you wondered and you wanted to know.

On Being Clean

Anne-Marie Levine

*For Teibele to be asked, as a matter of course,
(before making love to a demon) whether she is
clean is, even in its 19th century context, an
odious question.*
*__ review of I. B. Singer's
play, Teibele and Her Demon.*

The demon lover withdrew.
His phallus was still hard
and covered with her blood.

"There," he said, pointing it at her.
"Suck it off. Like a vampire."

She shut off her inhibitions,
thought of Germaine Greer,
and sucked.

The blood had no taste,
no odor,
almost no texture.

Which made it seem surprisingly
clean. Perhaps it was clean.

She had learned what vampires know.

This is Living

Amy Meckler

Some days, I feel especially childless
and my hollow pipe of body
echoes with apologies. I'm sorry
I never shaped you into more than
sorry your non-fathers and I
argued into dry cement and bare hangers.
I understand if you're angry.
Or maybe you think this is living—
the long slide down, then
eternity treading water.
You only saw the deepest
parts of me, and the cramps
as you packed up and filed out
are all I'll remember. It doesn't matter
that I didn't know how to keep you.
I know that excuse.
I'm also someone's child.

Period.

Cyn Kitchen

"Welcome to the land of the damned," my mother told me. I was sitting on the toilet, wondering what to do next, ill-equipped, ill-prepared, crampy, fifteen-years-old. The disgust on her face was unmistakable.

"Pad or tampon?" she asked.

"Uh, pad, I guess."

"Tape or belt."

"Tape," I said. "Definitely tape." But she'd already walked away.

• • •

Months later, the neighbor girl invited me swimming. It was day two of my period. I was still ignorant of the profound changes that bleeding imposed. I sneaked into my mother's bathroom, opened the cabinet next to the toilet and pilfered through her stash of feminine hygeine products. I'd never worn a tampon. Nothing had ever penetrated that part of my body, not even a thought.

Mom used these devilish little things they don't make anymore. It was shaped like a bullet, compact and hard. It was loosely mounted on the end of a sucker stick, a string hanging limp from its side. The idea was to shove the bullet in, then pull the stick out. I was determined to go swimming, so I studied the directions on the box. I placed one foot on the stool and grimaced as I put the bullet where it needed to go. The dry, fibrous material resisted my first several attempts. I was relieved and horribly uncomfortable when it finally stayed lodged inside me.

I followed Toni into the water. Instantaneously, a searing pain awakened every fiber in my body. It was wholly systemic, permeating every cell, every nucleus, every chromosome. Agony locked a vise grip around my head and screamed in my ears with unrelenting intensity. I couldn't breath.

"Something wrong?" Toni asked.

We were neighbors, but not that close.

"Uh, yeah," I said, gripping the side of the pool, waiting for the pain to pass, panting.

She stared at me. "What?"

"I used a tampon," I said. "I don't think I put it in right."

"Oh," she said, and dove under the water, headed for the deep end.

She was younger, not as developed, didn't understand.

The pain began to subside, but the feeling of fullness down there was more discomfort than I could ignore. I thanked Toni for inviting me but decided it was too much hassle to try to be normal and have a period at the same time.

• • •

I went to basketball camp in the eleventh grade. I sat on the floor to catch my breath while some other girls were on the court. I leaned against the wall with my knees pulled up. I stayed in that position for several minutes. I went to the bathroom during a break and realized there was blood everywhere. The others were too embarrassed to tell me. They were not too embarrassed to whisper and point.

• • •

My ex-mother-in-law kept track of my cycle. She marked it on her calendar, knew when it was due, that I was regular, what signals in my mood were clear indicators that it'd arrived.

I began to hide my period. I stashed the telltale indicators in my purse and later discarded them at the McDonald's drive-thru. I put on my game face so she wouldn't detect mood swings. I lied. I got good enough that even her son, who rarely touched me, lost track.

• • •

My mother said, "You'll hate it until it doesn't come." She was right. She also said, "A baby feels better going in than it does coming out." Right again.

• • •

No one told me that you bleed for six weeks after a baby is born. I'm telling you now in case you don't already know this.

• • •

I did not know what to do with a girl. I was afraid I would screw up a daughter. When the doctor said, "It's a girl," I felt more panic than joy.

• • •

My daughter started her period at a sleepover. She called me when she realized what was going on. I called in to work, drove to pick her up, left town, and took her shopping for the day. We stopped at a coffee shop and drank raspberry Italian sodas. We bought shoes and purses with sunglasses to match. We ate greasy burgers and salty fries for lunch. We had ice cream for dessert.

Here are some of the things I told her:

"You're lucky to live in the era of space-age absorbency."

"Ibuprofen helps."

"Swimming isn't that fun anyway."

"You'll get used to it."

"A period isn't necessarily the end."

I Have Been

Stephanie Silvia

I have been the burnt
    Good Luck New Year's dumpling
        that splattered out of the pan of oil
          onto the floor

The wine that sloshed and spilled
    onto the white linen tablecloth
        passed on for generations
          without a spill

I have been the bruise on the avocado
    the part of the banana that no one wants to eat
        the piece of soap no one knows how to get rid of

I have been the lump in the breast
    cut out by the surgeon's hand
the mud in the sandbox
    where the rain has been caught
the highest note of a wolf
    calling to be mated
the thorn on the rose
    the red drop of blood on the cotton sheet
the hook in the fish's mouth
    I have been the hungry gnawing

I have been the dirty water that went down the drain
    passing giant koi and baby alligators in the sewer
        on my way out to the river
          where I have grown

I have become the foam on the ocean wave curling toward the sun

I have risen
mist blown from the shore
on to the tip of the redwood branch

I am the golden light
I have become the golden words
I am not myself
I am the brightness and the gnawing

Before the Bleed

Eileen Moeller

I am sewn together with nylon cord,
threading through each cheekbone,
out my chin, and down the gorge
between my swollen breasts,
where it comes to rest
at the center of all gravity
within its nest of pelvic bones,
where a weight is hung, a pendulum,
and a magnet pulls it
tightly toward the ground.
.

Watch me flail my arms and legs
as spinal fault lines growl and shift.
I'm the moon's puppet now,
caught in the ancient shadow
dance, my hands made of wood.
I cannot smile; I cannot part my teeth.

Late

Therese L. Broderick

When it seems too late, I think
    not another pregnancy,
        this one so late in life

that I am older than my late
    grandmother when at forty-three
        she delivered her last child.

But lately women have been mothering
    later and later, so maybe I could
        give this baby a try

like I gave latex gloves
    a try and Starbucks latte
        and even Late Night Comedy.

But seriously,
    my only daughter is already
        old enough to have her own late

period, not to mention latent grief
    should I happen
        to die in childbirth.

So best not to keep thinking of
    a new layette which, luckily,
        I don't have to for too long

because finally, it does come late
    and what a good thing that I
        never mentioned it to him.

Entering the Elemental

Priscilla Frake

It stinks of fish and salt, this beast
that heaves itself onto the sand
and flops and slaps its way
to where you wait
while darkness knots
and constellates

inside. You have to be strong
to take on this muscled emotion
and not come to harm,
to navigate bulk and fury,
stubbornness, thickness,
a swimmer's body.

You have to be strong
to not lose your human head,
each month to dive
into dim worlds seething
with scales and eyes,
to come up breathing.

Then you can spill
the bloody dark, begin the sluggish
sloughing off of unconceived
potential. Be warned:
Each month it is you,
it is you who are born.

Elegy for a Past Life

Shaindel Beers

I miss the honest life we used to lead
scraping up odd jobs so we could see
a movie the next town over,
and stare for a few hours at people
on the drive-in screen who weren't
like us—who didn't wear too big hand-me-down
flannels and mud-caked boots—
and even if they were playing farm people,
had never known that pinching pain
in the sacral spine that paralyzes
as you heft the bale by the twine
and let it avalanche down to the ground.

For days, after seeing a show, we'd sit in the loft,
legs dangling over the bleating sheep below
and dream about the life we'd live
when we'd escaped. Back then at sixteen
I thought we'd make it out together,
and become writers, the only job we could imagine
where we wouldn't smell like shit or hay or cows

but too many months passed when I didn't bleed
and when we were safe, the test negative
and burned in the rubbish heap behind the barn,
you left, too afraid of being trapped
in a cornfield town
to wait for me.

Peak-Traveling Period

Shanna Germain

I'm in the back of the bus. The WAY back. Every time the bus takes a stomach-rolling turn to the right (which it does about every thirty seconds), the side of my head thumps against the cold window. The rice and beans from lunch rise in my gut and threaten to make an appearance in their new half-digested guise. I pull the seatbelt strap away from my stomach—I'm all for safety, but I'm even more for not throwing up on a bus full of near-strangers—and try to keep my eyes on the back of the guy's head in front of me.

We're on our way up the side of the mountain in the MiddleOfNowhere, Mexico, to spend the night on an organic coffee farm. Out of the two dozen "coffee people" on board, I'm the only one who has never been on a coffee farm. I'm just a reporter, along for my very first ride through the non-U.S. world. Everyone else's backpacks are loaded with extra socks and international cell phones and bottles of Mescal. My suitcase has a notebook, a copy of *The Idiot's Guide to Mexico*, three hundred dollars worth of "indestructible" travel clothes just ordered off the Internet, and twenty-six color photocopies of my passport, just in case.

In the midst of all these experienced travelers, I also happen to be the only female on the bus. And right now, as the bus takes another hard right on a clay mountain path that's about the width of a human being—a very thin human being—I'm definitely the only one who's worrying whether my expensive "no stain" travel shirt will work if I puke all over the front of it.

I'm also the only one awake. While my head is bouncing off the window, everyone else is drooling on their seat in Dramamine-induced sleep, oblivious to the huge truck that's squeezing by us so close I can read the lettering engraved on the door handle. Oblivious to the rivers of rain on the windshield. Oblivious to the fact that the side of the mountain appears to be melting in clay-colored torrents beneath the van.

I don't know why I'm the only newbie or the only female on the bus, but I do know why I'm who's in the way-back and wide awake. Because two hours ago, I had enough lack of life experience to politely decline the two things that I truly needed for this trip: fear and drugs.

I've had two long, stomach-churning hours to regret my audacity.

Two hours ago, we were somewhere in the outskirts of Oaxaca, Mexico. I'd been lulled to sleep by the smooth, straight roads (which I am sorry I did not know to appreciate then—if I had, I would have stayed awake, silently blessing every lack of bump and turn). I woke when David, our guide who was experienced in all things coffee and Mexico, put his freckled hand on my shoulder. "Last town on the straight and narrow," he said. I should have known something was up.

We followed David off the bus. "Welcome to" *something-something,* David said. Which someone told me later was the name of the town, but which seemed to translate roughly to "field with hut in it."

"Anyone want anything from the store?" David asked.

"The store," which could have translated to "hut with field around it," was a three-sided lean-to. Shelves ran from floor to ceiling, lined with dusty bottles of colored liquids, unlabelled plastic bags with spices or tea, bottles of sunscreen, and piles of plastic combs.

David came out with bottles of water and an open plastic baggy filled with what looked like dirty and crushed Bayer aspirin.

He handed me a bottle of water. "Dramamine?" he asked.

I shook my head. "Sorry," I said. "I don't have any."

"No," he shook his bag of pills. A little powder drifted out. "I'm offering you one."

Now, I may not have traveled much, but I did take Dramamine once when I was thirteen for a whale-watching trip. I didn't have motion sickness, but my friend did and I took it to be supportive. I learned two things: one, that it is possible for an excited teenager to sleep through an entire whale pod breaching thirty feet away. And two, Dramamine does *not* look like dirty, broken aspirin.

"Um, no thanks," I said. "I don't get motion sick."

"Great," he said. "Why don't you sit in the back then?"

Now, I'd like to stop right here and say that David wasn't being mean to suggest I sit in the back. At least, I don't think he was. He just thought I knew what the hell I was talking about. That's because I had "forgotten" to mention to anyone else on the trip that I have never been outside the United States before. (Other than a trip to Canada, which doesn't really count, because although I didn't take Dramamine, I did sleep through most of the trip—I was with my grandparents).

But on this trip, I'm surrounded by experienced travelers—older men whose breakfast tales have consisted of places like Burundi and Addis

Ababa and Choma (which I wasn't even sure was a place at first, and now that I'm writing this, I realize that I'm still not sure and perhaps had better look it up). No, in front of these men whose dinner tales consist of phrases like, *ate live worms* and *nearest hospital two countries over* and *woke up with a poisonous spider on my arm*, I am not about to admit that I am surprised to find so few bathrooms in this part of Mexico.

One man, a coffee roaster from Pakistan with a shaved head and at least six languages on his tongue, is the only one brave enough to sit in the back with me. He was also, if I remember correctly, the one who talked about eating live worms. Or maybe he'd eaten the poisonous spider he'd found on his arm. Either way, even *he* took his Dramamine and is snoring beside me. I turn my head to look at him. Mistake. The movement—bus sideways, head sideways, stomach who the hell knows which way—makes me face front quick. This man might eat *me* alive if he wakes up to find my vomit on his arm.

My eyes focus on the front just in time to see David stand up in the front seat. He grips both sides of the seats and turns carefully around to face us. His normally-pink face is pale, but he seems to manage the facing backward gig surprisingly well. I, however, cannot watch him face backward. The way the side of the mountain seems to race up behind his back—I have to close my eyes and look at the steady dark on the back of my eyelids while he talks.

"We're coming to the last bathroom before we head up into the mountains," he says. I hear bathroom, but what I think is: we haven't "headed up" into the mountains yet?

David continues. "So if anyone needs it," he seems to be talking directly to me, but I don't dare open my eyes to find out, "now's your last chance before we come back down."

Did I mention that we're spending the night at the top of this mountain? In an empty concrete warehouse at the coffee farm? Without electricity, running water or a coffeemaker? Translation: Now's your last chance to pee or puke without hitting your shoes (or shirt) for the next forty-eight hours.

I'm so thankful when the bus stops (and when my stomach does too), that I practically run up the aisle where everyone else is waking up. But my legs must still think everything's moving—I bump from seat to seat across the aisle, unable to walk in a straight line.

I don't really have to pee, but if this is my last actual toilet for the next two days, I'm damn well going to try. The woman in the front of the stand-alone wooden hut opens the door for me and smiles wide—she seems glad to have at least one woman on board to use her facility. "Gracias," I say as I slide a peso into her palm.

I enter and am alone in the semi-darkness for the first time in what seems like days. I strip and sit, determined to plant my butt on this non-moving entity for a while if nothing else. And then I look down. Even in the barely-there light, I can see it: the red badge of courage that spreads across my very expensive Ex-Officio dry-in-an-hour-so-you-only-have-to-bring-two-pairs underwear.

For one short moment, I am elated. "See," I want to yell, "I'm not a totally motion-sick newbie! It's just my period!" But then I remember where I am, and David's "last bathroom" speech and the elation settles into the pit of my stomach with the rice and beans.

I do have tampons and Midol (thank God for my superstition that if I bring something, then I won't need it. Although I do realize this red stripe blows that whole damn belief system out of the water). But the tampons are in my bag. Which is on the bus. With all the men.

I stuff a wad of toilet paper in my underwear. Then I slip out past the woman and step back onto the bus. Most of the men are back already, further proof of the old adage that they're just faster. A dozen pairs of eyes watch me walk all the way to the back of the bus, grab my bag and walk all the way back up front. Twenty-four eyes watching me climb off the van and go back toward the toilet. When I near the bathroom, I hold out my peso to the woman, but she waves me inside. "It's okay," she says in English. I am so grateful for someone who understands that I want to hug her, but I just rush in the door, pop a couple of Midol in one end and a tampon in the other (count: one down, six left), and rush back to the van.

I try to ignore all the eyes on me as I make my way back to my seat. I lean my head back against the fabric, wishing I was back in my own bed.

But then the bus lurches forward, takes a sideways swipe at the road, and there in front of us is the mountain, hiding its head in the clouds. It's nice to know I'm not the only one feeling that way. I keep my eyes on the mountain and rub my hands together quietly to warm them.

Three hours later, I'm standing in the very back of a pickup truck. The men from the bus are with me too, all of us huddling beneath a leaky plastic tarp. Having left the bus behind when it could climb no further, we're making our way up the last twenty miles of the mountain in the coffee farmer's four-wheel drive. It's been pouring here for days, apparently, leaving the roads looking like chocolate and caramel rivers. The air smells of forest and cloud. In fact, the air looks and feels like cloud. We can see right off the mountain from this angle. It is a shit-load of a long way down.

The truck lurches forward five feet and then slides back two or three. The tires on the right fall into something—a rut, a groove, a four-mile wide riverbed—and two dozen hands reach out for something solid to grab. Around me, the men moan as their stomachs try to climb up their throats again.

Despite all the twisty, turvy turns that made me feel so sick earlier, I'm delighted to realize that this—being some fifteen-hundred feet up—doesn't bother me at all. My stomach cramps, but I know it's just the period that's making me feel this way. I tighten my grip on the tailgate with one hand and press the palm of my other hand into my stomach. The way I feel right now is nothing new. I've handled this before. Finally, something that I know how to deal with. Finally, something I've done that none of these men have even thought about.

I might still be the only female on board and, yes, I'm still the only newbie. But we're all in the way back now and we're all wide-awake. And by the looks on the faces of the men around me, I'm no longer the only one worrying about spoiling my shirt. Or, for that matter, my underwear.

And just think of the great story I'll have to tell at breakfast on my next trip . . .

Stains Women Leave

Linda DeCicco Antonazzi

We yearn to leave our marks
yet spend our lives erasing them
blotting them out as soon as they appear
mascara on the pillowcase
lipstick on the coffee mug
the bloody brown of periods.

We tarnish everything
dropping mucous plugs
from watery wombs
each time a baby is born.

Even a good laugh, unexpected,
has us peeing in our pants.

Men mark their territory like dogs do
thinking nothing
of leaving up the toilet lid
grinding a cigar in the flowerpot
tossing a bloody wad of toilet paper
from a cut while shaving off
five o'clock shadows,

While we hide inside ours
Trying not to leave a trace.
Covering our tracks
Making a clean getaway.

Trying to pretend we were never there.

I Draw My Doctor a Picture

—after Sharon Olds
Robin Silbergleid

A red print like a butterfly hinging its wings—

the simile makes
what is happening to me
beautiful, a girl
in the bathroom checking

for bloodstains. How many
times? It began at twelve.

I stuffed paper-thin tissue in my pants
and ignored it.

These days it's all
I think about, shades of pink, brown, red

like the paints I mixed in art class.
These are colors I know
how to make, how to add a tinge
of white, a drop of black. When

the doctor says, *tell me*

about the bleeding, I have nothing
but metaphor. It was a butterfly

it was a bucketful of blackberries
it was raindrops on pavement
at the beginning of a storm.

Menstruation in the Time of Global Warming

Changxin Fang

This February morning
no snow on the ground
but broken thermometer—
air pollution, blood
on the linen, early
Valentine.

Sandstorm in a grocery bag,
lungs filled with down.
Trees inverted
arteries, copper wires
for veins, nerves
taut as harp strings.

Last week it was sixty degrees here.
Two weeks ago
the first snow of the year.

There is a terror in spring
like the terror of burning oil wells.
Outside, a girl plays in the grass,
her breasts budding early
like apple blossoms
in a greenhouse filled with light.

Over Easy

Amy Ouzoonian

Framed by a graph charting a woman's passage from
Menstruation to menopause
She demonstrates how to remove the little white eyes
From the case, cleverly disguised as a compact.
Jan and Sara, two severely retarded women
Have met with too many "accidents" and ended up "late"
At the other institutions.
It happens. Here, we'll take precautions.
It's true, what the other staff say, that
Jan doesn't even know what her vagina is for
Let alone understand why she bleeds every month.
And forget about Sara, she's not even potty trained
But she screams
When the male staff workers
try to come close.
Back at the home, I pop one white eye from the case
As Jan and Sara stare at dandelion heads
Covering the facilities yard with a plague of yolk.
Jan licks her smiling lips and rubs her tummy, thinking about lunch.
Sara asks Jan for the thirtieth time what they're having.
Jan giggles "eggs."
I call both
back in the dayroom
for juice and meds.

War Paint

Patti Dean

I rack up one-night stands as a front line singer on the road with a rock and roll band. Rock and Roll hotels are impact rooms—numbers slam-dunk sexed on a full tilt boogie prowl to create the perfect nightcap. Sex relieves the road's boredom, leaving red splotches on your chest and a semen cocktail as an inside job going-away present.

Transformation stirs at five p.m., after the talk shows end and the local news comes on—which town am I in again? I paint road warrior excitement where eyebrows no longer exist, eyelashes clump from days-old adhesive, and sallow complexion resists healthy glow due to lack of sun and excess of the amenities of an open bar and the local drug community. Makeup is a necessary art form and screams for attention between sets as the band plays fourth-rate road show rock and roll circus in stifling hot dance clubs.

Married businessmen check in on Thursdays. They enter the bar in groups, check out the band, and loosen up like little kids on their first away-from-home weekend sleepover. They are ripe for picking on Friday. They've seen your act, are tired of their herd, and are easily persuaded to take it to the next level.

The progression is an obvious visual: Eyes dart—case the room—what if you get caught—scared—ready to risk—laugh loudly with your other business pals—go ask that girl to dance—No!—don't get up—sit—the drink hits and the next thing you know you are on the way to the bar buying drinks for the entire table and seeding a nagging worry of how to explain the bar charges to the wife when the credit card statement comes at the end of the month—that hurdle cleared—it's a smooth ride to the finish line—how about the girl singer?

Most are tall, transparent, cerebral corporate business types stashing wedding bands wrapped around hundred dollar bills in their wallet. Married men pause—and say, "Your Room." You never go to theirs. They share a room with someone in the company to save money. "Your room" negates any payment for making a choice.

This one was different. Dark, short, stocky. Brown beard. Brown hair on his arms, knuckles, growing from the top of his shirt. Brown wide steady eyes. He held easy ground at the bar. Twice he danced with a local. Back to the bar and back to a steady gaze. This one wasn't married. He said, "My room."

As soon as the band finished the last set, I ran to my room and peeled everything off. I wanted nothing that was me in public. Makeup, four hours of work sweat, my ideas, what I thought was my personality—everything off. Wearing only a shift, I ran to his room.

He opened the door. The room in disarray. Clothes tossed in a pile on the floor. Towel thrown on the bed. His hair plastered down. Drops of water on his beard. He didn't smell of toothpaste, breath mints, aftershave and deodorant. The married man smell.

"Listen, I have to tell you I started my period today."

So quick, so deliberate, so expert, he reached between my legs and pulled my tampon out and tossed it in the corner. He pushed me back on the bed and his mouth opened, opened me wide. His tongue rammed deeply inside me. Accepting everything. When he lifted his head, his mouth shared taste and we both drank. Blood was our communion. Never taking his eyes from mine, he inched his fingers inside me, drew blood, and finger-painted warrior streaks under his eyes.

Sex during your period is always an adjustment: Oh, okay—well, let's just do it—for God's sake, grab a towel—don't stain my clothes.

The menu is limited. As I once overheard a woman complain, "Honey, that lowlife had the nerve to tell me, 'I don't do no shoppin' downtown!' I drop-kicked his fat ass down the street. Made skid marks as he bounced." Uh huh.

All through the night, we finger-painted masterpieces on undulating canvases, using every color. There was little talk. Deep wine-fueled moans and earth smells mingled with twisted, blood-stained sheets. A crime scene for the maid to clean in the morning.

He stayed one more night. My blood flow was lighter. This night we were quiet. Low murmurs. He smoked while I slept on his chest. His fur was soft. We slept and made clean getaway sex in the morning. No addresses, no phone numbers. Few if any promises can hold on the road.

That night, a sandy-haired, tall, brainy businessman with glasses bought me a drink. I didn't tell him I got my drinks for free. Bases covered, he telephoned his wife and recounted his day while I was in the shower.

Years later:

I went to an AA Women in Recovery Indian Sweat retreat. Women of every type and social strata were there. As the heat from the rocks made even the flimsiest bathing suits feel like winter clothes, we stripped our life experiences down to few words but much meaning for each of us. At one point during the long sweat, as we told our truths, some hard and some hopeful, one woman spoke of a man that she'd loved and called him a Young Warrior.

Breath stopped. A body memory in every woman there—whether experienced in this lifetime or not. The impact of a warrior on a woman's life. The warrior's power to awaken and open the female body's "Yes!" The power that peels back the skin and entwines the soul as arms and legs open to receive thrusts of life. That woman lifted us all up with her bravery in naming him Warrior.

The leader of our sweat nodded. Years ago, she'd spent three years of her life chained to a bed as a sex slave by a fellow Native American also damned by the credo, "The only good Indian is a dumb/drunk/dead one." Now she was a respected grandmother, called Auntie by her tribe.

Grace had finally bestowed on her the experience of a Warrior whose choices were brave.

The Mainstream

Barbara Crooker

That time of month.
All day long I am under
water in anticipation.

My stomach slogs and sloshes
like milk in a jug carted
over a rocky road.

The sullen moon pulls out
the balance;
the monthly tide returns.

Swaddled in water, cradled in salt,
we lived nine months in the current
before that first swim,

the gush and run
of the birthing flood,
when the water broke

on boulders and we fell
into the alien air.
Not fish out of water,

we survived, grew older,
watched the grass swish and eddy.
But once each month,

our quivering gills remember.
We swim again in the mainstream,
touching the current.

We know what is real:
birthwater, bathwater, milk & manna.
My woman's hair

rivers out behind
like tributaries
seeking the sea.

Bess Miller: Redwing, 1888

Katharyn Howd Machan

Full spring: she's gone back up
into the hills again, flanks lean,
thick fur dull brown from winter's

long slow sleep. She's given birth;
three or four or five mouths need
her milk, so now she has

to seek the grass most close
to sun, the richest green that's rising.
I watch her, mornings, keeping

track of how she noses
from beneath the barn, ears turned
for every sound, round back

emerging carefully,
teeth ready, claws prepared. I see
her venture into light's

cool grayness, silent, all
her breath for hunger's hurry. Back
where clover grows, where berries

unfold blossoms pale
as snow, I know she finds and feeds
and fills her swelling belly

just as I sit tight,
and hold my dresses still, and wait

as womb's blood seeps away

the certainty that I
will bear my young, despite my care,
my steady appetite.

River Blood

CB Follett

I think of blood,
moon-blood,
that collected each month.

Films in junior high,
the velvety Y of the womb
how it pillowed with blood

and waited. How the pinprick
egg set off from its ovary
and floated free

into the arms of the fallopian,
slid down the tube to the uterus,
cushioned and welcoming;

one egg per month, maybe two,
each with the potential
to look like me.

In the classroom, we watched the eggs
pause in the womb, awaiting acceptance,
but the gates opened,

lives moved on and out, the walls
sloughed their welcome into a river of red.
How many months that river,

one hundred and fifty before I was ready,
another one-fifty while I willed
the rivers to stop, begged each egg

to dam the flow, build legs and a heart:
river of hope, heartbreak river,
river without mercy.

Still Your Bridesmaid

Sarah E. Holihan Smith

The rabbit is restless,
and I'm the one who bleeds

because the only expectant mother
in the house is the rabbit.

That metallic cling cling is her feet,
her feet bunched up to her chest,
compact as a bird's nest in a tree.

As something hot flows
from the severed root of my tongue,

and whatever words I had wanted
to bring along were cut
so that I would swallow them whole,

she rings the cage with her feet,
her feet, cling, tink tink,

my mother-to-be.

History in the Making

Nancy Wahler

"Preserve our past," I scream through the jagged glass that was once a window to one of the area's finest homes, the Whitley-James, as I lob one of my missiles toward the street. My throat is raw. I have been screaming a variation of this phrase for over two hours now, protesting the demolition of another historical home. The wrecking crew, three stories below, whose boss is chomping his gum so zealously I can see his jaws moving from here, is unimpressed. However, the chain binding me to the radiator applauds my efforts through its loud clanking each time I shake my fist.

Morty is down there too, in his tan suit, white shirt and striped tie. He tried to come in after me earlier but changed tactics after putting one of his feet through a rotting stair. The new game plan seems to be trying to coax me out from the relative safety of the street. He keeps talking to the gum guy. I toss down another water-filled balloon, a yellow one. It splats near his Sebago loafers and he steps to the right as if the water is dog poop.

"Rebecca, get down from there." His voice has changed from pleading to annoyed. He knows the police will come soon and arrest me—again. Lucky he is a lawyer. What he doesn't know is my period started last night. That the cramps of failure are ripping into my abdomen as the hot rush of blood rejects my womb. The in vitro didn't work. This was our last shot. I turn forty tomorrow and we agreed we would stop.

But I won't stop trying to keep what they call progress from destroying everything that is beautiful. Sinking to the floor, the multi-colored balloons bobbling around me, I lay my head against the cool metal of my one supporter, the radiator, and allow myself to sob. It is technology that has denied me a baby. First, in the drug they gave my mother for morning sickness and now in this failure.

Sirens blare in the distance and tears blur my vision. Damn Morty and his self-righteousness. He had to admit on the adoption application that he had been arrested for possession. The computers would have told them anyway, he said. His offense was over twenty years ago but I know that's why they haven't given us a baby.

"Ms. Jacobs," a hollow voice calls through a megaphone, "this house is scheduled for demolition. If you do not leave of your own free will, you will be removed." Peeking over the wooden sill, I hope the blues of my eyes aren't visible. I don't want the two police on the street standing next to my husband to even know they got my attention. One of them looks like he ought to be in retirement with his portly belly and gray hair styled in the fashion of Bea Arthur from *Golden Girls*. The other one has black hair, wears his blues like a military uniform and, judging by his posture, it would seem that he is storing his police baton up his ass. Then I change my mind. If they want my attention, they can have it.

"Preserve our Past," I call again standing up, only to lean back to give them the finger, with both hands. The chain resumes its applause as I toss fluid-filled bombs down at their heads in a rainbow of mutiny. Morty says something to them and then stalks off to get into his white Acura. His shoulder length dark hair swings out for a second as he throws himself into the car. That hairstyle is the only thing that hasn't changed about Morty since we got married twenty years ago, although it has more gray now. My heart gives a queer ache of loss for the man who would have chained himself next to me even ten years ago.

The stairs creak below me and it seems that Officer Baton-Up-His-Ass has left the front yard. He must be coming up. The floor outside of the dormer room I am inhabiting groans as it takes his weight. Will he even notice the hand-painted ceiling on his way up?

"Lady, this doesn't have to be hard."

"Blow me," I say, realizing I don't really have the right anatomy to make such a request, but I think he gets my point because he sighs heavily and the wood of the stair groans again. Is he damaging that carved banister? Little upstart, he was probably learning not to pee in his pants when I saved my first house. The question now is, can he get me out of here without doing anything that will allow me to sue him?

When he walks in his eyes aren't hard. In fact, they kinda look like a cow's, all big and dull. He holds his arms out from his sides like he is showing a wild animal that he isn't going to hurt them. Maybe that is what I have been reduced to by my biological clock, some sort of feral creature. Then he takes me by surprise by charging toward me and cuffing my other hand to the radiator.

"What the hell? I hate to tell you this, but that isn't going to get me out of here," I tell him, rattling the cuff.

"Really? Thanks, but it is going to keep you from hitting me." He proceeds to read me my Miranda rights. I quote them with him for fun. My fun that is, as it is clear by his tense jaw that it is just as annoying to him as I intend it to be. Taking out a small saw he starts grinding away at the chain. If my ears could shudder, the screech of that saw on metal would do it. I try to pull free from the cuffs. Sometimes in old houses like this things are loose. The radiator does move slightly as he finishes and I lose my balance.

With the finesse of a seasoned hunter, he cuffs my hands together behind my back and muscles me to the car, like I am a deer he just shot. Will I have to ride on the hood?

• • •

Three hours later Morty and I are riding home in silence. The air-conditioning is blasting and the cool air is making my nose stuffy. He was already at the station when I got there. He doesn't even look at me as he waits at a stoplight.

"Could we make a stop?" I ask, fiddling with the smooth wooden prayer beads I wear around my wrist.

"Where? You have some red paint to throw on a fur coat?" His grip is so tight on the steering wheel that his knuckles have blanched.

"Now really Morty, that's more of a PETA thing. Besides, who would be wearing a fur coat in September?" I give him a sidelong look to see if he can tell I'm teasing him.

If he can, he doesn't care. The gray guardrail flashes past and I wonder when we became these people who don't know how to talk to each other.

"Where do you want to go?" he asks. I am confused for a moment before I remember I had asked him to stop.

"I need tampons," I tell him, watching for his reaction. It is barely visible but it is there. First his eyes widen then his brow furrows. Finally, his shoulders slump maybe a quarter of an inch. He reaches over slowly to take my hand, which is resting in my lap, as he clears his throat.

"When did it happen?" he says in graveside tones.

"Last night." His hand feels warm and soft next to my callused one. His used to have calluses too. The roughness used to make me shiver in delight when he ran his hands down my back when we were making love. I wonder when he lost his and why I hadn't noticed. "Are you using my lotion?"

"Maybe," he says and gives me a half-smile as he turns into our neighborhood, the restored houses smiling on me as we pass them to reach our Victorian.

"Lotion, ha—you're such a girl," I say, as it is one of our running jokes. Of the two of us, Morty has way more feminine characteristics than I do. Maybe he should be the one trying to get pregnant, he might be better at it. He certainly couldn't be any worse.

"It might be the smell reminds me of you," he says giving my hand a squeeze before he releases it to downshift. What an unbelievably sappy thing for him to say and yet, I love it. He pulls up in front of our brick rancher. "I've got to get back to work," he says leaving the motor running. "Unless you need me to stay?"

"No, I guess I'll be all right." The warm moment is gone. What am I supposed to do? Beg him to grieve with me? I can't quite bring myself to admit I need him right now especially when he clearly wants to get away. He gives me a quick, hard peck on the lips before I get out. As he drives away, I remember we never did stop for the tampons and my car is still parked on a side street in the Fort.

Standing there on the ultra green lawn, compliments of Chem-care, (he got his green lawn if I got another round of in vitro), I hear the phone ringing in the house. I barely get there in time to grab it before the answering machine does. It is Morty.

"Can you wait until I get home or do I need to come back?" He is referring to the tampons but doesn't call them by name. Now that is male.

"I can wait." It was really my way of telling him that the procedure didn't work without actually having to say it.

"Okay, I probably won't be home until around seven."

"That's fine."

"Becca?"

"Yeah."

"We're gonna be fine, you'll see. But I am sorry. Maybe we ought to get a dog."

"Yeah, that's the same."

"You know what I mean."

"Yeah, I know."

"But Becca."

"Yeah?"

"If we get a dog, you won't join PETA, right?" he says with a slight quaver in his voice for effect. It works since it makes me laugh.

"Maybe. See you tonight. 'Bye."

"'Bye." I hear the click and think I ought to go out and get some PETA brochures to spread across the dining room table for when he gets home.

Then I remember I don't have a car. I'm not going anywhere except to the couch. To what? Blubber and stare and feel sorry for myself? I set the phone down on the island in the kitchen.

A Dr. Pepper cold from the refrigerator helps wash down two Midol. While getting the drink I noticed a square package of cookie dough. The blue plastic rips easily and the first layer is gone before I can make myself stop. It is only after I drink a full glass of milk that I remember I am supposed to avoid dairy, caffeine and chocolate when having my period. A sharp stab in my midriff reminds me why. Come on Midol.

The phone rings and I pick it up on the second ring. I think it might be Morty checking on me. It's not. Caller ID reads Knox Co.

"Mortimer Jacobs?" a cultured female voice asks when I pick up the phone. Call me crazy but I'd think she would be able to tell the difference between my soprano and his alto. I wonder if it is one of the bimbos that works the front in his office.

"No, this is his wife." I say putting emphasis on the end of wife, as if that gives me a greater claim.

"Thank you," she says and hangs up before I can even ask if there is a message.

"Bitch," I say throwing the phone toward the island. It hits the ceramic floor with a crack that makes me wince. Morty will be pissed if I've broken another phone. Yes, I did say another, the last one I left outside in the rain. Didn't matter how many times I changed the batteries, I couldn't get it to come back from that one. The phone rings again and relief sails through me. It's not broken. Scrambling across the floor I answer it, standing up to lean against the fridge.

"Hello?" I say not even looking at the caller ID.

"Did I get any calls?" This time it is Morty.

"You must be psychic. Your girlfriend just hung up on me."

"Did she sound hot?" he says. The image of that front desk receptionist fills my brain, Maria or Marcia or something like that. She's twenty-two, curvy and probably as fertile as the proverbial Myrtle. Even though I started it, his joking stirs annoyance in my gut. It churns around with my cramps so that by the time it has crept up my throat to my mouth it is anger.

"Aren't you even going to deny it?" My head and jawline thud in response to my clenched teeth. They're dancing to the same tempo as my heart. The muscles in my arms ache to hit something but I just grasp the phone harder.

"Becca, you're being stupid," he says and tears well in my eyes. Somewhere inside my brain a small voice is screaming shut up, let it go, you're being irrational but what I say is, "I can't believe you just called me stupid."

"Bec—"

"Stupid, I guess that is what you would think. Stupid—for caring about the destruction of everything beautiful in this world, even a stupid old house; stupid for trying to stop the ripping away of our society's history; stupid for ever thinking I could ever be a mother or have a baby. Stupid, stupid, stupid. Thanks Morty I guess I am pretty stupid, I married you."

In the silence that follows, I hang up and set the phone down carefully on the island. The sweet rush of winning is quickly overcome by regret but the anger is still too strong for apologies. He shouldn't have called me stupid. He's the stupid one. He's the one who doesn't care. No one cares. Tears begin leaking down my face until I am crying, then the crying becomes sobbing.

Sliding down the refrigerator, my chest heaves as I cry. The handles of the refrigerator are digging into my back as my legs fold and I collapse to the floor. Raising my head, I hold my neck with my hands, letting out throaty wails as I rock back and forth, snot running from my nose. My chest hurts, my head is pounding, and still I can't stop. The release has become the master until the sobbing becomes moaning, I feel I can hardly breathe through the grief.

The back door opens and Morty comes in. His eyes widen as he sees me on the floor. I know my nose is swollen; my face is red.

"Oh my God, Becca," he says and his eyes fill with tears. I turn away not wanting to deal with his tears. But he gets down on the floor and enfolds me in his arms. Now we are both against the cool fridge. His chest is warm, his heart steady. I thought I was done crying but a new wave washes over me. In trying to ride it, I am pushed underneath again, choking. After a time, I lean back wiping my eyes and nose with the back of my hand.

"I'm getting snot all over your shirt," I choke out, half-laughing. Only the laugh becomes more tears.

"I've got more," he says, which reminds me of the fights we have had lately about his conservative clothes. "Can I get you a Kleenex or does that make me a conservative shit?" he asks me smiling.

"You're funny," I say, only it comes out like 'you'd fuddy' because of my stopped-up nose. He gets up and brings me a roll of toilet paper from the half-bath. After I have rid my nose of the corpses of millions of white blood cells in their gelatinous coffins he tips my chin up with his forefinger.

"I have some good news," he says. I lean back still taking shuddery breaths and raise one eyebrow to let him know he has my attention.

"I got a stay on the Whitley-James house," he says and breaks off. "No, no, don't cry again." My eyes are already filling and he is ripping more toilet paper off the roll and handing it to me.

"I don't know if . . ." He pulls me back into his arms and kisses the top of my head, probably the only dry spot on my body. "Stop crying or I'm going to call them back and tell them to level the whole thing."

"Morty, I— " he puts up his finger to stop me, like he is about to make a point in court and doesn't want to be interrupted.

"That was what the lady was calling about today. To tell me it went through. It's close though and it still may not qualify as a historical landmark." He leans back against the fridge and closes his eyes. The lines on his face smooth out and for a moment the twenty-year-old I married peeks out at me from underneath the graying hair. I lean over and kiss both of them full on the mouth. His lips are soft until they curve upward under mine.

"What's the smile?" I say, trying rather unsuccessfully to find a dry spot on his shirtfront to lay my head.

"Good thing I've got a girlfriend at the courthouse," he says. When he looks at me I am not smiling. "Still not funny?" he asks.

"No." I get up and smack him lightly on the head. "What do you want to go get for dinner?"

Three months later, we are at the site of the Whitley-James again but this time I am standing on the street holding Morty's hand instead of watching him from inside. The house did not qualify and the appeals we filed were rejected. They are about to level it. The machinery of destruction roars behind us.

"I hate we lost," says Morty, his hand squeezing mine. The house has become even more special to me since it's what brought my old Morty back. Plus, six weeks ago we snuck in pillows and made love underneath the vaulted ceiling. The cherubs in their clouds smiled down at us. Now, it seems like the columns quake a bit as the wrecking ball approaches.

"I know I said I wanted to be here but I can't watch this," I say, turning and leading him down the cracked sidewalk away from the destruction. The majestic trees form a cool canopy above us. Watching him from the corner of my eye as we walk, I think how lucky we are.

"So," I say, lightly touching my stomach, "I'm thinking when the baby comes, it should be named Whitley if it's a girl and James if it's a boy." His body seems to freeze as if he is a rabbit sensing danger. After all our failed tries, I can understand the wariness. Hence the six pregnancy tests I took.

First his eyes swivel over to me, taking in the stupid grin I can't keep off my face, then his whole body turns. As I face him, his eyes pass my sore breasts, dropping to my stomach that gives no outward sign of the little heart that is fluttering inside, safe in my blood.

"Really?" he says and I nod. Morty drops to his knees and wraps his arms around my hips. Pushing up my shirt he kisses me right on my abdomen. Chillbumps cross my skin but his lips are warm. This time, his tears are wet against me. I hug him back, my arms draped over his shoulders, not caring about the people who are passing, giving us stares.

"You were right Morty, that day on the phone, we would have been fine." He nods, his hair tickling my belly button in his agreement. "But I'm so glad that—" Tears are building in my throat too, choking off my words.

Standing up, he puts his hands on either side of my face, his fingers in my hair just above my ears. He kisses me then and it is full of love, passion, devotion and the salty taste of tears. Pulling back he looks at me and his brow furrows.

"Should you be out of bed?"

"I'm not at-risk," I say. Far from it, I'm so buoyant, it seems like if I began leaping I might fly.

"I want you to take it easy." His hands are behind me now, ushering me back toward the car as if I am an old lady.

"Okay Morty." He needs time to adjust. There's a protest rally scheduled at the courthouse for three o'clock. Maybe I won't tell him about that yet.

The Red Album

Jill Kelly Koren

1

My best friend got her period
At twelve, thought she was
Wetting her pants.
Her mom bought her gray
Sweatpants to celebrate.

2

My first period came at
Sixteen, a smattering of blood
I thought I should have
Sweatpants, too.
So I asked my mom for some.
She laughed, bought them
Anyway.

3

The next period waited a year
To show up. I didn't mind.
My body had to wait until
My ankle was broken
To have enough of a break
From a gymnast's grueling
Routine to gather the strength
Needed for bleeding.

4

My younger cousins nearly faint
At the sight of hairy women
Washing out reusable pads

In the campground bathroom
At Lake Monroe
After dancing all night with men
Who wore skirts but no deodorant
This was too much to bear
They never went back
To Sugar Hill

5

Rag
Tampon
Maxi
Mini
Super-absorbency
O.B.
Pad
Feminine Napkin
Panty-liner
Glad Rags
Nothing—
bleed into old underwear

6

I remember seeing my mother's
Underwear floating in a pink pool
In the bathroom sink
Once, I wore a pad before
I even knew what it was for.
I felt like a thief.

7

Never mind the red tent thing
He knew when she walked in
With that cowboy hat on
That they would be fucking
Before the night was over
She knew when the CD
Started over, started bumping
Right about now
Funk soul brother

That they would get it on
She didn't bother to mention
That she was still bleeding
And he didn't ask
And he didn't notice
She walked home the next morning,
Past Starbucks and Smoothie King
Still wearing her cowboy hat,
Sore and sad.

8

Boyfriend wanted to watch me
Take a tampon out.
He'd never seen it before.
He watched, fascinated.
I didn't understand.

9

Bloody underwear in the shower.
I always thought it the best place
To rinse it out, and then,
Who cares if it hangs there
For a day or two?
A woman might be tempted
To think that if she were dating
A woman, things like this might
Be easier, a girlfriend would
Understand.
A woman might be wrong.
The girlfriend hated the bloody
Underwear in the shower,
Hated it so much she started
Hating me, too, for taking up
Her space, for trying to be
The flower. Do you even try
To please your lovers? she spat
Back in an angry stream
Of words.

10

Leading a class trip
Of seventh graders
Our last stop was Jacksonville:
The Beach
We'd been waiting all year
Maria and Diana approached, shy
They were on their periods
And couldn't swim
I explained about tampons, they
Were excited, but needed
To call their parents for
Permission
The math teacher—a Latino
Who knew the customs—
Called me off, saved me
From a fury I could not understand
Lest I be held responsible
For the loss of two virginities
To one small cotton plug

11

Holed up in a hotel, my husband
Of more than three years
Chases our toddler
Into the bathroom while I
Am changing a bloody tampon
I don't bat an eye, but he
Raises an eyebrow with mild curiosity.
It is the first time he's seen it,
But he is no girlfriend
He doesn't wince at the sight
Of bloody underwear
In the shower
He lets me bleed
In peace, he is
In tune with the rhythm
Of these cycles:
They are his own.

Five of Cups

Marty McConnell

for the incident of blood which is not
your birth. for the sweet, imperfect tempest
that could have made you. for the nights
you bathed in wine, raucous drinking songs
in the belly, for you less miscarried than
unwished, I have no ready prayers. no
offerings but the usual application of heat
to the abdomen and back, no lullaby, no
mourning song. you were less you
than a notion, hoped-against, unnamed.
this month's pain lays me flat and—
yes—grateful. hungry as the devil
and barbed as sawgrass. good spill,
nothing owing, I watch you like a silent
movie, like seabirds in the distance, circling.

Adam Refuses the Sacrament

Teneice Durrant

During those first seasons
of dust and rock,
before the pain of concentrated
testosterone, before
I was allowed to choose
a landscape, I welcomed
this clot. Color was
the only indicator
that I was alive in your world;
I bled gardens
like ripening fruit.
And when I sought a female
sanctuary, you lied to Cain
and Abel, told our sons it
was bad luck, would wither
your stunted crops, would scare
the cows, those dumb animals.
You made them afraid
of whatever they can't create,
and me, afraid of their hands.
Even now I long to find
Lilith, baptize each other
in crimson holy water.

Blood Ritual

Demetrice Annt'a Worley

Humid air swaddles my hot body.
With one bare leg draped over
the back of the porch swing,

I slowly sway in rural blue-black darkness.
Close-bitten nails. Chipped red polish.
Fingers folded flat against belly, I count

Twenty-eight days since the last full moon.
On the eastern horizon,
a billowy thunderhead,

thousands of feet high, expansive
as the distance between *quicken*
and *termination*, stations itself.

Pulsating yellow-pink, and purple flashes
illuminate the gray-white cloud,
transient brilliancy.

A white flash quivers
through it. My skin tingles.
I listen for a thunderous rumble

to determine the lightning's
closeness: *One thousand one,*
one thousand two, the swing stops.

My moist hands press down on my womb.
I inhale heavy ionized air, smell
dewy soil's pungent iron odor.

Woman, Water Tower, Man

Loreen Niewenhuis

As she sipped at her second glass of wine, she felt her head loosen on her neck. It felt good.

A water tower in transit looks like a giant martini glass on a flatbed truck. It is assembled on site.

He found himself saying *baby* aloud for no reason, in the shower, in the car. It was something he could not stop.

On her third glass of wine, she began to tilt her head as she sipped. The red wine left a stain on the corner of her mouth.

The assembly takes weeks, as all of the seams must be sealed and the motor installed. The water tower is painted on site.

The *baby* was as one would say to a lover; he did not have one. The *baby* was his longing made inadvertently verbal.

Toward the end of the third glass of wine, her head lolled as she sipped. The wine left a red crescent stain, like half a smile, on one cheek.

Once the tower is complete, they hook up the pump and turn it on so as to begin pumping the water up the shaft of the tower and to fill the bulb at the top. It takes weeks to fill.

He began to clear his throat compulsively to mask the word as it came out of his mouth. If he held it in too long, it came out in a string: *baby, baby, baby.*

She looked like a clown, grotesque, drunk, her mouth half-painted, her head rolling around on her neck. There was no one to tell her to stop, to slow down, to love yourself.

It is the weight of the water in the elevated bulb that makes the water pressure for the town. The pumping continues because the water is continuously used by the town.

This morning, in the shower, he heard himself say *come here, baby* and he crumpled to the tile floor; he cried. He let the water touch him, then he got dressed and went to work.

The bartender took her glass away and called a cab after taking two twenties from her purse to cover her tab. He knew a cabbie who was a woman, so he called her to be safe in getting the drunken woman home.

The last thing painted on the water tower is the name of the town. They call in a specialist for this who checks with the city clerk to get the proper font and to see if they want a slogan, smaller, underneath the name.

He is wined and dined by a visiting saleswoman that night because he is in charge of making a big purchasing decision. She intimates that she will do anything to get this account, so they go up to her hotel room.

The woman cabbie helps the bartender slosh the woman into the backseat of the cab. He hands the lady's purse over to the cabbie so that she can find her address and, later, collect her fare and large tip.

If there is no catwalk around the bulge of the water tower bulb, then the painter of the town's name must use ropes and pulleys to suspend himself. He outlines the letters using the welded sheets of metal as a grid.

He is astonished just to touch her skin, the saleswoman's skin. The touch of skin on skin is enough to silence the words that bubble up from his soul, wanting and longing and wanting, but they have sex all night because he is a starving man.

The cabbie hopes that the passed-out clown will not puke in her cab; she had just cleaned it Monday. She wonders how one gets to be a passed-out clown, how anyone gets so lonely that they will put themselves in a situation where they must trust strangers to care for them.

The painting of the name and slogan go quickly once the letters are outlined on the grid of the welded panels of metal. The painter travels all over the country painting large letters up close like this, not seeing his work until he is safely back on the ground.

He devours her, ingests her, imbibes, swallows, inhales, mouths her all over; he would become a cannibal this night if he could. He wonders if he ate her flesh if that would satisfy the words that bubble up constantly; if her flesh would become the internalized *baby* he longs for.

The cabbie finds the address by shining her spotlight on the rows of brownstones on Elm Street. She pulls out a keychain and her fare with hefty tip, then opens the back door of the cab to find that the woman is not on the seat.

The painter of town names feels a looseness in the ropes and pulleys and forces himself to remain calm. He tries to think of the next job—if he can only remember the name of the next town—as he reaches for the dangling hook of his safety line.

It is the middle of Saturday when the man awakens, horrified, in the hotel room, alone, smeared with blood, surrounded by bloodstained sheets. He sees the contract with a note: "Sign it, Stallion. Sorry about starting my period."

The cabbie pulls the clown drunk off the floor of the cab and hauls her slight arm over her big shoulders. She drags the rag mop slip of a clown drunk up the three stairs to her front door.

The painter of town names cannot reach the safety ring without swinging in the loosening ropes. He begins to swing gently, then gives one more push to reach the ring.

The man signs the contract and puts it in his briefcase before going in the bathroom to take a shower. When the water touches him, he feels the words filling his mouth again.

The clown woman drunk pours easily into her bed and the cabbie looks around at her lovely place. The cabbie tries to wipe away the stain on the clown's soft face with her calloused finger.

The hook of the safety line bounces off the loop and he makes one more swing for it. On the backswing, however, the ropes let loose even as he is poised with the hook to save his own life.

Baby, baby, baby, come here, baby, baby, he cannot stop the words as he smears the traces of her blood off his arms, his stomach, his penis. He curls on the floor of the shower.

The cabbie turns the clown woman so she won't inhale her own sick.

The painter has never seen his work like this, in fast-motion pullback.

The man sobs, lets it out, and vows this will be the last time he ever cries.

The cabbie makes sure the door locks on her way out.

The painter becomes a red stain.

The man never cries again.

Tampons

Ellen Bass

My periods have changed. It is years
since I have swallowed pink and gray darvons, round
chalky Midols from the bottle with the smiling girl.
Now I plan a quiet space,
protect myself those first few days when my uterus lets
go and I am an open anemone. I know
when my flow will come. I watch my mucous pace
changes like a dancer, follow the fall
and rise of my body heat. All this
and yet I never questioned them, those slim white handies.

It took me years to learn to use them
starting with pursettes and a jar of vaseline.
I didn't know where the hole was.
I didn't even know enough
to try to find one. I pushed until
only a little stuck out and hoped
that was far enough.
I tried every month through high school.

And now that I can change it in a moving car—
like Audrey Hepburn changing dresses in the taxi
in the last scene of *Breakfast at Tiffany's*—
I've got to give them up.

Tampons, I read, are
bleached, are
chemically treated to
compress better,
contain asbestos.
Good old asbestos. Once we learned not to shake it—

Johnson & Johnson's—on our babies or diaphragms,
we thought we had it licked.

So what do we do? They're universal.
Even macrobiotics and lesbian separatists are hooked on them.
Go back to sanitary napkins?
>   Junior high, double napkins
>   on the heavy days, walking home damp underpants
>   chafing thighs. It's been a full twelve years
>   since I have worn one, since Spain when Marjorie pierced my
ears
>   and I unloaded half a suitcase of the big gauze pads in the hotel
trash.

Someone in my workshop suggested tassaways, little
cups that catch the flow.
>   They've stopped making them,
>   we're told. Women found they could reuse them
>   and the company couldn't make enough
>   money that way. Besides,
>   the suction pulled the cervix out of shape.

Then diaphragms.
>   It presses on me, one woman says.
>   So swollen these days. Too tender.

Menstrual extraction, a young woman says.
I heard about that. Ten minutes
and it's done.
>   But I do not trust putting tubes into my uterus each month.
>   We're told everything is safe
>   in the beginning.

Mosses.
The Indians used mosses.
>   I live in Aptos. We grow
>   succulents and pine.
>   I will buy mosses
>   when they sell them at the co-op.

Okay. It's like the whole birth control schmeer.
There just isn't a good way. Women bleed.
We bleed.
The blood flows out of us. So we will bleed.
Blood paintings on our thighs, patterns
like river beds, blood on the chairs in
insurance offices, blood on Greyhound buses
and 747s, blood blots, flower forms
on the blue skirts of the stewardesses.
Blood on restaurant floors, supermarket aisles, the steps of government
buildings. Sidewalks

                                        Gretel's bread
            will have
                            like
                    blood trails,

crumbs. We can always find our way.

We will ease into rhythm together, it happens
when women live closely—African tribes, college sororities—
our blood flowing on the same days. The first day
of our heaviest flow we will gather in Palmer, Massachusetts,
on the steps of Tampax, Inc. We'll have a bleed-in.
We'll smear the blood on our faces. Max Factor
will join OB in bankruptcy. The perfume industry
will collapse, who needs
whale sperm, turtle oil, when we have free blood?
For a little while cleaning products will bloom,
409, Lyson, Windex. But
the executives will give up. The cleaning woman is leaving a
red wet rivulent, as she scrubs down the previous stains.
It's no use. The men would have to
do it themselves, and that will never come up
for a vote at the Board. Women's clothing manufacturers, fancy
furniture, plush carpet, all will phase out. It's just not
practical. We will live the old ways.

Simple floors, dirt or concrete, can be hosed down
or straw, can be cycled through the compost.
Simple clothes, none in summer. No more swimming pools.

Swim in the river. Yes, swim in the river.
Dogs will fall in love with us.
We'll feed the fish with our blood. Our blood
will neutralize the chemicals and dissolve the old car parts.
Our blood will detoxify the phosphates and the
PCBs. Our blood will feed the dry, tired surface of the earth.
We will bleed. We will bleed. We will
bleed until we bathe her in our blood and she turns
slippery new like a baby birthing.

Premenstrual Craving

Cindy Childress

I am isolated
in a cluster of beach rocks beaten to fine grains.
Starfish suffocate on my spine
each time the tide recedes.
Dunes change shape in the wind.
Lilies wither, flourish, wither, flourish
unaware of lava molting below the surface
waiting for a sacrifice.
Fat calves and princes do little to quench the thirst
to find myself in some other body of water.
I am hungry to digest myself,
eruption burning inside and out,
an effort to rise above the sea's level.

Wednesday, 3:56 a.m.

Sally Bittner Bonn

with arms I pull my body through lake
five, eight, more feet below the surface
underneath roots of lake weed dangling
I breathe and travel great distances

long and belly-down in bed I awake
warm and rich brick-brown liquid
begins to seep from my tendrils

my autumn print sheets
accept this new organic leaf
as one of their own

I prefer to sleep naked
on the Tuesday nights I know
these Wednesday mornings come
unencumbered, uninhibited, the red tent

some morning dreams are empty
hold the deep squeeze inside
stumble to the bathroom yet unpainted

The Last Time

Jane Yolen

I didn't mean to mourn,
I meant to laugh,
But my bloodline
Dribbled away so slowly,
So silently,
I hardly noticed it had gone.
The biological clock having long since
Stopped ticking,
There was no alarm.
Only silence
And a kind of wistful death.

The Evolution of the Facts of Life

Julia Schuster

I sat at the kitchen island with my nine-year-old daughter, watching her slurp angel hair pasta through the most perfect pucker I'd ever seen. Spaghetti sauce droplets joined the freckles that littered the dunes of her cheeks and looked like footprints left by angels after a night of dancing through her dreams. She's too young for this, I thought. It's too soon. But I had no choice. I realized that I must tell her the truth and not hedge on the details. It was approaching too quickly for my taste, but better to head off the flood of questions before she filled in the blanks on her own.

My mind floated back to a time in my youth, a time of bubble baths and sponge rollers, go-go boots and David Cassidy. I was nine and a half—not just nine, and not nearly ten, but a full, yet immature, nine and a half. I had played outside all day, climbed into the neighbor's tree house, fought off pirates that looked remarkably like my brothers and painted daisies on the walls of my tool-shed clubhouse—a normal 1967 spring day.

After a dinner of meatloaf, fried okra and mashed potatoes, Daddy left for the bowling alley to join his team for the league championship. And, as usual, my brothers, John and Arthur, abandoned the kitchen before Mother could include them in clean-up duty. I scraped the dishes while Mother pulled on her rubber gloves and filled the sink with hot water and Palmolive liquid. Seeing her in those yellow gloves made me wish again that Daddy would finally break down and buy her a dishwasher for her birthday. We were the last of our friends to "hold out." It was time. It was way past time.

When Mother cut me loose, I toyed with the idea of going back outside to play—Daylight Savings Time had just started—but instead, I made the girly choice of sinking neck-deep into a humped mountain range of Mr. Bubble suds, while still wondering what my brothers meant when they teased me about taking a bath with a "man." The tub was deep, water warm, air steamy. I scooped up handfuls of bubbles to make a beard and mustache, then sat up and constructed puff sleeves and a dress bodice out of the iridescent pink fluff. John knocked on the locked door a few times, yelling for me to hurry up; I ignored him. Arthur was the next to disturb my leisure; I ignored him, too. Being boys, I figured, if they needed to pee they could go outside and find a bush.

When my hands and feet had pickled and the water cooled, I stood up in the tub and splashed myself to rinse off the soapy residue. The coolness of the water trickled down my torso, mingling with the pink bubbles in a river that followed the curves of my flesh. I leaned forward at the waist to wrap my hair in a towel and noticed that the body river had darkened to a ghastly red at the top of my inner thighs. My breath caught in my chest as I watched this crimson fountain cascade from some secret place hidden in the vortex between my legs.

The shock stood me upright so quickly that a wave of dizziness washed over me. I grabbed the shower curtain for support. Then, coughing sounds that took no form, *ma, ma, ma, ma, ma*, I danced back and forth in a panic, legs splayed, the water's agitation rocking and sloshing with my distress. My lips formed the word "Mother," but only baby-babble came from the effort. I jerked another towel from the rod and high-stepped onto the tile floor. Red droplets rained down and splashed onto lily-white grout. I threw open the door and dashed out, but in the hallway, my wet feet lost traction on the glossy hardwood. I slipped and fell, skidding on my rump into the far wall, a pink imprint of my right hip marring the cream-colored plaster. I scrambled to my feet, towel flying.

When I burst into the den, Mother's shaming look and startled yelp, "What in heaven's name?" alerted me to my nakedness. John and Arthur sniggered as I fumbled with my towel and my face warmed to match the color of the dribble between my legs.

"I'm dying!" I finally managed, securing the towel under my armpit. "There's blood . . . blood everywhere. Call an ambulance. I need help!"

No one moved.

A silence usually reserved for hospital waiting rooms enveloped the room as a small puddle of pinkness collected around my feet. I reached down and tucked the towel high between my legs, crossing them to keep it there. Mother shot a look of retribution toward my brothers that said, "Leave now or die," and to my amazement they stood and exited by the nearest door, obeying with more haste than I'd ever seen them implement.

"Mother!" I moaned. "Do something, please!"

She rose from her chair and moved slowly to the telephone table, taking a

large arcing route around me as if my plague might be contagious. Lifting
the receiver, she dialed my sister, who was thirteen years my senior, already
married and living away from home. The punctuated cadence of the rotary's
dum-ba-da-dum-dum revolutions became a mournful accompaniment to
my dismay.

"We need your assistance," Mother said when my sister answered. "Yes,
it's Becky. She started. I think it would be better coming from you."

I wondered then if my sister also suffered from this horrible ailment.
What other reason could there be for "it" to "come from" her? Mother
"uh-huh'ed" a couple of times, and "Yes, yes'ed," a few more, then replaced
the receiver and turned toward me.

"Get dressed," she said, without inflection. "Just put an old washrag in
your panties until Sissie gets here. She'll bring what you need." She almost
looked up at me when she said, "You're awfully young for this, but I guess
I should have . . . oh, well, it's too late now." Her eyes glanced instead at
the floor, the window, the wrinkles in her hands. Then she walked back to
her hysterically floral chair and sat down as if all was well with the world.
An Andy Griffith rerun was on television. She focused on it, and within
seconds she was chuckling with the studio audience, while I stood motion-
less in the middle of the floor, dripping, my body towel sagging, my hair
towel slipping off the left side of my head.

Sissie appeared in my doorway before the *Mayberry* credits ran. I was
curled up on my bed in my robe with three washrags in my panties and a
bath towel pressed between my legs—just in case the massive abdominal
hemorrhage I was experiencing couldn't be contained by the washrags—
and wondering why my usually doting mother was now treating me as if
I'd farted at one of her Christian Women's Club luncheons. Sissie flew to
my side, God love her. Her arms around me had never felt so good. She
held me, and didn't say anything until I had cried myself out.

"What's wrong with me," I asked, when the hiccupping sobs subsided.
"Am I dying? Do you have this . . . this . . . this illness, too?"

She smiled, but didn't laugh at me. "No, sweetie, you're fine. This is
normal. You just started your period. You're a woman now."

I guess the blank expression on my face alerted her to my stupidity.
Period? And what did bleeding profusely have to do with being a woman
I wanted to know. I'd heard rumblings at school about the "womanly
mysteries" I would learn about in the health class I'd have to take in fifth
grade, but nothing was mentioned about dribbling blood or washrags in
panties. Information that startling would have certainly gotten around.
Why hadn't anyone prepared me for this?

"Mother hasn't told you anything, has she?" Sissie asked.

I didn't even know what "anything" she was talking about.

"Oh, good grief," she said, shaking her head as if she were the mother. "I would have thought she'd learned her lesson with me. Mother's been post-menopausal since you were born, you know. But she didn't warn me either. I was lucky, though. Most of my friends started theirs before me. They clued me in before Mother ever got around to coming clean with the facts."

What on earth was she talking about? Started their what? And what facts? It felt like the female members of my family had been abducted by aliens and now Martians inhabited their bodies and were speaking some language I could not understand. Then, ceremoniously, Sissie presented me with a brown paper bag, recognizable as being from the Rexall drugstore near our house. She put such effort into the giving of this odd gift that I was surprised she didn't sing out, "Ta-da," when she placed it in my lap. I peered in, reluctantly, then pulled out a large rectangular box marked "Kotex" and a smaller pink one with "Tampax" written discreetly on the front.

"Don't tell Mother I bought the Tampax," Sissie whispered, cupping her hand around her mouth as if someone might hear. "She thinks they cause cancer, but they are the greatest things ever invented for women. You'll see what I mean."

I opened the cancer-causing Tampax box with two fingers, afraid of what it contained, and wondered why my sister would give it to me as a gift. I dumped it onto my bed. But before I could survey its contents, Sissie scooped up the paper-wrapped cylinders. She shielded them with her body as she stuffed them back into the box, as if spies lurking in the shadows of my closet might deduce some top secret biochemical information if she didn't protect it from their unfriendly eyes.

I have to admit that by this point I was beginning to wonder if insanity might run in my family. Sissie ushered me into the bathroom, where she gasped at the blood trail I'd left. Then, stepping gingerly, she ignored it as best she could, locked the door behind us and proceeded to reverently extricate one of the Tampax cylinders from its box, placing it strategically on the edge of the sink. She then opened the Kotex box and unfurled an inch-thick sheet of what appeared to be Styrofoam with long tails of gauze on each end. Reaching deeper into her bag of contraband, she extracted an elastic contraption with dangling metal barbs.

"These are killers, but once you learn my special knot, pad slippage will be reduced to a minimum," she said, pointing at the odd fasteners.

I glanced down at the assortment of "menstrual aids" and wished I could disappear. This session was not advancing in a direction I felt comfortable with and I began looking for means of escape. Sissie had blocked the door, of course. I gave my robe belt a securing tug.

"Don't just stand there, young lady," she said, a raised finger punctuating her command. "Drop your drawers and let's get this over with. You're a woman now." She lifted the toilet lid, revealing a Tidy Bowl abyss.

Even though Sissie had seen me naked thousands of times, (changed my diapers more often than Mother had, I'm sure,) a surge of modesty came over me. Its quiver agitated the cramping muscles I now recognized in my abdomen. I raised the hem of my robe just past my knees, reached under it, grabbing the leg elastic of my panties with my fingertips, and wiggled them down. My robe eased down with them, but when my panties passed my kneecaps, the three washrags I'd used to absorb the hemorrhaging fell out onto the floor. A new kind of embarrassment warmed my cheeks. I scrambled to pick them up. Then, finding no acceptable place to deposit them, I hurled them in the wastebasket and wiped my hands off compulsively on my robe. "Ugh," I groaned.

"Sit, sit," Sissie commanded, not even allowing me my moment of disgust. A hand on my shoulder guided me onto the toilet seat. Holding it at eye level, she peeled the tampon paper back. Its cardboard tube reminded me of the orange sherbet push-ups I used to buy from the ice cream man. "Spread your legs and fish around down there," she said. Once again her finger took motion to demonstrate and point the way. "There is a hole . . . one you've never used before . . . It's there. You'll find it. Go on. This goes in that hole." She handed me the tampon, but I didn't take it. Its braided string dangled between her fingers. "It won't hurt much. Just push it in."

Every muscle below my waist contracted involuntarily. "Gross" was the only expletive that came to mind. Oh, sure, I knew about "the hole" she meant, but I wasn't about to let on that I had examined myself while bathing a few times, even while snuggled privately under my covers. And, yes, okay, it felt kind of nice down there. Self-gratification was normal, I justified. But I hadn't mustered the courage to confess my bodily explorations to a priest, so I certainly wasn't going to reveal them to my sister. Besides, the selfish pleasure had now lost all its appeal.

I considered my options for a moment. Learn this and get it over with, or become a hermit until I hit Mother's "menopausal" age. It made sense, really. Plug the hole, stop the flow. Simple fundamentals of physics. But at my rate of "leakage," and the tampon's obvious absorbency limitations, I'd be trotting to reload every ten minutes or so. Taking the tampon from Sissie's hand, I did what I knew I must. I held my breath and aimed. Once, twice. I knew it was down there somewhere. But where had it gone? It was here just yesterday, I thought.

"Take your time," Sissie offered, leaning in a bit too close. "A little to the right."

Her proximity was making me nervous. "I can't do this!" I shouted, looking up, and fumbled the tampon. It slipped from my fingers and splashed into the bowl. Gaping between my splayed legs, my sister and I marveled at how the cottony center sucked in ten times its body weight of Tidy Bowl. A blue dome bulged out the top of the cylinder, expanding, expanding, until the cardboard applicator couldn't contain it. It ruptured like a tube of biscuits and unfurled itself.

"Oh, no . . . no," Sissie almost screamed. "Get something. Quick, quick! Get up!" She searched the countertop for something to use to fish it out. My hand moved toward the flush lever. "No, don't flush it. Daddy will kill us. It will clog the pipes." My hand retracted. She was right, of course. It was bad enough to be straddling bloody splatter; a blue flood of toilet water would have put me over the edge.

I winced when she grabbed Arthur's toothbrush. She considered her choice for a moment, her eyes moving from the toilet bowl to the toothbrush and back again. Then she chose Daddy's double razor instead. Twisting the handle back and forth, the razor's mouth opened and closed like hungry tongs. But she soon thought better of that idea, thank God. Finally, she threw open the door and dashed out, without closing it behind her. I waddled over and pushed it shut. But within seconds, Sissie returned triumphant, Mother's best flour sifter in hand. She approached the potty like a surgeon with hands and instrument raised. I lifted the lid to give her maneuvering room and in one grand sweep, she scooped the soggy tampon out of the bowl. It joined the washrags in the trash as we both let out a whoop of success.

It took several more tries for me to get that damned tampon in place. By the time Sissie finished introducing me to the bodily orifice I had initially thought had no purpose but my own pleasure—to which we then poked, probed, excavated and embedded a Tampax within, and saddled me with the sheet of Styrofoam, looped and tethered with such precision around those metal barbs that she swore it would never slip, and I swore this odd flotation device could keep me afloat indefinitely if the water ever got that high—two hours had passed. Our dear Mother had never darkened the door.

Finally, I kissed Sissie good-bye, but I didn't thank her. I shuffled, bowlegged, back to my bedroom and collapsed onto my bed, sure that I'd never again have the desire to climb into our neighbor's tree house, fight off pirates that looked remarkably like my brothers or paint daisies on the walls of my tool-shed clubhouse. I was certain that life, as I knew it, had ended that day.

"Mom? Mom, you okay?"

My daughter's words jerked me back to the present.

"Mom, let go. You're crushing my leg."

Ah, the strength of memory, I thought. "Sorry, honey." I patted her leg.

She looked at me with wide nine-year-old eyes, and I was sure she was wondering if insanity runs in the family. I knew that look well. Her best friend had showed up at school wearing a bra yesterday. Yes, she was too young for this discussion, but better to know what's coming and not be traumatized needlessly like I had been. After all, once I learned "the facts" and understood them, the knowledge taught me what a miracle this crazy body of mine really is. Of course, not even perpetual therapy had enlightened me as to why some mothers can't bring themselves to talk to their daughters in a loving and open way.

I lifted a corkscrew strand of her golden hair off her cheek and tucked it behind her ear. "How about if the two of us go shopping on Saturday, maybe get a bite of lunch, make it a girls' day out?" My fingers lingered in her hair.

"Sure, whatever," she said. "But you're not going to get mushy, are you? I mean, you know how you are." She smiled and I knew she really liked my mushy moments.

"No, I promise. Just thought we needed to spend some time together, maybe buy your first bra, talk about sex, and boys, and menstruation, how Tampax don't cause cancer, and how the evolution of thinner, more absorbent Kotex has changed the way women view their monthly cycles. Simple stuff like that."

"Okay, sure, Mom. Whatever."

She didn't look up from her spaghetti. Had she heard me? Or was her mind on more important things like what she'd wear to the mall. I decided that I'd better stop by the bookstore, or Google "The Facts of Life," and do a little research. Things might've changed since the Sixties—but then again, nah!

Gospel of Mary Magdalene
Madeline Artenberg

I Mary Magdalene opened my heart to the Lord,
allowed Jesus to part my soiled loins.
His voice entered me, shook my breasts,
rumbled through my body. Inside,
He faced demons that ate at me every day:
despair, fear, shame.
Jesus cast them out,
wrote the Gospel in my cave
and the words *You are saved*
and I was.

My womb is a vessel that holds Jesus' words
as once I held His sacred feet,
washed them with my hair.
He has commanded that I lay myself open.
Enter and read what He has writ,
What is hidden from you, I will proclaim to you.

Yet, men accuse me,
hiss that the folds of skin between my legs
must harbor sin,
that a woman's body holds secrets.
I was given tongue and lips
with which to spread the truth:
Reveal what is hidden deep inside.
It will save you.

Yet, these men would rather honor penitents
proclaiming pain as most holy penance,
rasping their skin until boundary
between body and heavenly air melts.

If bless-ed is the scourged blood of the penitents,
bless-ed is my blood poured forth each month,
bless-ed is the dying and resurrection I host each month.

I say unto you,
Let the Lord flow through each of us
like tributaries joined at one source.

My path to Him is through the tingling in my nipples,
twitching of my feet.
I allow Him to enter me, rock my hips,
I tremble,
more truths appear upon my womb
my breath comes faster
I am in a hurry to receive the Lord
angels fly away with my thoughts
nothing separates me from Him
and I am come to Heaven in liquid moan and yell
      Oh Jesus Oh God Yes Yes
      Oh Yes.

The Bleeding

Robin A. Sams

Something stirs in me at night, an eternal
pounding
pretending to be a heart thrown hard
against the daylight. But it is something
beyond simple image and metaphor.
I wake up with my hair holding onto the first light,
entwining it in the mass of coppery elf-locks.
My hands on my belly, smooth and big with myself,
I am waiting for the monthly gift and the monthly ache.
It will be soon. I know it from the yearning pull
between my legs. And when it comes
bleeding, bleeding, double-check the bleeding,
my body is ready, but I am stretched thin.
My mind untwists with infant screams in the middle

of the night and waking dreams
of my lost children. I am losing more
three days every month, and the incessant pull
that it brings makes me ache.
My heart is in the right place, but something
is picking apart my lust. I need something, something
other than truth. I need a good night's sleep.
But each night, I am left with a barren bed
And these dreams that cry, "Mother!"

For Cycles

Stacia M. Fleegal

The laws of geometry are clear on this:
one dip, curve, disjuncture in a line
and the line is defunct, no longer
itself. Flawed, a god with a broken spine.

Let's celebrate circles, then, the shape
everyone knows cannot be perfect,
personification of earliest knowledge:
day to night to day to night again.

April

Ruby Kane

This month instead of liquid I bled solid.
In my underwear I found
my Great Aunt Annie's amethyst pendant,
the one I lost before my mother could bequeath it.
My father's torn canvas sneakers,
molded to the boomerang toes that kept him out of Korea.
A stem of lilacs from Grandpa's yard in Woodside,
The rat Grandma killed with her bare foot—
that was just the first day.
After breakfast I passed Grandpa's yellow cab
right into a black thong. Talk about cramps.
That night I found a mouthful of pills with
vowelled, exotic names carved in:
thorazine and
valium and
imipramine.
A six-pack of Bud, and a mug still frosty from the freezer.

Tampons just got in the way. Pads were useless.
After the cab ruined my favorite pants,
I stayed home to deliver.
A manuscript of my father's memoirs
discharged day three, meticulously typed
and tied in yellow string.
His brother's medical degree got lodged in my cervix and had to be re-
trieved.
It caused an infection.
There were keys day four,
a metal top you pump to spin, a kite of unknown origin,
false eyelashes, and a basketball.
Day five I reached inside, looking for something
gone.

May

Ruby Kane

I have miscarried you for years,
tucked you in my pocket
when you wanted a piggyback.
I should have draped you on my shoulders:
stole.

Where you're stuck
could house embryos.
It could feed something.
Instead, you take up space
and I shrink to fit.

I clutch you like roots hold dirt,
stubbornly.
What survives this climate
gives itself to damp,
but knows its center in the
mud,
and holds.

Welcome to Our World

Suzanne Grossman

If men could menstruate, as Gloria Steinem wrote, they would convince women that sex was more pleasurable at 'that time of the month.' Instead, a woman's period remains an awkward intrusion to getting it on, particularly with casual relationships. A few years ago I had an encounter that made me think twice about having sex for the first time during my period.

I met a singer-songwriter through a friend, and liked him, but did not take him very seriously. He had just moved to NYC and was more focused on his next gig and how his army pants looked in the mirror than he was on relationships. We had been dating off and on casually for a few months when he called me one end-of-summer day to hang out.

Singer-songwriter's Brooklyn apartment was a ten-minute drive from mine. When I got there we went straight to his room. He immediately lay down on his bed with his body alongside the pillows and gave me a come-hither look. Oh, I thought, it was that kind of call. Did I want to make out with him? He looked sexy lying there, one hand under his T-shirt, the other propping up his head of longish black hair. There was no good reason not to. It's not like I wore a sleeveless tank top and lip gloss for nothing.

Singer-songwriter and I started to kiss. He had nice hands and a smooth body. Our kissing became intense quickly and he began to unzip my jeans. At this point I realized I couldn't hold out much longer without telling him some unfortunate news—I had my period. I silently cursed my body's bad timing.

As he reached for my underwear, I debated in those few remaining seconds exactly how to bring it up. Should I use the word "period"? Maybe. Do I say, "I'm menstruating"? Too clinical. What do other women say in this situation? Regardless, I knew it would be a mood-killer so I settled on:

"Um, so, it's kinda that time of the month . . ." Thankfully I got it out before his hands creeped farther up my legs.

"Oh. Okay." He retreated from my pants and instead started to unzip his own.

"I don't think so. I have to get something out of this too." I hadn't gone to his apartment to service him!

"Okay, so what do you want to do?" he asked. Good question. I ran through the list of options in my head. There weren't very many. "Well . . . we could just have sex." It wasn't top of my list of things to do, but it was doable. I started to warm to the idea. Yes, sex in the past had actually been quite nice with my period, very slick. It seemed easier than finding creative ways to get us both off.

He paused and avoided my gaze. "I don't know . . ." Oh, he's one of those, I thought. For some men I'd been with sex and periods were no big deal, but others were more squeamish.

"Haven't you ever had sex with a girl who's had her period before?" I asked. He didn't respond so I pushed on, "What about with a girlfriend? You have had a long-term relationship haven't you?"

He squirmed. "Yeah, well, it's been awhile. And even then, we just, no not really. It's just not my thing."

Apparently I was mistaken in my assumption that all couples eventually had period sex.

"Plus what about my white comforter. I don't want to mess it up," he added.

"All you do is put down a towel," I told him. "It's no big deal. Really." I had done this plenty of times in the past with boyfriends who preferred sex to a monthly week of abstinence.

He was not convinced. "Okay, we don't have to," I said. I could take it or leave it, and he was the one who started this whole thing anyway. I sat up and made like I was getting dressed. When I started to pull on my jeans he jumped up and went to the closet to grab a towel—an old, red Ralph Lauren Polo towel to put on the white down comforter. Ha! A mini-victory for me, I thought. I'm no sucker who was going to please a man without getting pleased herself.

I'd never had sex with singer-songwriter before and it puzzles me now why I chose this particularly messy time to do it with him. It had to be related to the sexually liberated girl-power phase I was in: Yes, I can have casual sex with singer-songwriter and not get attached, and he will still respect me afterward. But could I do it while having my period? Of course I could!

So he put on a condom and we set about doing it. I was trying to enjoy myself and thought he was too until I looked up and realized he was actually a bit freaked out.

He stopped suddenly and said, "I'm sorry, I can't do this. My brother's a doctor but there's a reason I'm not. I can't deal with blood."

The condom was bloody, he was bloody and so was I. "No worries," I told him, trying to act unfazed. "Go get cleaned up. I'll wait." How could I have forgotten that sex makes my period flow like water? I was slightly embarrassed that it was my body that had caused the mess. But it's not like I hadn't been there before, and there was a part of me that thought, deal with it. Sex is messy regardless, period or no period.

When he headed to the bathroom, I took a look around. Feck!! His pure white down comforter had a giant bloody stain that had soaked through the towel! (Who has a white comforter anyway?!) I had once permanently stained an ex-boyfriend's mattress, but at least he had known me for a few years first. Could I cover it up and sneak out of there? Then I would be the girl who got blood on singer-songwriter's comforter and ran away.

There was no getting out of it. I went down the hall and sheepishly told him, "You're not gonna be happy." He came back to the room and handled the news surprisingly well. I had expected him to freak.

Instead he said, "Oh whatever, I'll just buy a new one, it's only a hundred or two hundred."

"Wha?" I cried out. "No, no. You don't have to do that. We can definitely get the stain out." I knew singer-songwriter struggled to make a living and I was feeling mighty guilty.

So he dragged the blanket to the bathroom and set about scrubbing at the red splotches with soap and water per my instructions while I got dressed. I decided it was time for me to make my exit.

"We'll be laughing about this one day," I told him in the bathroom.

"I already am," he said, still scrubbing. I wasn't sure I believed him but I was relieved.

"You know," I said, "this is what women have to deal with on a monthly basis—stained underwear, sheets, pajamas, pants. Welcome to our world."

"Really? Wow." This clearly had never crossed his mind. "That's rough," he commented. He appeared to have a newfound appreciation for women, and our hidden bodily concerns. I offered to take home the red towel and wash it for him. He consented since he already had the washer full with the comforter and was late for a show. He gave me a big hug, and I headed out of there, fast.

I e-mailed singer-songwriter from time to time after that evening, making funny references to the red towel I had yet to return, but we never connected, and I've heard he has a girlfriend now, so it's probably not appropriate to bring it up anymore. I still have that towel, and in fact I used it just the other day. It brought a smile to my face; I like that it's red.

Though it will never be top of my list, I haven't given up on casual sex during my period—a single girl in the city's gotta take advantage of opportunities when they come along, and thankfully, most men just go with the flow.

Matisse's Red Studio

Sonia Pereira Murphy

Your studio shakes the dye of hunger
And of shame.

I garden blue cells beneath my dress.
You say it's a sign of the season.
I say it's an empire of breasts
At the hanging posts.

Swing low.

Were you in this room when her silk belly
Burst like so many wet fruit flies?

Big bear, you grope and plunge.

She said you illegally bathed
The brushes in the river.

We part like fingers.

I lie on your red floor.
I like the scent of it all,
I purr out my approval.

The Biggest Difference

Dana S. Wildsmith

More than breasts. More than folding in where
men hang down. More than right brain versus left.
More than which parts get shaved, legs or chin.
Even more than whether a gut means
beer or baby. This circumstance:
waiting for your period to start
and not being sure that it will. No
man has ever seen his future
in the white crotch of his underpants.

Oh, the promises! Never again
the opening yes, no matter what,
you vow, praying for stains, swearing to
bear with grace five days of cramps, six,
an entire week of the twisting fist
in your bowels. Thanks be. Each tampon change
am act of holy office. Over and
over the red flag of redemption,
the smear that saves you. More than x
or y, this occasion: your life handed
back to you in a wad of fiber.

Not the First

Marsha Smith Janson

I stand at the back door, one hand on the glaze
of cold glass while outside the sky
behind bare trees in the orchard is blushing,
a stain spreading from unripe
to trumpet vine red, mimicking a mouth,
mid-kiss. Not the first kiss but deeper.
I'm bleeding. A shaft of light
has traveled from rim to floor
where canyon wren is canyon music.
There is ache, there is opening.
Seep becomes flow.
The water condensed from flowers
has made its way. I need someone
to come inside and say yes to every version:
seeds, no seeds.
Now on the hillside, on the terraced slope,
the day's room has darkened.
Still the after-image of trees stays
with me, the espaliered and those others
whose thick and low-sweeping limbs
have been so long propped
by small, notched sticks
that they've grown together, fused
into the same rough skin.

The Hut

Robin A. Sams

I should be secluded in some
hut somewhere far away
to rage and weep and bleed.

I am eating fat
for the gross-ness of it,
for the way it makes my thighs
feel like blobs rubbing, rubbing
together squeezing the pain
of too wet in between.

This is not the Earth Mother flow
of years past.
This is the flow
of death throes of obstacles
tipping time's weight forward
of overgrown grief and fury
and dissatisfaction.
This is the flow of winter earth
stomping out summer heat.

Light Heavy
spot . . . . soak
The turmoil of sore labia
push-pressing cloth.
I am pale,

wishing for silence
for the hut
secluded, where my scent
would absorb incense

where naked I would
pound out the hormones
for another month.
But here I pound inside
my head, shout hoarse
the thin walls and unsealed doors.

I am buried by the rush
beloved cycle.

Random Wiccans

Tab Curtis

It was arguably the worst decision of my life and, as such, I remember it perfectly. I felt gorgeous, perfect Laura looking at me, waiting for a response to her question. She had just asked me to go on an overnight camping trip with her on Saturday. My jaw tightened as the thirty-four reasons I shouldn't go with her scrolled through my brain. I had to work at the gas station Sunday afternoon. I'd promised my friend Dan that I would help him move Saturday. Laura had broken up with her girlfriend of two years just two weeks ago. And, most damning, I was seconds away from starting my period.

Since I was fifteen, I have suffered an unholy fear of spotting. I trace it back to an unfortunate high school incident involving white jeans. I often use both tampon and pad, yet still find myself running to the bathroom to check my status every fifteen minutes for the first three days of my curse.

I carefully weighed the reasons for rejecting her proposal, finally determining that helping Dan move was a bit more socially acceptable than admitting my crimson paranoia. I opened my mouth to politely decline while suggesting an intimate gathering in the near future when, to my horror, I heard myself utter a single word: "Sure."

Did I mention that Laura was gorgeous? Tall, reddish-blond hair, sleepy green eyes, strong jaw, and huge hands—just this side of man-hands. Irish Amazon. Woof. "Cool," she said. "I'll pick you up at your place at three, cutie." She gave me a shy smile then walked back to her friends at the other end of the bar. Fearful that I had started my period while she talked to me, I left my half-empty beer on the bar and bolted downstairs to the bathroom.

I spent the next day apologizing to Dan and getting together my camping gear, which hadn't seen daylight since 1982. At 2:48, I examined the items spread out on my apartment floor: stainless steel mess kit, folding shovel, mallet, compass, one roll of toilet paper and a musty Partridge Family sleeping bag. I shoved all the items save for the sleeping bag into a battered duffel bag, along with roughly four pounds of feminine protection, and went to check my tampon.

"Hey, cutie," she said as she swept into the apartment at 3:02. She hugged me tightly for a few beats too long, kissing me softly on the cheek as she pulled back. "Ready to go?" I nodded, gesturing toward my gear. She reached down and stroked the multi-colored sleeping bag. "Oh," she chuckled. "You're just too cute."

The hand-drawn map she handed me consisted of a star next to a byway called, disturbingly enough, Rabbit Hash Ridge Road. I played the part of navigator and, 18.2 miles east of Floyds Knobs, we found a red sign nailed to a tree marking the campsite. The deserted field was about two acres square, bordered by trees on all sides, with the exception of the narrow gravel drive. A small hill in the middle of the field was its only distinguishing feature. Her ancient Datsun groaned as she jerked it into 'park.'

I turned when I felt her meaty hand on my thigh, only to be rewarded with a gentle, teasing kiss. She wrapped her paw in my hair, pulling me closer before breaking the kiss. "You know that I broke up with Kate," she said. I nodded. "She was just . . ." she sighed. "Just never *there* for me. You know?" Fearing an embarrassing confession if I dared open my mouth, I nodded again. "But I think you're really cute."

"Me, too," I said, trying to keep from hyperventilating. "I mean—I like you."

She ran her finger along my jaw. "Too cute," she said.

"I have to go to the bathroom," I said, feeling the blood rise in my cheeks. After brushing my pocket to check for a fresh tampon and a Kleenex, I silently cursed the menstrual gods then followed her into the field. "Where do you think I should go?"

"Anywhere away from the road, I guess," she replied.

I walked toward the hill in the middle of the clearing. On the opposite side of the rise, I spied a toilet seat lying next to a large metal spoon. Curious, I lifted the lid to find that it covered a two-foot-deep hole. "World's tiniest latrine," I mumbled. I checked to ensure that she couldn't see me then squatted to check my tampon saturation status. No spotting and the string felt dry, so I opted to conserve my supply.

Laura was pounding the last of the tent stakes into the ground. I grinned, imagining those hands kneading my thighs. "Looks like you got it covered," I said.

She stepped back to admire her work. "Kate and I used to go camping a lot." I winced. I was startled from my self-pity by the sound of the mallet hitting the ground. "I brought something." She pulled a small envelope from her front jeans pocket. "You know, to make it more . . ." She produced two small squares of paper from the envelope. "Special." She handed one to me. One side of the paper was blank. The other had a smiley face with a bloody bullet hole in its forehead. "Cool, huh?" she asked as she slid the paper under her tongue.

"Uh-huh." I debated slipping the paper into my pocket. But then I looked at those green eyes and giant fingers and I knew that I would slaughter a puppy if she asked me to. I recited a silent prayer to the menstrual gods as I slid the hit of acid under my tongue.

We busied ourselves for the next couple of hours moving our supplies into the tent and gathering wood for the evening's fire. "Didn't you say there were other people coming?" I asked.

"Yeah, just my ex and some random Wiccans," she said nonchalantly. "I guess they're a coven."

"Huh?" I dropped the cooler I'd been carrying beside the tent. "Kate's a witch?"

"Not *Kate*." Laura chuckled. "Raven."

"Who?" I sat on top of the cooler. "I don't know anyone named Raven." I moved my hand slowly in front of my face. "Hey, I'm seeing trailers. Are you feeling anything yet?"

"Not yet." She waved her hand across her face then shook her head. "You know Raven." I shook my head. "Black hair. Nose ring. Hangs out at Discovery."

"Oh my God," I said in a low voice. "Does she look like Butch Patrick?"

"Who?"

"Butch Patrick. You know—Eddie Munster." I shook my head. "You *dated* Eddie Munster?"

Laura knelt down in front of me and took my hands in hers. "Hey," she whispered. "Are you okay?" I suppressed the urge to giggle. "Have you ever dropped acid before?"

"Loads," I said, sliding my palms against hers. I clenched my thighs. "Buckets of acid." She sighed and patted my knee. We both looked up at the sound of a car's engine. "I've gotta go to the bathroom," I said. I walked into the tent and shoved another tampon in my pocket, grabbed my roll of toilet paper, and headed for the hill. I found no spots in my underwear but decided to change my tampon anyway. I wrapped it snugly then dropped it into the tiny pit, tossing in a handful of grass to hide the telltale chrysalis.

I saw Laura talking to the other driver, who I now recognized as Raven. I grimaced as Laura laced fingers with Eddie Munster. "Hey, cutie," she said, smiling at me. "Raven's here."

"Hi," I said, raising my hand in a half-hearted wave. "I guess you're responsible for the, uh, accommodations?"

"Oh, you mean the toilet?" She gestured toward the hill. "Nah. I think Rael did that." She looked around. "I thought he'd be here by now—we need to get ready for Circle."

"Circle?" I asked, staring at Laura. I tried to ignore the waves breaking around her face. Raven rolled her eyes then walked to her car.

"It's a Wicca thing," Laura said, taking my hand in hers. "You sure you're okay?" she asked. "Your pupils are *huge*."

"I need to show you something in the tent," I said, pulling her along by her hand. We ducked under the canvas. "It's just over . . ." I spun around and kissed her. She ran those giant hands up and down my back then pulled me closer.

"Laura, come help me build a fire." Raven's voice echoed through the tent. "I want a tofu dog before Circle."

"Sorry," she whispered then turned to leave. After feeling my pants for damp spots, I shoved another tampon in my pocket then walked out to join them.

I tried not to drool as my Amazon built a raging bonfire then grilled me a tofu dog. I sat, staring into the flames and gnawing on the half-frozen tofu dog, for what felt like days. I was startled out of my reverie by an aged Chevette. "Rael!" Raven waved at the car. A tall man wearing—I swear—a black cloak emerged from the vehicle. The passenger door opened and a dwarf carrying a pumpkin spilled out of the car. I closed my eyes, sure that the vision would dissipate. "Mind if I put this here?" the dwarf asked as he dropped the pumpkin at my feet. I touched it with my toe, convinced that it wasn't real. "Where're the girls?" the tall man asked.

"Should be here any minute," Raven said, poking the fire with a stick. The words had scarcely left her lips when a green Ford Ranger pulled up. Two disheveled women emerged from the truck. "Sorry we're late," the driver said. She was a tall woman with wiry red hair. "Traffic."

"Whatever." Raven rolled her eyes. "It's almost time." She stormed off toward the far line of trees. "Don't forget the lantern," she yelled over her shoulder. The driver ran back to the truck and grabbed a Coleman lantern then ran after her.

"Hey, Laura," the truck's passenger, a bottle blond, said. "Long time, no see."

"Oh, um, hey." Laura smiled awkwardly.

She stood too close to my Amazon. "Heard you broke up with Kate."

"Yeah," she said.

She gripped Laura's wrist. "You have my number," she said in a low voice. I growled, envisioning the blonde skewered on a tree branch.

My Amazon and I watched the group wander off into the trees. "Will you be okay while I go to the bathroom?"

"Are they coming back?" I asked.

"Not for a while."

"Then I'll be fine." I tossed my last bite of tofu dog into the fire as I watched her walk away. I went into the tent and checked my crotch for dampness. I patted my pocket to ensure I had a tampon then walked back outside.

I was sitting on the pumpkin and staring into the flames when I heard chanting coming from the woods. *We are part of the goddess and to her we shall return* . . . I walked into the trees, following the voices, and glimpsed a flash of light. I advanced slowly, hiding behind a tree. I peeked around the side and saw Raven sprinkling the ground with water from a thermos. The two women from the truck stood on either side of her and, mercifully, the tall man and the dwarf stood with their backs to me. Did I mention that everyone was naked? I looked down, thinking that perhaps my own clothing had dissolved. Relieved to find my outfit intact, I turned back toward the camp.

I stopped when I saw the bonfire through the trees. I shifted on my feet, feeling a telltale trickle of liquid on my thigh. I glanced toward the latrine but decided the trip would take far too long given the dire circumstances. Looking around to ensure privacy, I squatted next to a tree. I made a quick tampon change, realizing too late that I had no toilet paper. I looked around for anything I could use to wipe myself. My gaze settled on a thick cover of leaves wrapped around the tree. I ripped off a handful and wiped vigorously.

I ducked into the tent to get another tampon. Laura lay huddled in my sleeping bag. "Where have you been, cutie?"

"I, uh, took a walk," I replied, edging toward my tampon supply.

She tossed back the flap on the sleeping bag. "Why don't you come make me warm?" I kicked off my shoes then crawled in next to her. She wrapped an arm around my waist, pulling me closer, then kissed me deeply. She trailed kisses up my jaw, pausing to nibble on my ear. "Did I ever tell you," she whispered, "how horny acid makes me?" I groaned and rolled her on top of me. I needed to feel those gigantic hands all over me. She kissed down my neck, her muscular fingers pawing at my breasts. I ground my pelvis into her, urging her on. She slipped her other hand past the waistband of my jeans.

I grabbed her forearm. "I'm on my period," I said.

She stilled her movements and looked down at me. "Does it bother you?" she asked. I shook my head. "Doesn't bother me, either." She leaned forward, running her tongue along my lower lip. Her hand resumed its delicious motion, evoking a moan from me. Suddenly, her movements stilled. I looked up at her. The light from the bonfire gave her face an eerie glow. I felt her hand leaving my nether regions and sliding up my body. "What is *this*?" she asked, holding aloft several limp leaves connected by a vine.

I felt the blood pounding in my ears. "My, um, my . . . bush?" I said then burst into hysterical laughter.

"Gross," she said then rolled off me and stormed out. Debilitated by bursts of uncontrollable laughter and menstrual paranoia, I didn't leave the tent the rest of the night. Snippets of conversation floated in from the fireside, including an animated debate about whether Native Americans used garlic when roasting pumpkin seeds, but I knew that my Amazon was lost to me forever. I envisioned twenty-foot-tall ovaries pulsing, drowning the campsite in a vermilion tsunami. And I smiled.

We said about fifteen words to each other on the drive back. She pulled up to my apartment then turned to face me. "I think maybe it's too soon for me to date," she said. "I mean, I just got out of a relationship and, well, you know . . ."

I nodded. I *did* know. I grabbed my gear and got out of the car. I watched her drive off, dreading the next time I would see her at the bar. Probably with the bottle blonde. I headed up the stairs to my apartment, pausing halfway up the steps as a burning itch ripped through my privates. "God damn it," I mumbled under my breath. "Poison ivy."

Blood-Cycle Brooding

Rachel Dacus

One more unpeeling of the womb,
close enough to the final time
that I can relish the tiny tearings,
the way muscles unclasp
from what might have been—
Once more, the shredding of a bed
that waited fruitless five times seven
years for an egg and dart
to decorate its aching lap.

Once more a blood-gravity pulls
me into a planet's centripetal spin,
the dropping-down cramp
mimicking birth-pang,
open mouth delivering
a new poem, breath
heaving and rasping.
And what do I have left
from all those empty moon-circles?

Scraped squeaky clean, the blood-room
has birthed generative words.
They sleep twitching in their cradles
or sun themselves nude on public rocks.
Tribe after diatribe of oaths and chants
spilled from lips too like another portal.
Yes, in this blood-tide of verbs
I brought myself forth
through a mirror, witched awake
out of the pounding dark.

Tracking Orbs

Connie Wasem

You can see the rings
with binoculars, he said, pointing
to Saturn. *It's so close.*
She sets up the telescope tonight
in her yard. She wants to see it all—
red swirls, dark bands, icy mist—before
the planet moves on.

The twinge a woman feels
when her egg launches
into the darkness of her tubes
is called *mittelschmerz*,
the "middle pain" of protest
against the dark void,
the meddling ache that shrieks
for a moment: *I want life.*

"It takes Saturn twelve years
to circle the sun. He's called
the Dark One because he's that
space in the mind where all things
troubling are dumped.
When he draws
close to the Earth, he causes
obstacles and delays."

The calendar becomes
her chart—the days' squares
scribbled with basal temperatures,
the numbers circled for days
of blood, X's for sex.
X's, O's, #'s—it's
all about timing.

The blood
relentlessly comes.

I was twelve. The blood
looked brown
which confused me.
Mom wadded some paper
towels, then drove me
to my lesson. I sat
on that hard piano
bench and bled.
I've bled nearly
thirty years since.

The fear that made her
back down and say *leave me*
alone becomes a space
to be filled. The darkness grows
crowded with wanting,
becomes a meddling ache
that cries: *plant me*
in bed, give me seed.

"Wrap a river stone
in a length of blue cloth.
Tie it next to her
womb to draw
out the dark
spirits that cause
the delay."

She can't fix Saturn
in her sights, that fleck
of burning orb
lost in the star-crowded sky.
The telescope
wobbles in her fumbling
hands, which grow
impatient as Mercury
tonight.

The Seminar

Alison Hicks

Sun-spun floorboards,
outside a tree bursts orange-red.
Familiar thickness in my lower back;
Metaphysics and Epistemology:
what we might know
and how we might come to know it.
Full-paned light, heavy ache,
the professor's incantations,
roomful of young men, hair flopping over foreheads,
bending to hear, Aristotle, causes of the oak.
Blood runs through me like sap,
closing ears to argument,
bright roots pushing through earth.

Girl Talk

Susan Christerson Brown

When my thirteen-year-old daughter invites her friends for a sleepover, it means enough girls to carpet the den with sleeping bags and to fill the kitchen table even with its extra leaf. The latest extravaganza began with the first arrivals shooting basketball in the driveway while waiting for the others to show up. They swarmed each car that stopped in front of the house, taking possession of duffel bag, sleeping bag, pillow and passenger. The pile of gear slumped inside the front door grew, along with the commotion outside.

Finally the door burst open one last time and they all pressed in. It was like the lid popping open on a box crammed with hair accessories—a riot of colors and textures and personalities. The bright, poufy bows vie for attention, a stray hairpin goes flying, strands of ribbon tangle through the no-nonsense barrettes, headbands insist on their space, and the simple covered elastic ponytail holders nestle quietly at the bottom where they are sought out almost every day. Wild curls and straight tresses, ponytails and baseball caps, barrettes and braids, their voices and energy filled the house as soon as they stepped in the door.

I always learn something when I talk with them, but I learn even more when they forget I 'm there. The kaleidoscope of their conversation spins in constant motion, combining and interpreting their experience. Listening helps me see their world.

They stayed up late making jewelry and talking, revealing a surprising sense of history and of their own privilege. As they chose their beads I heard:

"People in the thirties couldn 't afford to do this. "

"Yeah, and things only cost like five cents then. "

They were optimistic realists:

"This is going to be a really cool bracelet. "

"But they never look as good as they do in the book. "

They appreciated each other 's accomplishments:

"That is so awesome, how 'd you do that? "

And acknowledged them with a flourish:

"We're so talented and special!"

These girls are smart and funny:

"It looks like a blue raspberry."

"It has meaning!"

And self-aware:

"Last year I liked all the shows on Nick Junior—this year I think they're *so* dumb."

At the mercy of a social system beyond their control, they find support in each other:

". . . and he said 'She likes you,' and I was like '*shut up.*' I don't like him. I mean I like him, but . . ."

"I know what you mean. You don't like him, like, *like* him . . ."

"Yeah, you like him like friends."

They carry the imprint of their mothers:

"You could've put my eye out!"

They have to sort out a scary world:

"Have you seen that movie . . . ?"

"My parents said, 'You can't see that, you won't be able to sleep at night.'"

"It's not scary. It's about this clown that eats kids."

Silence. Then uncontrollable laughter.

"It's not a real clown, though."

They shatter the cliché of sentimental girls:

"My dog is very stupid."

"So's my dog."

"So's my dog."

"So's my fish."

"This girl down the street, her gerbil got out today and the cat ate it."

They map the *relevant* geography of their lives:

"I've lived in five different houses in my life."

"I've lived in four."

"I've lived in two."

"I lived in California."

"Did you have your own room?"

They have different approaches to the big questions:

"Tracy thinks everything is interesting. Like how did we get here?"

"My mom drove me."

"My parents had me and that's all the details we need."

"I walked."

In one evening they connect old friends and new, weaving the bonds of shared experience.

They opened the lid on a cheese pizza delivered that night, shining like a full moon, and opened their lives as well. As if to transcend the chatter of ordinary conversations, they reached for the pulsating stories at the center of their world, sharing hidden knowledge about their families:

"I have two brothers but my mom had a miscarriage in between."

"My mom had a miscarriage before I was born."

"If my mom hadn't had a miscarriage there would be five in our family."

At thirteen, they recognize those glimpses of the past shaping the present. They sense the power of stories seldom spoken, and of forces seldom named. One by one they encounter the life force beginning its monthly cycle in their own bodies. Armed with knowledge, they are nonetheless claimed by mystery.

They drew close together around the table that night, considering the power within the bodies of the women they are becoming. Losing a baby, or having a baby, alters history. Life or death can happen within a woman's body. Perhaps they recognized an issue on which much of their own lives will turn. Certainly they grasped that everything changes depending on whether there's a baby. Or not.

Banks of the Nile

Judy Lee Green

When the banks of the Nile were overflowing
butter wouldn't come.
My grandmother couldn't churn.
She couldn't work in the garden, pickle, or can.

Butter wouldn't come.
Food spoiled if touched by a woman's hand.
She couldn't work in the garden, pickle, or can.
Attendance at church was forbidden at high tide.

Food spoiled if touched by a woman's hand.
Her eyes could not gaze on a newborn's face.
Attendance at church was forbidden at high tide.
A bleeding woman could weaken a holy man.

Her eyes could not gaze on a newborn's face.
She couldn't wash her hair or bathe in a tub.
A bleeding woman could weaken a holy man.
She kept away from fire and water.

She couldn't wash her hair or bathe in a tub.
She couldn't walk among the living or the dead.
She kept away from fire and water
when the banks of the Nile were running red.

She couldn't walk among the living or the dead
when the red flag was flying and rags were ablaze.
When the banks of the Nile were running red
a bleeding woman was banished for five or six days.

When the red flag was flying and rags were ablaze

My grandmother couldn't churn.
A bleeding woman was banished for five or six days
when the banks of the Nile were overflowing.

Affection for Normal Taboos

Monica Mody

The two children stand before the mirror
brushing teeth. The younger on tiptoe, making faces.
The girl scoops up her paisley linen nightdress and
sits down to pee. Sees slime on the inside of her panties—
        a spittlefilm of angry rust. "I have a terrible, terrible
        disease," she thinks. "I must not tell my brother." She
        sends him hurrying out to get their mother.
        Mother locks the door and kneels before the girl.

In my dream I kneel before you. You have a cunt and tiny pale breasts.
When I bring my mouth close to the moist pink, I see white tassels—for
me a promise of sweetness, they remind me so much of the phirni at Nasir
Iqbal—remember you refused always to taste it, every Thursday without
fail? I don't. I gaze up into your gray sea eyes and tell you about the flecks
glistening in your cunt, bend down, and lick. This happens last night.

That night, you tell me I've bled thrice since we met. I shimmer that it is
you who counted. Months pass. We stop meeting. The shadows between
us grow, silences collect under chairs. You don't know any more when I
take a flat cotton pad and place it firm between my thighs, when my belly
swells with ache. Still I count each cycle
               like a prayer bead, like a passing cloud.

What clouds this blood is shame.
      "Don't enter the kitchen or cook."
          "Don't sit with the gods or pray."
      "Speak *softly*." "Don't touch . . ."
      "Hide that unclean body!" "Kill it."

The pious are not dead. To stop them selling their rank *ittar*, you need to
be cussed. Slop magenta ablaze scandal on that thing-called-shame and

swing it around and strut through every corridor. Or be that child running in without qualms, shattering everything, every norm, because the
world is new and the world is his.

> The world does not notice, when one day
> the girl decides to not tell. The black koel sings
> noiseless between her legs as she moves in
> sacred kitchens and temples. Where the lovers
> > had danced their *ras* smitten and sensuous,
> > where he had combed her hair, picked out
> > a thorn from her petulant feet, the girl se-

curely
> > folds up the proofs of her bleeding and slips

them
> > in the front pocket of her knapsack. In the house of
> widows her godfearing hosts, no one finds out.

No one knows she walks amongst them. The body needs its mischief
but brickwater is often invisible and you barely hear the sharp clicks of
touchwanting. My first love was young and brash and would have, but
I did not let him put his tongue there. The truth is not always seen—
unless I tap my feet you don't see my impatience. The wind too does not
tell tales, and yet for every blood drop, there must be a young green leaf
growing new on some plant, somewhere.

The Blood Poem

Glenna Luschei

They told me about blood.
It didn't come red
but in dark clots of plum.
They told me about birth.
I would be twisted
from the thorax
like a box elder bug.

Can't we live together
in a golden ring shining?

Moist Adagio

Changxin Fang

Almost that time, cervix
yawns like a camera shutter,
red eye of the mimosa opening
and closing. A loosening
in the uterus. Spring rain.

This time last month
my head ached, stomach
full of homunculuses
having a field day.
In the morning,
when you withdrew,
there was blood everywhere,
poppy blossom in the middle of the bed,
the pillows streaked with it.

I scrub my sheets, hang them
by the window to dry. I am
a clock in the linen,
its edges on fire,
body stretched thin
as a curtain. When the night came
my bed was still wet,
pockets of melting snow.
Your voice on the phone
is disembodied:
a violin singing under water.

Dogwoods At Forty-one

Willa Schneberg

Although her period is heavy as usual
and requires two tampons and a pad,
she pauses this time
before flushing
the blood-clotted cotton
down the commode to watch the red
dye the water.

At forty-one she is surprised
she is happy with her queasy stomach
and swollen breasts,
although she never wanted children.

Now it is not enough for her
to observe dogwoods profuse
with pink and white petals
from her window,
she must take them inside,
filling every glass in the house
with their short-lived beauty.

Novel Excerpt: *Flood*

Crystal Wilkinson

July 1962

Four days after she has given birth and two hours after the storm slows to a good downpour, Lucy Goode Brown wakes to rain beating against the windowpane. The smell of squash is still with her. She remembers the fuzzy green stems, the five-fingered leaves reaching out, but mostly she holds in her mind the yellow bodies curved, long-necked and graceful, their fullness heavy on the vines around her as she pushed the baby out. Years later, this image will return to her again. She will be slicing squash in the kitchen and there will suddenly be clarity and even a little fear about the kind of woman she has become. She will always mourn some parts of her former self, the woman she thinks she used to be. She will only then be curving toward the kind of mother she wishes she could have been all along.

This afternoon, in her own bedroom, she is fully awake. In fact this is a new alertness, the kind she had before she was ever in a family way. She reaches down somewhat surprised that the taut mountain that had been the child's is now wobbly and loose under her hand and back to being hers alone. She is aware of her hip bones now, the hollowness of her belly, the tightness of her engorged breasts. She rolls to Joe's side of the bed. She misses that extra weight there in the front of her that kept her oddly off balance for all these months. Now, she feels hollow underneath her navel, a riverbed drained. This burden of emptiness has descended upon her. This feeling, this particular sort of worthlessness, after carrying a baby so long, is being felt for the last time. It seems odd to her that this vessel of hers, built just for this purpose has performed this miracle for its last time.

She stands, feels a gurgling between her legs, which reminds her of her first menstrual blood, and smells the rusty tang. She hears family moving about the house, the rain's persistent tap-tapping. A welcomed coolness has come with this rain. Her body is stiff, a little weakened. She shuffles across the room like a woman twice her age. She fully opens the window, which is already cracked a few inches and leans into the sill. A muddy pool of water forms at the end of the walk, growing wide, like a tiny brown pond. And even Lucy, a woman who will later consider herself too busy for daydreaming, is taken by the outdoors until the clamor of her own house grows as faint as secrets whispered into a cupped ear.

The neighbors are out on their porches, fanning themselves with cardboard flaps and newspaper. With the rain has come gnats and mosquitoes, the sound of skin slaps echoes two houses away. But they will all celebrate the gardens, their backyard tomatoes and the second round of kale greens now holding water in their curly leaves. The zenias and begonias will perk up bright in pinks and reds. And on up the road, across Mission Bridge, toward Diamond, the old farmers in the country are nodding with the quiet pleasure that a good rain brings. They have crossed their black arms; their chests are swollen with pride; their snowy heads held up high beneath the shelter of barns and porches. Some will stand fully in the rain and let it take them. The crops will green up again. The garden is glistening wet, the remaining squash turning their necks toward the water.

Below Lucy's window, a girl and a boy chase each other around in a circle up and down the road. The girl's hair has gone home already, bushing out around her plaits. Lucy can't quite make out whose child she is, one of the Jenkins girls, maybe.

A woman with a coat over her head trudges down the hill. Lucy can't see her face. *It could be me*, she thinks. She imagines herself with her Grandma Tookie's beige raincoat over her head, unnoticed, walking up the hill in the downpour, across Mission Bridge away from town. *An invisible Goode woman, imagine that.* Her eyes tear up, spill out like thimble-sized oceans. What would happen if she jumped? Would anybody care?

She hears the ruckus of evening again on the other side of her bedroom door—the end of supper, voices muted low, chairs being scooted out. Behind that door are clothes to wash, a white sudsy sink of dishes, children to feed, a husband to love, a mother to please, a grandmother to praise . . . But in these moments she relishes being alone, though she recalls her time beneath the squash vines as a sort of loneliness too. Her arms are damp from the open window, droplets on her skin like sweat. It's nice and quiet and cool and she imagines herself in the water, splashing around like a muddy child then takes back to her bed.

Joe's dresser drawer is cockeyed, a few of his socks bunch up at the edge of the wood and hang over. A necktie, the red one with a blue zigzag like a lightning bolt, reflects itself in the metallic pool of the looking glass. Another tie, a gray one, sprawls from the drawer and dangles far enough downward to reach the third drawer. There is a pile of work clothes on the floor and his pajamas are thrown over the back of the chair in the corner. Lucy breathes in the moist air that settles around her, then takes in one deep-lunged breath.

She will scold Joe later when he is beside her in the bed. "Joe," she'll say. "Daddy," she'll say then stop and smile . . . "Baby," she'll begin again, "with Kiki and this new one and Dinner on the Grounds coming up . . . and Mama and Mom Mae getting up in age . . . and Daddy . . . Sugar, could you just do a little bit for yourself?" And then she'll place her fingers together like she's just asking for something tiny, something small, just a pinch of something. And she'll cut her eyes just right. "Joe . . . Will you? . . . I'll do the rest . . . Ain't I always done the rest?" She won't know what to say really, exactly how to say it. Then Joe will get that hard look on his face like he's preparing for a quarrel and she'll iron it out, smooth it all out with a light kiss on his collarbone right next to his Adam's apple. That place right there like a little hill and valley where she likes to rest her lips. Her lips won't be dry then. They'll be the tiniest bit wet. And then he'll know what she means. They can't make love yet but that one kiss right there will tide him over, smooth it out like an iron to a sheet. From behind her she'll scoop his rough hands around her jiggle of a waist and he'll press his chest to her back without a word about her softening body. That's how they'll sleep.

But that won't be the way it needs to be said, Joe. I won't say, Why can't a grown-ass man pick up his own damn britches? I don't want to be picking up after you, with one more person to take care of, pretty as she is. We need a new baby like we need one more eye or toe or mouth, Joe. But I won't say that either. I won't say nothing.

Remember when we got married? Came up to this room and didn't come out for a week. Had your big old eyes right here for me to look into. That scar running clean through your eyebrow like my very own beacon. You was just mine. Two legs, two arms, one silly heart. That's what we was. She laughs. Oh, how that sounds. Now you scattered out all over, your head turned in every direction. Your heart? Don't know where your heart is now. You belong to the whole damn world, all of creation. And don't get me wrong, I would wash your dirty drawers till kingdom come if you could save me from this. This . . . drowning. Feel like I am in Mission Creek. Just about gone. Circle me back to that old feeling again, Baby. Just once, Daddy. And don't think I wouldn't do anything in the world for my babies 'cause I would. Mama and Mom Mae too, and there's at least a hundred and fifty people in this town that I'd give my right foot for.

The tears well up again and Lucy falls, gully-washed into her own kind of grief.

While Lucy Goode Brown sleeps toward healing, Mom Mae comes in and changes the rusty padding between her legs and tests her forehead for fever. "'Bout time to feed this baby," Mom Mae says low but Lucy sleeps on, her closed eyes darting back and forth. Mom Mae wipes drool from her granddaughter's mouth and calls Tookie in to change the pillowcases which are sour with sweat.

"Fever's most gone," Mom Mae says and wipes a streak of dark thick blood from Lucy's thigh before covering her back up.

"Ok for Joe to stay tonight?" Tookie smoothes the fresh pillow and places it under her daughter's head.

"Yeah, long as Joe ain't got no man ideas. She ain't ready for that."

Tookie says nothing. Lucy begins to stir in her sleep but doesn't wake fully.

"In my time, we put the men out for at least six weeks."

"Um huh," Tookie says but thinks a husband belongs in the bed with his wife, even in times like this. She squeezes both of her daughter's feet through the sheet before she leaves.

In a dream, Lucy climbs a ridge following a path to a pond. Her plaits are freed and her hair coils out around her head like black snakes set loose. Her palms are splayed open, held skyward as if in prayer. A gust of wind ripples across the water and the mysteries it holds are more important than any one thing Lucy can think of. She quells the urge to jump in, to swim to the other side just to see if she can. She remains at dusk, then through nightfall. She sits on the water's edge and it is churning like a river at flood time now and rising. At nightfall ants are crawling up her calves and there is a snail on her knee, a frog nestled in the crook of her arm. She tries to fight them off but more come. It is after she grows resistant to the pinching bite of the mosquitoes and after the dance of the lightning bugs in her hair, after that, stillness settles in her. The water continues to chop but in the darkness her own churning stops and her attention is folded inside out. She has almost finally lost herself. *Good, good*, she thinks. *Good*. A barred owl hoots. Above her is an endless blanket of stars, a world larger and more glorious than herself. And yet even with this knowing there is still a tiny pulse of trepidation throbbing in the distance.

Lucy wakes, not knowing how long she has napped this time or that her mother and grandmother have been in and out of the room to check on her. The sheets are stale again with her sweat. She doesn't remember her dream, not in any exact way, but her heart races like she's afraid of something. She shifts her weight to the side. The day is nearly gone, a fleshy orange out the window, now, even though it is still raining. Lucy hears the baby crying behind the closed door, the squall in her ear, a sweet ache. Her breasts throb, then tingle, and she can already feel the milk straining through her crusted nipples first in slow drops, then faster, running down the rise of her belly and pouring into the crevice of her navel like a flood. Later, when the she thinks of herself like this, Lucy's skin will goose up and she will find herself in awe of the miracle of motherhood.

Tookie brings the baby in but Lucy refuses to feed it.

"Come on, honey," she says. "Every living thing got to eat."

"Then she'll learn early then won't she?"

"Lucy, girl, you ain't making no sense." Tookie brings the baby closer then. Her left hand is on her breasts where streams of clear blue milk still drip down the sides of her bra and her right hand is down below where nobody should be touching this soon.

Joe crawls into the empty space beside her. He notices right away where her hands are placed and says, "Baby, you okay? Need anything?"

"Need a lot."

"You want me to get you some ice water? That fever . . ."

"No."

"Hungry?"

"Not for what you talking about."

Joe Brown clears his throat because even in the dark he can see Lucy's hand moving around in that place. The smell of women's blood is filling up the room. Even under the circumstances, though, he didn't want to get an erection, his penis is hard and throbbing against his thigh and he longs to touch himself even more than he wants to touch her but he doesn't. He just lies in the dark, listening to her breathing beside him. He knows and she knows that he knows but neither of them speak another word.

In his memory years later, long after she is dead from a silent heart attack, he will still remember that Lucy's smell had taken up the entire room that night and remember the rain pinging on the window and how they laid like that for a long time and how her hands were still on herself in those places when the sun came up and how he'd watched her sleep then, sleeping just like that with her hands, now unmoving, there atop that sweetness.

Main Attraction

Sonia Pereira Murphy

I bleed.

Salty, milky,
My sour cerulean week travels
Topsy-turvy, spiral-mango,

Each month
In the bluest orbit
Of a pink grotto.

And the birds stare.

The bees zimm,
The breasts break
Out of jail,

Tender as my sprained ankle.

Circus artist,
I can go and go and never stop.

I can perform for six nights
And still stand.

"A woman's months are slippery"

—*Isaac Babel*

Why Women Have Enough of Blood

Stella Brice

Sometimes
when I lurch outside my body's
frame,
it's not so easy to take—
this collection of blood
that groans
from my pelvis.

Deep drops make an
evidence trail to the bathroom floor
(now red
& black & white).

A gang of blood
drives down the eye of my
drain.

A 5-day collection of blood soaks into
                              wing after wing.

"A woman's months are slippery."
said Babel.

Are slippery?

Ha!

Are the Middle of War!

Are my own harvest
        of murder without
        slashes
        or blades
        or imported arms.

So,
all practiced &
goose-like I squeak: I wipe my own blood
from the floor. Why would I want to kill you
                           & wipe yours?

In the Hood

Melissa Guillet

Three words:

Red
Riding
Hood.

Like I was some can they could pop open—
Pffffzzzz . . . .Soda pop!

Those Internet wolves
And their convenience store flowers,
Meeting me at the strip mall.
Wish we were playing cops and robbers.

Here's my basket full of eggs.
One breaks open,
Now I'm fertile.
Shiny red.
New.

Inverted scissors save me now—
Hands insert into fallopian fingers.
Squeeze shut.
Shed the baby out.

The Issue

Amy Ouzoonian

You'll notice at first,
it's not so gluey or
even copious in its strength
to remain on your hands
long after the issue
has occurred.
It's not like ketchup at all
or red Jell-O or the strawberry
jam you saw caked on
the girl's thighs in the photograph
at that show in Dresden. Draining
through to your panties is a chance at
motherhood; a face looking from
your bedroom window.
It's what you can manage
as each drop dissolves possibility
and you wipe it away from you
clean as the white
of a child's
unopened eyes.

The Promise of Blood

Jana Russ

Wild-eyed with fear,
she feels the birth.
First a hoof,
a white nose, then
an hour or more to wait.

In the end we pull
this slick new thing
into the world. Lead her
to the moon-curved udder,
watch thin milk spill
down the infant face as
placental blood
still weeps from the dam.

White rags collect
that slow red flow.
Barn cat washes one
pale paw,
sniffs, waits—
as we all do once we've
been bled—
for the bounty of milk,
the small mouth at the teat,
the cramp of an unused belly.

Afterward, walking the path
of river-polished stones
back to an empty house,
the waiting bedrooms, dark
with their own secrets, I feel

my own blood rising—
a response to the night, the moon,
the clench of a womb past bearing.

The blood will come.
Thick ropy strands
that trickle down my thighs
uncontrollable and
unforgivably female.

As if All Must Fall

Tomara S. Aldrich

with this single egg
and its fluid home of soft red
loosening so fast
I can feel it taking me down . . .

     is it different now?
more with her
to love every inch
hold fast, pull me up
with her fingers settled into me,
my thighs rinsed in red?

I never bled on the sheets before,
but my underwear lay damp
discarded beneath the bed's edge
where she left them,
I slept, that catching
layer gone.

     Should it be different now
because I can tell her
how the pain grounds me like a palm
at the small of my back
into wet earth

or that I've imagined
     letting one stay
amidst its pillows, to grow,
already less to come
than have already fallen.

PMS is like . . .

Chezon Jackson

. . . one big ol' run on sentence where thirty or forty thought patterns run into one and you question where exactly you can throw in a comma or a period or an exclamation point and when you think about it, the exclamation point has gotta be the cutest punctuation because it's a straight line with a dot underneath to drive home the point of exhilaration or aggravation like when you were young and your mama would say: *"You are getting on my last nerve* **exclamation point** *"* and you would visualize yourself crawling up her spine clinging like a rock climber to the last nerve she has left and she would break you from your concentration with a warning like *"You better get out of my face* **exclamation point** *"* and your eyes would jut around the room looking for the nearest escape before someone in the house would pull you aside and say *"Baby, don't worry about her, it's just that . . ."*

PMS is like . . .

. . . cooking for four hours a family-uniting feast only to find that your uncle *who last month was named Michael, but this week is a militant Muslim named Malik* announcing that he will not eat your **quote** *slave-inspired-collard-greens cooked in the same high-blood-pressuring pork scraps left over by the man* **exclamation point end quote** yet is now devouring your garden salad, sprinkled with your homemade bacon bits, off the lap of that Caucasian female who came with LaShanda from church, who just for the record, did NOT get an invitation, yet had the audacity to invite the guest who keeps asking if you have any raspberry vinaigrette salad dressing and a mineral water but instead of taking every emotion you've ever experienced and shoving it down their throats, you turn on your heels to fetch tap water in a wineglass, a second bottle of hot sauce and a set of mismatched playing cards for your great-aunt who ain't dealing with a full deck herself and just as you pass your room full of coats and sweaters of friends and family members you wish would go home, it's then that you remember your grandmother's words of wisdom: *"*Babygirl, you are a strong black woman and you gunna be all right **exclama-**

tion point and you believe her because she always knew that . . .

PMS is like . . .

. . . sitting down because you need a good soul-cleansing sob but when you think about it, what do you really have to cry about . . . you have your health and shelter . . . so you wonder, do you whine because you have nothing to weep about or do you cry about crying because the more you think about it the more you realize that men are not socially allowed to cry out because someone in history thought it wasn't masculine for men to be visually vulnerable and men for centuries have been following in his foolish footsteps and so you take it upon yourself to CRY FOR MEN EVERYWHERE because they have unutilized tear ducts and you cry and you cry and you cry right up until the time you hear your man come home and you turn on *Lifetime Television for Women* hoping it will camouflage your emotions before he asks: "Baby, what are you crying about **question mark** and even though you know honesty is always the best policy all you can manage to sniffle out is NOTHING **exclamation point** and he looks at you like you're cousins with crazy and you know that you're not, it's just explaining PMS to him is like explaining the African-American experience to a bigot . . . **he just wouldn't get it** . . . because he doesn't understand that

PMS IS MORE THAN JUST A **PERIOD**
exclamation point

so instead, like millions of women everywhere, you settle for the exact same elucidation: you wipe your eyes, pop a Midol and move on with life.

period.

Section III:

Waning

At the Softs, the Silks

Margo Berdeshevsky

It comes like smudged lavender paint,
a cave that invites coma, the solo viol,
luring me in. It pretends song, stroking.
The change comes, and it is a woman's
time, and it is not the dark led toward
day, and it is not the day. I'll understand
it when I am old. Now I am only changing.

It stretches with no edges, to the yellows
of old fields, old summers, old sun.
It is still smudged, lilacs, still crushed
jacaranda, a thousand tumbled spirit
petals, lost on a late rain floor. It is
still whispering its unhealable extravagance.

I came this way, the straight-spined girl,
wide-thighed and too intelligent. I came this
way as a would-be faun, too fat for the great ballet.
I have arrived at the mouth of the change, ravenous
cave, calling space and chill air, best friends, hills,
the disappearing promises of mist : my love.
My love, I have arrived at the cries of not knowing.

Not ready for my own flirtatious hips, crazed
gypsies, aging, how this long hum of woman-spin,
crooned by all the other changelings at the walls—
how we are too amazed by the sandpapers of
madness, by the silks of petals.

Sharp silver, at the dull
metal sleeps, even though the moon was
fully conjured. God, go to work on other

breasts. Mine are naked to these days.
Mine are mute kin to northern nights. Mine are
blanched. There is white voile at the window,
a world of other muses. I have only
to politely murder this one.
Certainly her Father will understand.

• • •

Out of the white mouth, blankly, no explaining
: Yes, you can. Out of the wrinkled eye,
one touch to mine : Yes, you can.

My love, send me jonquils, on a glacier plate of clean, pale night.
Send a tundra cloth to cover me, this little, I know—
My love, this slope-shouldered marble
is cut.
This now. This past. This northern light that calls burn-white to
cells, that spin in latitudes of steams. Their lavender forgettings
are like caged leaves.

What a good girl am I, hiss, to the alert listening of the go-round-horse.
Bear me to Petersburg. Or Africa. Or forest.
Ride me to hell between loins of a thirsty stag, galloping.
Break these bones into marrow for tomorrow or kiss me,
God, kiss me. Oh, still the carousel, it was ever too fast.
I am ice, and you a carved staff across the sheer, leaning.

My love, this Monday chime, this time bowing to chants
from our mothers' ragged memories, all their quiet wombs set me
free. These chittering trees tune, and tune,
instruments the wind prepares, to teach us how to change, or sing.

In the long shade, how we are thirsty
birds, even in the rain.
I am the woman who asks.
The silent actress. The lost myth.
I forgot how to weave water. Or silk. From sand. Or dried milk.

Blood Soup

Linda Parsons Marion

February cold cracks
marrow deep, no potion
of lavender or lanolin
softens the blow.
Past fifty and done
with my monthlies,
I let it flow: tiny refusals
dot towel and dishcloth,
seep into celery rib, turnip,
onion skinned for winter
broth, tinge of time's sting.

Period

Priscilla Frake

My daughter started bleeding today,
on the same day that I did.
It is her first period,
and my last before chemo.
My ovaries are about to be silenced;
hers are just starting to speak
of discomfort and riches.
We are in a foreign house,
in a country no longer native,
far from home.

My mother is dead,
my aunts are dead,
betrayed by estrogen.
Alone, I prepare to enter
the world of darkness
under the world. My blood
will be drawn out,
not according to the moon,
but weekly,
in order to check my counts.

My daughter protests the blood
that sweeps away her childhood.
What can I tell her?
She can't deny her new breasts
anymore than I can turn
from this poison road
or refuse to claim
my own reluctant
power.

Red Hot Chili Pepper Surprise

Jane Vollbrecht

"Do you think God has a gender?" Patrice flapped the large paper fan she was holding even harder in hopes of giving Corrine the benefit of the breeze.

"Is there a right answer? I'd just as soon save myself the aggravation of having you contradict me twelve ways from Tuesday if I get it wrong." Corrine dipped her washcloth in the pan of ice water on the table beside her, wrung the cloth, and pressed it against both wrists before draping it over her forehead.

"I didn't ask if you *know* what the gender is—I asked for your opinion."

"Does it look to you like I'm in the mood for a hypothetical discussion about something we can't possibly hope to reach a conclusion about?" Corrine raised her head from its resting place on the chaise lounge, then lifted her bottle of water and sucked down a big swallow. "Why should I care if God has a gender?" She set the bottle on the wide arm of her chaise and let her head drop back on the upper curve of the backrest.

Patrice double-checked to be sure Corrine had the washcloth over her eyes before she made a face and silently aped her partner's words. Sixteen years ago, when she and Corrine had first gotten together, their eight year age difference hadn't seemed like a big deal. Now that Corrine was forty-nine and she was a mere forty-one, the gap felt much wider. Of course, Corrine's less-than-joyful trip through the early stages of menopause wasn't helping anything these days—most noticeably, Corrine's sense of humor and her tolerance level for darn near everything.

Corrine had started having hot flashes four months earlier. Patrice was glad they had first hit in the winter and almost always at night. All she had to do was fling the backdoor open and get out of the way as Corrine went racing by, shedding whatever articles of clothing she could while remaining sufficiently covered to avoid being arrested for indecent exposure by the DeKalb County Police. After the surge passed, Corrine would come back inside, her face bright red, the hair at the nape of her neck moist, her shirt wet—often wringing wet.

After several weeks of next to no sleep for either of them, Patrice went online and researched natural products that might help the worst of the symptoms. She sure as heck wouldn't be fool enough to suggest Corrine see a gynecologist to get an estrogen patch. She had no desire to find out if Corrine could make good on her threat to reach down Patrice's throat and yank her ovaries out past her tonsils. Nope. She only advocated natural treatments, or she mentioned nothing at all. So far, the only thing the dong quai, black cohosh and evening primrose oil seemed to be doing was making a few bucks for the health food store in Toco Hills.

Now that it was spring in Georgia, even the footrace to the back porch several times a night wasn't doing much good. Thirty-degree weather had been far more effective than sixty-degree weather in counteracting the hormonal flames. And the flashes were coming during the day now, too. Which was why, at nine thirty on a Sunday morning in April, Patrice was on the patio in her bathrobe, sitting next to Corrine, waving her palm-shaped fan and struggling to find a conversation topic that would distract Corrine through the worst of the swell that had turned her face crimson and her exposed skin dewy.

They hadn't been inside a church to attend Sunday services in more than a dozen years, but they had made an agreement about how to keep religion in their lives: if they had at least one serious conversation on Sunday that used the words "God" or "the Creator" in an appropriate context, it counted the same as if they'd actually gone to a building and sat through a liturgy.

"What about a sense of humor? Do you think God has a sense of humor?" Patrice could see the red hue fading from Corrine's cheeks, meaning the blaze was dying down.

"Must have. Why else would men's genitals look like they do? If that's not a joke, I don't know what is."

Good sign. Corrine actually laughed out loud as she gave her answer. And good point, too, come to think of it. Plus, now they'd had their requisite "God" discussion and could relax for the rest of the day.

"How bad was this one?"

"Somewhere between pepperoncini and chilaca."

Patrice had read up on the medical explanations of what happened during hot flashes. She knew they were triggered by falling estrogen and rising follicle-stimulating hormone, and that when they occurred, the blood vessels in the skin of the head and neck opened more widely than usual, bringing an influx of blood, thus producing the heat and redness, but that intellectual cognizance didn't really tell her how they made Corrine feel. To better Patrice's understanding, they had devised the "Corrine Dozier Chili Pepper Ranking Scale" to rate each flash. Patrice still couldn't fully empathize, but it helped her to know whether to have the shower running—cold tap only—afterward, or if she should consider hauling out the garden hose.

This one was way down on the low end of the scale. If things ran true to form, this was just a warning tremor. The real seismic shift and at least one aftershock would be arriving momentarily.

"And you know what else tells me God has a sense of humor?" Corrine swung her feet to one side of the chaise so that she could sit up and face Patrice. She laid her washcloth on the table.

"What?"

"I'm forty-nine and hitting menopause, my thirty-year-old daughter is pregnant, and her eleven-year-old daughter started having periods this year. That pretty much gives us the gynecological equivalent of covering all the bases. When the three of us are in the same room, we have enough mood swings to hold our own home run derby."

Patrice knew better than to comment one way or the other. It was one thing for Corrine to make wisecracks about the Dozier women's varying temperaments, but quite another for Patrice to seem to have an opinion on the matter. One thing Patrice was sure of, age in years was an ineffectual way to gauge Corrine's granddaughter, Cassidy. The calendar might say she was eleven, but it was eleven going on thirty-four.

"Oh, crap," Corrine said.

Patrice could see the color creeping up Corrine's neck.

"Here comes the inferno." Corrine lay back down and stretched out on the chaise.

Patrice resumed fanning for all she was worth. There were still a few ice cubes floating in the basin on the table and Corrine's water bottle was still half-full, so all she could do was sit by, silent and supportive, as the lava cascaded over her lover's upper torso.

"Damn, it's a scorcher," Corrine growled. "Give me that washcloth."

Patrice refreshed the cloth in the ice water and laid it on Corrine's face.

"This one's at least a poblano or a serrano. Maybe even a chiltepin."

Oh, oh, this will get ugly. Patrice fanned furiously.

"Double damn." Corrine yanked her T-shirt up, all but exposing her breasts and used her other hand to catch the sweat beads forming on her chin. "If God's a woman, she's got some explaining to do about these freakin' hot flashes."

Patrice kept fanning, Corrine kept perspiring. Three minutes later, the conflagration abated. Corrine flung the washcloth into the pan and huffed out a sigh. "This is so much fun. Take notes, dear, your turn will come."

Again, Patrice opted not to reply. It wouldn't matter if she agreed or disagreed. Until the wave of the last vibration rolled by, there was no point.

"Time for the final act." Corrine snatched up her washcloth, squeezed it quickly, and held it to her left temple. "An anaheim, or maybe a potent jalapeno."

"Good. That should be the end of it for a while." Patrice continued fluttering the fan toward Corrine, just in case.

Corrine let her arms fall so that her fingertips were touching the flagstone patio on either side of her chaise and breathed deeply for a minute or two. "What's left to do to get ready for Ramona and Cassidy?" Corrine's daughter and granddaughter were coming to Patrice and Corrine's house for Sunday dinner. Ramona's husband, Tom, never joined the women's Sunday gatherings. He'd rather watch whatever sporting event was on TV than listen to the four of them discuss whatever female topics they picked for the day. The arrangement seemed to suit everyone just fine.

"Not much. Since Ramona has sworn off all meat while she's pregnant, we're just having a rice, lentil and cheese casserole for the main course, and that's ready to put in the oven. I've chopped some broccoli and cauliflower to steam. I'll throw a green salad together just before we sit down, and there's a loaf of that good dark bread from the bakery. If Cassidy pitches a fit that there's nothing she likes, I've got some turkey franks I can nuke for her."

"What about dessert?"

"Fresh strawberries and homemade oatmeal cookies. Ice cream for anyone who wants it."

"As always, you are my hero." Corrine stretched her arm toward Patrice and patted her calf. "By the way, when I talked to Cassidy on the phone last night, she told me she's having her period. God only knows what kind of state she'll be in this afternoon." Corrine rose to a sitting position. "Thanks for helping me survive another trip through the jaws of Hades."

"Think you're about ready to go back inside?"

"Yeah, that should about do it for this morning's visit to the edge of hormonally-induced insanity."

Shortly after noon, Patrice heard Ramona's Saab pull up out front. She watched from the top step of the stoop as Ramona and Cassidy walked across the lawn. She was struck yet again at how seeing the two of them was like watching a home movie of Corrine in reverse time. Their gaits, mannerisms, voice inflections, postures—everything they said and did left no doubt they shared Corrine's bloodline.

Corrine had married at eighteen, given birth to Ramona at nineteen, and become a grandmother to Cassidy at thirty-eight. Along about age twenty-eight, Corrine had left her husband (she still referred to him as "Tofu"—nothing but a meat substitute) and taken up with the woman she sat next to in the Trinity Lutheran Church's choir. That union didn't last, but her attraction to women did. Five years after her fling with her favorite contralto, she met Patrice; they'd been together ever since.

Ramona was fourteen when Corrine and Patrice hooked up—not exactly an ideal age for a child to have to accept her mother's live-in lesbian lover. There had been some turf wars to be sure, but eventually, Patrice and Ramona made peace with each other's place in Corrine's life. When Cassidy was born, Ramona had asked both Corrine and Patrice to be in the delivery room with her. The memory of cutting the umbilical cord could still reduce Patrice to a puddle of tears. She couldn't have loved Cassidy more if she were really her grandchild.

Because she'd never known things to be any other way, Cassidy had an easy time accepting the notion of having two grandmothers on her mother's side of the family. In fact, she felt sorry for kids who didn't have both a Gran (Corrine) and a Meemaw (Patrice) under the same roof.

Conversation over dinner focused on Ramona's round belly—only ten weeks until little Madison Adele would make her appearance. After dinner, they migrated to the living room. Ramona propped herself in one corner of the sofa, and Corrine claimed the other end. Cassidy sat between them.

"Thanks for the nice meal, Patrice." Ramona patted her abdomen. "Any minute now, baby shakes will grab her pogo stick and make her presence known. She hasn't figured out she's supposed to take a nap after she eats."

"You were the same way, Mona," Corrine said. "I was sure you'd come out of my womb carrying a bottle of Pepto-Bismol." She shifted on the sofa. "Is it hot in here?"

Before any of the others could assure her it wasn't, Corrine spoke again. "Habanero heading for Szechwan. Call the fire department." She leaned forward and tugged her shirt off.

"Big, bouncing baby on board," Ramona countered as her stomach started to visibly move.

Without a word, Cassidy laid one hand on her mother's undulating midsection and placed the other on her grandmother's glowing upper chest. Patrice watched from her seat across the room. She'd have sworn she could actually see a strip of genetic encoding stretching like an indestructible band among the three generations. Several moments passed.

"This is so cool," Cassidy said in a hushed voice. "Aren't you glad we're not boys? They don't get to have any of the real fun." Cassidy grinned, then continued, "I mean, think about it. We make babies inside our bodies, and then when we get old, we've got a way to burn off the stuff that can't be used anymore. The whole deal is just so incredible."

Wait till you've had to fight three days of unrelenting cramps. Patrice kept the thought to herself.

Patrice looked at the mother-to-be and felt she could read Ramona's mind. Unless she missed her guess, Ramona was thinking something like, "Try racing for the bathroom at the start of every day for a trimester of morning sickness or experience the thrill of feeling you're pushing a bowling ball through a drinking straw in childbirth. Then we'll talk."

Patrice saw the look on her partner's face and assumed Corrine's unspoken comment probably ran along the lines of, "Yeah, a laugh a minute. I might be the first woman to spontaneously combust, courtesy of unrelenting hot flashes."

Patrice had been ready to leap into action with cold compresses or ice water to help break the fever of the hot flash, but Corrine shook her head as if to say, "I'll ride this one out on my own." If there were any of the usual peaks and valleys of subsequent surges, Corrine kept them to herself.

Patrice was content to observe from outside the group while the Dozier women chatted with each other on the sofa for the rest of the afternoon. More often than not, though, the three just sat silently, communicating without words about things that couldn't have been adequately described anyway.

That evening as Patrice and Corrine were getting ready for bed, Corrine called from the bathroom, "Hey, where did you put the tampons? Looks like I'm getting my period. I haven't bled for three months or more. Menopause is just one surprise after another."

Surprise?

Earlier that day, Patrice had witnessed the turning of the spokes on the wondrous wheel of womanhood. She understood now that there really was no such thing as an ending or a beginning—just an enduring circle, one generation to the next. No, Patrice concluded, the onset of Corrine's period wasn't surprising in the least.

lies about progeny

Marty McConnell

and then, one morning, finally, blood.
just when you thought the moon
wasn't yours anymore, that six years
of chemical postponement had convinced
the emptiness of its permanence,
the walls of their right to quiet,

you're wrong. and nothing lies quiet,
you watch the bowl fill with blood
in ribbons and clumps. the permanence
of the body terrifies; you're not the moon
or her cousin, you do not burn, convinced
though you were of penalty years,

years without touch in trade for years
of damage, of affairs, of traitorous quiet.
you can't look in subway carriages, convinced
of your need for punishment, for the old blood
to be drawn off, the veins cauterized, the moon
given a name you can't learn. wanting permanence,

you are cursed with a permanence
you could not have anticipated. years
of uncertainty, of stutter and stop, the moon
refusing to give up her face, gone quiet
and unrecognizable, denying you the blood
exorcism you craved. now, unconvinced,

you sit. draw from the body the long convincing
cord. call it a small god. call it a permanent
sin. the only product of your penance is blood.
there are days you set aside for crying, and years
when the only effective tourniquet is quiet.
you try magic, you try to draw down the moon

but the moon won't come. the moon
is a cold stone, looking away. convince
the body it is a planet. our orbit is quiet.
solo. cycle is its own kind of permanence.
don't want what you want. in years
to come, you won't. what you'll want is blood

on the moon, water fast on its way, blood
of gratitude, the convincing permanence
of solitude, the good quiet unreeling of years.

Red, Riding

Michele Ruby

Little Red, riding hooded,
comes by the moon,
basket brimming with cherries,
with grapes the color of blood,
tomatoes ripe to bursting,
seeds swimming in their sacs,
pomegranates like rubies.

I, the grandmother, will have
none of them, will turn her away,
will refuse those goodies too raw
or too fresh. Come back, I'll say,
when you've learned to bake,
when you know the flashing heat
of the oven, and can turn
old fruit into pie.

Her basket is meant for the wolf—
his breath baited with sweet wooings,
his rough tongue ready. Embrace his hunger;
wear him like a fur, I'll say. Use him:
tour guide, thrill ride. Take the trip
through the wolf. Soon enough,
you won't be able to afford the ticket.
Soon enough, you'll be bloodless and calm.

A Death in the Family

Ellaraine Lockie

I check toilet papers for
the pinkish stain
that announces its arrival
My time of the month
Link to the moon
Mankind enabler
A period fading into
a question mark
Soon to be an unpunctuated blank
Ovarian governors wither on
fallopian vines
An oncoming death in my
family of organs
Death by a berserk body-clock
that no repairman can fix
Forty years of dependable dates
with my most feminine old friend
have become surprise visits
No calls first
Just discourteous drop-ins
Surely an Emily Post violation
but not nature's
Her way of surviving the fittest
Giving babies I'll never have
to my daughters
and their daughters
My body rebels against the bias
Fights a noble retirement battle
opposed by hormonal brigades
A futile war

that mutates into mourning
Evolves to acceptance
Changes to contentment
Satisfaction when the pink stain
announces its cramps
leakage, smell, messy sex
On someone else's paper

On Menstruation and Euphemism

Zola Noble

On my tenth birthday in 1956, my mother gave me a little booklet published by Kotex called *Now You are 10*. It explained menstruation and the changes I could expect in my body. I loved my mom for that booklet. I thought she was smart and wise and open-minded, and she had acknowledged that I was growing up. Considering that she learned about menstruation when she found bloodstains in her underpants, I think my mother did quite well by me. But I waited impatiently another two-and-a-half years for the event that would confirm my womanhood: the onset of my monthly periods.

That's the term we used for menstruation—monthly period or simply period. Later, I learned a new term when my best friend told me she couldn't go swimming because her granny had come to visit. I took her literally. Since then, I've learned to be more savvy about language substitutions for the word menstruation. They are legion.

Perhaps the earliest euphemism for menstruation appears in the book of Genesis in one of my favorite Bible stories. Jacob's sojourn in the land of his father-in-law Laban becomes difficult when disputes erupt between his shepherds and Laban's. Jacob decides to end the problems by returning to the land of his father Isaac. Fearing Laban's protests, Jacob departs by night taking his two wives (Laban's daughters) and his many children. Unknown to Jacob, his favorite wife Rachel has stolen her father's idols. Insulted at the secret departure and angry about the missing idols, Laban storms after Jacob's caravan and searches tent after tent for the idols. Lifting the flap to Rachel's tent, he sees her sitting on a pile of camel skins concealing the idols. "Come on in," she says, "and search all you want. But you'll have to excuse me for not getting up, 'for the custom of women is upon me.'" Her father allows her to stay seated, conducts his search, and leaves empty-handed. The gutsy Rachel keeps her secret.

Thinking about Rachel's gentle euphemism for menstuation, I Google searched the two words. Up popped www.MUM.org, MUM being an acronym for Museum of Menstruation. Euphemisms scrolled down my computer screen like coins falling at my feet from a slot machine in Las Vegas. MUM is a veritable treasure trove of information about menstruation compiled by Harry Finley who creates, writes and maintains the site. In fact, if you want to print the alphabetized list of favorite euphemisms for menstruation contributed by Web site visitors, you'll end up with ninety-five pages.

Perusing the euphemisms on MUM, I began to see categories emerging from the list, interesting patterns that created a mosaic of thought about menstruation. The euphemisms ran the gamut from innocent (granny visits) to vulgar (fluffing it).

My junior high friend isn't the only one to receive visits from Granny, I discovered. Though the visitor is sometimes the unwanted guest, he or she might also be anonymous or simply the visitor. Visitors also have names. Besides Granny, there's Aunt Aggie, Aunt Martha, Aunt Sally or Aunt Tilly, and the most popular, Aunt Flo. Men come to visit, too: Herman, Clyde, Charlie, Freddy, George, Cousin Tom, Cousin Pierre, or the more bawdy Cap'n Bloodsnatch. After all, men are the ones who bring all the trouble to women, one contributor suggests. I would not welcome Mr. Grumpy or Mr. Cranky Business. I think I'd rather see smiley Red Skelton, who also made the list. Also a noteworthy visitor is Little Red Riding Hood (blood) who comes through the woods (the body). Then there's Big Red or Big Red Monster. The most sinister, I suppose, is a visit from Carrie. Now, I haven't seen that film because I can't sleep after scary movies. Was Carrie's problem related to her monthlies?

The next most popular set of terms listed on MUM evokes water images, especially damaging ones: the dam has burst, the floodgates are open, it's Hoover Dam, I'm flooding, the flood is of biblical proportions, the banks of the Nile are overflowing, it's monsoon season. Also, I'm a human waterfall, I'm chasing waterfalls, I'm flowing like a hydrant, or I'm emptying. The term depends on the amount of flow. If the flow is lighter, terms might indicate as such: drainage, draining, drippy faucet or drip drop. Or it just might be raining down south. Images of the tide can be included here: it's the tide; it's high tide; the tide's out; the tide's in; it's crimson tide, or in southern California, surfing the crimson tide. Reading these terms, I begin to feel a little seasick.

The ebb and flow of nature out of control are mild terms compared to some euphemisms contributed by people who obviously have no qualms about calling a spade a spade, so to speak. If the words blood or bleed and crotch or vagina offend your sensibilities, you may not want to read on. These harsher terms include the bloody beast, the bloody mess, the bloody snot, Bloody Mary and blood is fighting its way out my vagina. The contributors of these terms believe if you bleed, say bleed: I have the bleedies; I'm bleeding like a stuck pig (code word, B.L.A.S.P.); I'm bleeding freely from the crotch or bleeding out my vagina. It might be bleeding uterus day (code word, BUD) or bloody vagina (code word, BV). Or a woman might say she's hemorrhaging. Any of these expressions don't mince words. If a euphemism is an inoffensive term substituted for an offensive one, these terms hardly fit that definition. The word menstruation seems gentle by comparison.

More delicate euphemisms listed by MUM contributors include the terms girl, lady, female and woman. Examples: She's being a girl, being girly, has girl issues, or it's girl time. She's being a lady, having lady days, has a lady parts problem, or it's lady business. She's being a woman or womanly. She's being female, or it's feminine biology. These terms land more gently on the ears. They reveal acceptance of the biological processes as a natural part of being a woman.

Some women, not so accepting, view menstruation as illness. This is understandable for the many women whose menstrual periods are accompanied by cramps, headaches, leg pain, and the like. They might use expressions, such as, I'm feeling blah, I'm incapacitated, I'm under the weather, I'm unwell, I have cramps, I've come sick, I have the misery, I have girl flu, or more dramatically, I'm dying. Some even say they could cure the plague, a reference rooted in a time centuries ago when people believed drinking menstrual blood cured the plague. I really hope no one tried this.

Though many MUM contributors use negative terms, others look on the bright side. A menstrual period confirms they're not pregnant. They might say I have good news. I'm happy and bleeding. I'm in celebration. Thank God! The apparatus worked (be it the pill, the condom, the diaphragm, and so on). Other positive sounding euphemisms might be uttered seriously or sarcastically: it's my special time, my happiness, the joy of womanhood, or my cup of joy is overflowing. Some call menstruation the gift. Or they say they're decorated with red roses. Or more crudely, their snatch box is decorated with red roses.

Besides red roses, many MUM contributors focus on the color red in other ways: it's code red, I have the reds or the mean reds, my red flag is up, it's my red-letter day or redheaded cousin or redheaded aunt. (There are those visitors again!) Another expression is Jenny (as in genitalia, not Jennifer) has a red dress on. A surprising one, for me, and a real stretch of the imagination are the euphemisms in which the red color connotes communism. Examples: the commies are coming, the communists have invaded the summerhouse, I'm falling to the communists, the red army has invaded or it's my cousin from Russia (another guest).

Time is also a factor in euphemisms concerning menstruation: It's . . . time, calendar days, cup week, that time of the month, the wrong time of the month, the monthlies, the monthly bill, the monthly troubles, the monthly visitor or I'm having my cycle.

Travel terms, such as riding and driving, also engage the euphemistically inclined—and usually have vulgar connotations: I'm . . . in the saddle again, riding the red pony, riding the cotton pony, riding the rag, on the bus, driving the red car, driving through a forest, driving through a redwood forest, driving through the bushes.

Usually menstruation is a time to abstain from sex. Lots of euphemisms listed on MUM imply this: I'm closed for business, closed for maintenance, closed for the holidays, out of action, too wet to plow, not user-friendly, or I can't go swimming, the kitty is sick, and I'm broken. Some women might say there are strings attached, which refers to the string from the tampon. And finally, the line is busy, please try again later. Not all couples abstain from sex during menstruation, however. Their euphemisms are equally revealing: I will swim in the red river, but I won't drink from it; I like a little ketchup with my steak; I like my meat rare. Hm. I'd say, no, thanks!

Euphemisms for pads and tampons abound with MUM contributors, as well. Collectively, they are called girly products or FHP (feminine hygiene products). Pads are called Band-Aids, french bread, cotton ponies, cooter pads, jam and bread or manhole covers. When you put on a pad you diaper up. A tampon might be called a bullet, a cigar, a cooter plug, a torpedo, a cotton tail, a cork, a dead rat, a mouse mattress or Dracula's tea bag. Implied in some of these is the string for removing the tampon. Inserting a tampon is called by some blowing a fuse. Wearing a tampon is packin' dynamite. Using two tampons is the double-barrel technique. These terms sound deadly to me, but they also reveal a woman's ingenuity, resourcefulness and sense of humor.

One friend's story about how she came to call a tampon a french plug illustrates that sense of humor. She related that she and three friends traveled around Europe in the '80s. One of their concerns was having the right size electrical plug for hotel rooms in various countries, so they could use their hair dryers and curling irons. As they were riding a train through France, one of the women remembered extra plugs for outlets in France that she carried in her purse. Wanting to share them, she reached in her purse. "Does anyone need a french plug?" she said. Instead of the electrical plug, out flipped a tampon and fell on the floor near some men across the aisle. Ever after, the women have called a tampon a french plug.

Whether it's a substitute term for a pad or tampon or one for menstruation per se, the euphemisms we use reveal our attitudes toward a natural body process, one that is at first welcomed by young girls as confirming their womanhood, but through the years as their enthusiasm wanes, the process becomes dreaded at most, an inconvenience or an annoyance at least. The psychological implications of all this are beyond my ken. But it does indicate, perhaps, denial of or unwillingness to celebrate our womanliness. But it could be, partly, that we just can't pronounce menstruation. That word does not roll off the tongue easily—one of my friends pronounces it ministration—so we substitute other more colorful, creative and fun terms.

Many years have passed since my mother gave me that little booklet on menstruation and the excitement of becoming a woman surged through me. So many years, in fact, that the granny visits have ceased. There are no more floods of biblical proportions, no more monthlies, no more B.L.A.S.P., no more bloody beast, no more lady days, no more miseries, no code red. Am I glad? You bet! I am nonetheless thankful for those lady days, but my life has entered another phase. Every day is good news. And if the time is right, there are no strings attached. I'm no longer packin' dynamite. I'm traveling light. However, there are drawbacks to this freedom. Now if I'm not in the mood, I can't say, sorry Dear, but it's that time of the month.

Work Cited

Finley, Harry. "Words for Menstruation." *Museum of Menstruation & Women's Health.* 2006.

The Blood At 45

Andrea Potos

These days she announces herself
more than a week before her arrival—the tender,
extra flesh, the long, unravelling carpet of fatigue,
as though she yearns to be noticed—

beauty queen,
nearly vintage, who knows her reign
is expiring,

at her feet—
a withering brood of roses.

Waning

Maureen Tolman Flannery

These are heartfelt couplings,
the last few chances for our mingling flesh
to draw some uncalculated factor
into the already complex equation.
My dwindling power to call forth independent life
is balance to those early years when I, a new wife,
fecund as a rumor, bore you more than we had bargained for.

Now one son, in the rutting season of first romance,
can smell love the way a coyote noses wool's lanolin
born on a timber wind with a hundred other scents.
And our daughter, last born, stands already at the rim
of womanhood like a hang glider waiting for the right gust
to carry her airborne upon the future.

And we know each other's bodies as our own,
their only surprise the periodic rise of new keratoses,
brown and scaly as though we would slowly
kiss each other back into toads.
Each time now I assure you I could not conceive.
Then again I flow through one more moon tide,
my body clinging to fertility like a weather-beaten farmer
reluctant to give over his fields.

A tender and blessed love thrives in the darkness
while our unconscious collaboration with the gods
is waning like a harvest moon. But as we thrust
toward fearless years of reckless sex,
there courses in us both, in lieu of lush fluids of fertility,
a secret sadness.

No more amber-haired babies will hover like sea birds,
poised to descend and trouble the waters we enter into.
The last of our lovely ones has been remembered unto life.
No more formless unborns tread starlight
beyond the hard matter of our love,
hoping to catch us off guard.

A Life of Blood

Donna J. Gelagotis Lee

Mood
as steady as a seesaw.
Then, sleep slips . . . starts

slipping . . . I
medicate. I think,
maybe it's . . .

and sure enough,
the body
releases its bloody

flow—and I am
surprised at my dis-
pleasure—hoping to have

dissed it—sixty
is looking good!—if
I'm not harboring

a genetic landmine
that trips off—
don't believe

it gets better
unless you plan to beat
time with a stick,

your muscles
to plump up your skin,
unless you plan

to pass this ir-
regular time
with fortitude

until you regain something
of what you initially lost
in service to a life of blood

Unlikely Testimonials

Julia Watts

As many readers of women's magazines know, advertisements for feminine hygiene products have often relied on testimonials by famous women. In the Seventies, perky gymnast Cathy Rigby demonstrated that Stayfree maxi pads were compatible with an active lifestyle. In the Eighties, even perkier gymnast Mary Lou Retton did the same for Tampax, while sultry-voiced actress Brenda Vaccaro lent some of her gravelly glamour to Playtex tampons.

What is less known about the history of feminine hygiene advertising, though, is that not all women whose images and words appeared in these ads were athletes and actresses. Over the course of the twentieth century, several famous women artists, writers and musicians have provided testimonials for feminine hygiene ads. Until their recent discovery, however, most of these ads, which appeared in obscure and long-out-of-circulation magazines, had been forgotten. Due to the ravages of time, it was impossible to reproduce the ads themselves to appear in this publication; however, in the interest of preserving these vital pieces of women's history, a description of the artwork in each ad, followed by the ad's actual text, appears below.

Gertrude Stein

[The ad shows a full-body photo of Stein, smiling affably. She is smoking a cigar but is wearing a skirt—a helpful cue to readers who otherwise might not recognize her as female.]

The text reads,

Gertrude Stein for Goddess Sanitary Napkins

A woman has a dot.
It is the dot at the end of this sentence.
The dot is her sentence.
The dot is red.

Cotton will stop the dot.
White cotton will stop the red dot,
Will catch the clot.
The clot
that is
the dot
that is the woman's sentence.

Under these lines, the following slogan appears:

"Goddess Sanitary Napkins—for the Modern Woman!"

Georgia O'Keefe

[O'Keefe didn't provide any words for this ad, but the page is dominated by the painting she created for it: a vivid, pink, blue and lavender flower that appears to be on the verge of blooming—with a single string of white cotton dangling between its petals.]

The text reads, Vampax Tampons—Let your femininity blossom.

Dorothy Parker

[The ad shows a close-up of a sardonically smiling Parker, sporting bobbed hair and a chic hat.]
The text reads,

Algonquin Round Table wit Dorothy Parker says,
"Men seldom make passes
At girls with red asses."

To avoid unsightly "accidents," heed the wisdom of everyone's favorite funny lady and use Goddess Sanitary Napkins.

Frida Kahlo

[Like O'Keefe, Kahlo provided a painting but no words for an ad for Vampax Tampons. The painting depicts Frida, splayed naked on a bed the white sheets of which are stained a vivid red. Frida's uterus and ovaries float in the air over the bed, spraying blood all over the room's white walls.]
The text reads,

Girls, don't let this happen to you!
Use Vampax Tampons.

Janis Joplin

[*The ad shows Janis wearing nothing but bangles, rings, love beads and a smile. A tampon string is visible between her thighs.*]
The text reads,

Man, you know when you're out on the street lookin' for a little action with some dude or chick who looks like they've got it goin' on? But then you feel that trickle down between your legs that says the floodgates have opened and your hopes for a little action have just dried up? Well, that might be how it was in our mama's day, but it doesn't have to be no more. Vampax Tampons can stop that flood just like putting your finger in a dyke, and you're good to go, honey. So don't let your period drag you down like a ball and chain. Use Vampax Tampons, and get it while you can!

Prose Bios

ADRIENNE ANIFANT graduated from Mount Holyoke College. She has an MA in Writing and an LL.M. in Human Rights and International Law. Her fiction, essays and book reviews are published in Ireland, England and the United States She lives in New York City. When she got her first period, she ran outside in joy and inspiration, her feet hitting the black macadam, her tears hidden by the cool evening rain.

SUSAN CHRISTERSON BROWN earned her MFA in Writing from Spalding University and has published work in various journals and collections, including *The Louisville Review*, *Tobacco: A Literary Anthology*, *The Journal of Kentucky Studies*, *The Journal of Family Life*, and *Spirituality & Health* magazine. She received the Alice A. Dunnigan Award for creative nonfiction and an Al Smith Award from the Kentucky Arts Council. She is currently a student at Lexington Theological Seminary. Her cycles have helped her understand that human life is subject to rhythms older, deeper and more powerful than we can fully apprehend.

LYNN RAYE CAMPBELL is an engineer whose first love is words. She wrote secretly beginning at age eight. Finally, at age thirty, she got up the courage to take a writing class. This resulted in her becoming a founding member of the Byliners writing group, which has met continually for over eighteen years. "Blood Brother" is her first published essay. Lynn got her period early and then only once a year for the next eleven years. She wonders if that was practice for approaching menopause.

TAB CURTIS was born and raised in Kentucky, but has managed to overcome. She is a sporadically employed systems analyst but spends most of her working hours editing her fiction. She currently lives in Chicago-land with her lovely girlfriend, their surly dog and a cat that just may be the

Antichrist.

PATTI DEAN is a rock-band singer, former stand-up comic and comedy writer for nationally known comics and an actress off-Broadway. She produced, wrote and edited an award-winning documentary on stand-up comics in Seattle. She is the author of a children's musical focusing on disabilities and has produced and written various cabarets and plays performed in Seattle, Baltimore and New York. Her short story "Women's Clothes" was published in the anthology *Love and Sacrifice* as a companion piece to the international movie *London Voodoo* by Zenfilms. She is currently working on a film script of that story with Zenfilms for feature film production. Patti writes, "My father was determined that his four daughters all be daily joggers. Coming from a family of all boys, he never got that we were strange birds indeed with our periods and cramps every month preventing us from keeping up with the regimen. We're still not telling."

K. COLEMAN FOOTE is from New Jersey. Her writing has appeared most recently in *Crab Orchard Review*, *Homelands* (Seal Press) and *Babel Fish* and is forthcoming in other anthologies. She received a 2007 Hedgebrook Writing Residency, an MFA in Creative Writing from Chicago State University and was a 2002–03 Fulbright Fellow in Ghana. She's grateful for the invention of self-stick pads with wings, which have spared her from the rags used in Lele's days!

KATHLEEN GERARD'S writing has been widely published in literary journals and anthologies. Her work has been nominated for *Best New American Voices*, a national prize in literature, and her prose was awarded the Perillo Prize for Italian American Writing. In addition, several of her essays have been included in the *Cup of Comfort* series of books and featured on National Public Radio. Kathleen was the last born in her family, but the first of her middle school circle of friends to get "that thing at the end of a sentence."

SHANNA GERMAIN is a poet by nature, a short story writer by the skin of her teeth and a novelist in-training. Her award-winning writing has appeared in places such as *Absinthe Literary Review*, *American Journal of Nursing*, *Best American Erotica 2007*, *Tipton Poetry Review* and *Salon*. Shanna travels a lot, and "Aunt Flow" seems to tag along on every trip, even when she hasn't been invited. Visit Shanna online at www.shannagermain.com.

ELAINE K. GREEN is an avid reader, freelance writer and New Orleans native. About her menstrual cycle, having passed fifty, she's glad that "period" of her life is over.

SUZANNE GROSSMAN is a Brooklyn-based writer, musician and activist. Her family was heading to a Mets game in 1987, when the mysterious cramps of her first period set in. Her grandmother, a big baseball fan, kindly stayed home with her.

CHEZON JACKSON (chezonjackson@gmail.com) has used poetry to punctuate her life's sentences since claiming writing as her life's passion at the age of eight. Beginning in 1997, and continuously through pre- and post-menstrual cycles, she has performed humorously human poetry up and down the East Coast, including at the National Black Arts Festival and International Woman's Day Celebrations and on numerous television and radio stations. She's also opened for celebrities such as Kindred: The Family Soul and the Grammy award–winning hip-hop duo OutKast. Between her performances and volunteer work teaching the joys of creative expression through poetry, Chezon self-published her first collection of poetry entitled, *Can Schizophrenics Ride in the HOV Lane?* She remembers, distinctly, the day she got her period, she did not immediately feel like a woman, as legend and myth had predicted. She just felt like a little girl with soiled underpants.

CYN KITCHEN teaches creative writing at Knox College. Her work has appeared in places such as *Carve, New Southerner, The Dead Mule, Minnetonka Review* and *Louisville Review*. Her essay, "Period," is part of a book-length manuscript, *The Cynical Kitchen*, which is currently in the book-proposal submission process. Cyn is in the relatively peaceful Nothing Years between the eras of Childbearing and Hot Flashes, and she thinks this is quite fine.

TSAURAH LITZKY is a widely published poet and writer of erotica. She is also a playwright and a writer of art criticism. Her erotic novella *The Motion of the Ocean* was published by Simon & Schuster as part of *Three the Hard Way*, a series of erotic novellas edited by Susie Bright. Her poetry collection *Baby on the Water—New and Selected Poems 1992–2003* was published by Long Shot Press. Tsaurah has published eleven poetry chapbooks, most recently *Crazy Lust* (Snapdragon Press). She is on the faculty of the creative writing department at the New School in Manhattan, where her ongoing course *Silk Sheets: Writing Erotica* is now in its tenth year. Tsaurah no longer gets her period, but she is happy to say she continues to be sexually active. Still, she misses her periods, how they connected her to the moon and the ebb and flow of the tides.

LOREEN NIEWENHUIS received her MFA from Spalding University. Her short fiction has appeared in *Blood and Thunder* and *Words of Wisdom*. She is currently putting the finishing touches on her novel *Tumor Board* and is beginning a new novel set in Atlanta.

ZOLA TROUTMAN NOBLE is an associate professor of English at Anderson University in Anderson, Indiana, where she teaches writing. She has been published in *Highlights*, *The New Southerner*, *The Smithfield Review* and various local publications. She received her MFA in Writing from Spalding University and is a member of the Writers Center of Indiana. She remembers going down the steep back staircase of the farmhouse in Nebraska where she grew up to tell her mother, who was working in the kitchen, that she had started her first period. She was twelve-and-a-half and was tingling inside about becoming a woman.

Author/educator **NANCY PINARD** has an MFA from Queens University and serves as a trustee for the Antioch Writers' Workshop in Yellow Springs, Ohio. Her novels *Shadow Dancing* and *Butterfly Soup* appeared in 2000 and 2006, respectively. Her stories have appeared in literary journals such as *Thema*, *The Beloit Fiction Journal* and *Dos Passos Review*. "The Blue Box" is her first published essay, the story of how she denied the advent of menstruation until after the birth of her children.

TONI POWELL recently retired from a career in academia where she taught organizational psychology at Barry University in Miami. Although she presented and published research studies in several professional journals, this is her first foray into fiction. Toni's early experiences with menstruation are harrowing. Her two younger brothers, both of whom had newspaper delivery jobs, delighted in tormenting her by stealing her unused sanitary napkins, printing her name clearly on each pad, attaching one of them to each newspaper, and hurling the newspapers-with-pads onto neighbors' front steps.

JULIA SCHUSTER'S award-winning short stories and poetry have appeared in numerous commercial and literary publications, including anthologies *On Grandma's Porch* (BelleBooks), *A Cup of Comfort for Sisters*

(Adams Media) and *Living by Faith* (Obidiah Press). She was the 2006 first-place honoree in fiction in the Kentuckian Metroversity Literary Competition. She holds a Master of Fine Arts in Writing degree from Spalding University in Louisville, Kentucky. Julia lives in Memphis, Tennessee, where she teaches junior high religion and creative writing at a private Catholic school. After enduring menstruation for thirty-five years, and benefiting from it (two beautiful daughters), the postmenopausal Julia can't think of one thing she misses about her monthly menses. Can anyone say "Freedom?"

ELIZABETH G. SLADE is a Montessori educator who has co-written the workbook *How to Raise a Peaceful Child in a Violent World*. She writes for LEGO's parenting column and is a frequent contributor to "Parent to Parent" in the *Hampshire Daily Gazette*. Her anthology selection is an excerpt from *Rest Stops*, her novel-in-progress. She received her MFA from Spalding University and is a member of the Fairview Writers. She lives in Western Massachusetts with her spouse and three children. Elizabeth did not get her period until she was fifteen and in the months prior was convinced she was a boy.

L. MAHAYLA SMITH is an air force brat who was born in occupied Japan, has lived all over the U.S., in Europe and in a war zone in Sri Lanka. She has been happily residing in downtown Knoxville, Tennessee, since 2004. Her writing has been published in professional medical research journals. Her inspiration is her offbeat family, students and patients, fiction writing classes at UTK, and the remnants of Julia Watts' Fall 2006 intensive fiction workshop, now known as Writers Without Class. She enjoys travel, hiking, fishing, reading, cooking, spending time with friends and following the band Pearl Jam on tour. With regard to menstruation, she's been there, done that, and is selling the T-shirt to the highest bidder on eBay.

NILDA VÉLEZ is a New York City public school teacher and author of *Negrita*, a novel about the dangers of not looking Puertorriquena. She received her MS from Mercy College and her BS from New York University. Nilda got her period the same day her cousin got a Barbie pool. She was sure neither she nor Barbie would ever swim again.

JANE VOLLBRECHT has five novels in print: *Picture Perfect, Heart Trouble, In Broad Daylight, Close Enough* and *Second Verse*. Her short stories have been included in the anthologies *Call of the Dark* and *Romance for Life*. Jane retired from Federal Civil Service in late 2004. She lives in the foothills of the Georgia mountains. Her hobbies include playing the piano, tending her gardens and watching the wildlife on her property. She got her period shortly before her tenth birthday and had what she hopes was her final period over her fifty-fifth birthday, making menstruation one of her most constant (and least helpful) companions for more than eighty percent of her life.

NANCY G. WAHLER is a licensed clinical social worker turned stay-at-home mom turned writer. She has been published in *A Knoxville Christmas* and has written a middle-grade fantasy novel for which she is seeking representation. She got her period at age twelve but is still waiting for her breasts to develop.

CATHY WARNER, wife, mother, writer, pastor and Amherst Writers and Artists certified workshop leader blogs at http://holyink.blogspot.com. Her writing has appeared in *Not What I Expected* (anthology), *Alive Now*, *PoemMemoirStory* (Pushcart Prize nominee) and other literary journals. Cathy's first period arrived on her first day of high school when she was wearing new white pants.

JULIA WATTS is the author of eight novels, including *The Kind of Girl I Am*, *Women's Studies* and the Lambda Literary Award–winning *Finding H.F.* Her most vivid menstrual memory is from her college days when she started her period unexpectedly while returning from a College Bowl tournament in North Carolina. She was the only female in a car full of nerd boys and felt awkward asking the driver to stop at a convenience store. She felt even more awkward when she found that the convenience store sold no feminine hygiene products. Nor did the second convenience store she spotted. Nor did the third. By the time of her successful foray into the fourth store, her shyness disappeared and she returned to the car brandishing her Tampax box like the Holy Grail. The nerd boys applauded.

VICKIE WEAVER has published short stories and is a 2006 Pushcart nominee. *Below the Heart*, her novel-in-progress ("Staining All the Way Down" is a chapter), placed in the top ten of the Parthenon Prize 2007. She earned her MFA from Spalding University and taught for Indiana University East. In 1964, Vickie was wearing a red blouse and a red skirt the day she got her first period.

CRYSTAL WILKINSON'S short stories have been described as "story poems." She is the author of two books, *Blackberries, Blackberries* (2000) and *Water Street* (2002), both published by Toby Press. *Water Street* was a long-list finalist for the prestigious Orange Prize and was short-listed for a Zora Neale Hurston/Richard Wright Foundation Legacy Award in Fiction. *Blackberries, Blackberries* was named Best Debut Fiction by *Today's Librarian* magazine. She has been published in the anthologies *Confronting Appalachian Stereotypes: Back Talk from an American Region* (University of Kentucky Press, 1999); *Gifts from Our Grandmothers* (Crown, 2000); and *Gumbo: Stories by Black Writers* (Doubleday, Harlem Moon Press, 2002). Her work has also appeared in various literary journals, including *Obsidian II: Black Literature in Review, Southern Exposure, The Briar Cliff Review, Calyx, African Voices* and *Indiana Review*. She is a faculty member in Spalding University's low-residency MFA program and is currently serving as visiting professor in residence for Morehead State University. Wilkinson was the 2002 recipient of the Chaffin Award for Appalachian Literature and is a member of a Lexington-based writing collective, The Affrilachian Poets. She now resides with her partner, artist and poet Ron Davis, in Midway, Kentucky. She got her first period at the early age of nine and remembers whispering to her grandmother, *"I think I'm dying."*

ASHLEY WRYE is a marketing director in Nashville, Tennessee, for a national nonprofit. She lives a double life as a writer by night. Her nonfiction work has been published in many newspapers in the South and Midwest, and her fiction has appeared in the literary journals *The Trunk* and *Generation X Journal*. Ashley is a proud graduate of Indiana University and an avid fan of all sports teams with "Indiana" somewhere in the title. The first time she had her period, Ashley cramped so badly she refused to walk anywhere for two days. That complaint didn't work the second month.

Poetry Bios

LINDA DeCICCO ANTONAZZI has finished her first novel, *The Fig and the Flower*. A former journalist at the *South Bend Tribune*, she is in her tenth year teaching high school English. *Notre Dame Press* published her book, *SLF Album: An Informal History of Notre Dame's Sophomore Literary Festival*. Her poetry has been published in *Flying Island, No Exit, Common Ground Review, Curbside Review, Poetry Motel* and *Spire Press*.

TOMARA S. ALDRICH graduated from Keene State College in 1998, and received her MFA from Hunter College in New York City in 2004, where she was the recipient of the Mary M. Fay Award for Poetry. She currently lives in Brooklyn and teaches writing in the city at Hunter College and LaGuardia Community College.

MADELINE ARTENBERG performs frequently in New York City, including at the Bowery Poetry Club. Her work appears in print and online journals, such as *Absinthe Literary Review* and *Margie*. She has garnered poetry awards and her book *Awakened* (with poems by Iris N. Schwartz) was published by Rogue Scholars Press, 2006.

LANA HECHTMAN AYERS has authored three poetry collections, *Chicken Farmer I Still Love* You (D-N Publishing 2007), *Dance From Inside My Bones* (Snake Nation Press 2007) and *Love is a Weed* (Finishing Line Press 2006). She lives in the Pacific Northwest where she is a manuscript consultant.

MARKIE BABBOTT is working on her first book of poetry. Her poems have appeared online in *Perigee: Publication for the Arts, Literary Mama* and *Poets Against the War* (Selected for "Poem of the Day, 5/03"). She is a member of the Fairview Writers. Babbott is a clinical psychologist who lives with her partner and two children in Western Massachusetts.

ELLEN BASS's poetry books include *The Human Line* (Copper Canyon Press, 2007) and *Mules of Love* (BOA Editions, 2002). Her poems have been published in *The Atlantic Monthly, The Kenyon Review,* and *American Poetry Review.* She teaches at Pacific University and at writing workshops in the U.S. and Europe. www.ellenbass.com

SHAINDEL BEERS' poetry, fiction and creative nonfiction have appeared in numerous journals and anthologies. She is currently a professor of English at Blue Mountain Community College in Pendleton, Oregon, and also serves as Poetry Editor of *Contrary:* www.contrarymagazine.com

MARGO BERDESHEVSKY's poetry collection, *But a Passage in Wilderness,* was published by The Sheep Meadow Press (2007). Her honors include the Robert H. Winner Award from the Poetry Society of America, The *Chelsea* Poetry Award, *Kalliope's* Sue Saniel Elkind, places in the Pablo Neruda and Ann Stanford Awards, 4 Pushcart Prize nominations (and a special mention citation in 2008) for works in leading literary journals including *New Letters, Agni, The Southern Review, The Kenyon Review, Poetry Daily, Poetry International, Pool, Nimrod, Women's Studies Quarterly.* A "visual poem" series, *The Ghosts of Versailles,* was seen at the Parisian *Galerie Benchaieb.* Her poetic novel, *Vagrant,* will be published next. She currently lives in Paris.

SALLY BITTNER BONN is a poet, performer and teaching artist. *Walking Woman* is the most recent of her two chapbooks and her work has been included in several anthologies. Sally teaches at Writers & Books and at schools throughout her community. She lives with her husband in Rochester, New York.

STELLA BRICE received her degree in English Literature from Rice University; she has worked, variously, as housecleaner, tarot reader and performance artist. Her writing has appeared in *Frank, Fine Madness, Southern Poetry Review* and many others. Online, her work can be found at *Right Hand Pointing, Radiant Turnstile* and *Clean Sheets.* Her poems have been anthologized in *Tierra Cruzada/Crossed Land* and *The Weight of Addition: An Anthology of Texas Poets.* She is a winner of the John Z. Bennet Prize and is co-editor of the literary journal *Art Club.* Her first collection of poems *Green Lion* was released last spring.

THERESE L. BRODERICK is a freelance poet and teacher residing in Albany, New York, with her husband and daughter. Her poems have won national and local awards and have been published nationally and locally. She maintains an "Ekphrasis" blog at poetryaboutart.wordpress.com.

AMALIA B. BUENO is a poet, writer and researcher who was born in the

Philippines and raised in Hawaii. Her poetry and fiction has been published in *Bamboo Ridge, Katipunan Literary Journal: Voices of Hawaii* and online by Our Own Voice and Meritage Press. Her short stories are forthcoming in *Honolulu Stories* (Mutual Publishing) and *Growing Up Filipino II* (Anvil Press).

CINDY CHILDRESS won the Marcella Seigel Memorial Award and the third place Christina Sergeyevna Award. Her poetry is published in Panowama, Third Wednesday, Touchstone, Rock and Sling, Epicenter and others. She teaches at the University of Louisiana at Lafayette and is completing a creative dissertation for PhD in English.

CATHRYN COFELL is published in such places as *Prairie Schooner, MARGIE* and *Cream City Review.* She holds two Pushcart nominations and the Wisconsin Academy's Outstanding Poem designation for two consecutive years, among other awards. *Sweet Curdle* (Marsh River Editions) is her fourth book, with a fifth forthcoming from Parallel Press.

BARBARA CROOKER has published poems in magazines such as *Calyx, Earth's Daughter's* and *Skirt!*; anthologies, including *Worlds in Their Words: An Anthology of Contemporary American Women Writers* (Prentice Hall) and *Boomer Girls* (University of Iowa Press); two full-length books, *Radiance,* which was a finalist for the Paterson Poetry Prize, and *Line Dance* (both from Word Press).

RACHEL DACUS's three poetry books are *Another Circle of Delight, Femme au chapeau* and *Earth Lessons.* She serves as contributing editor for Umbrella magazine (www.umbrellajournal.com) and is on the staff of the Alsop Review. More of her work can be read at www.dacushome.com. She blogs at http://dacusrocket.blogspon.com.

TENEICE DURRANT is a poet and graduate of Spalding University's Low-Res MFA Program. In 2006, she was a finalist for the Joy Bale Boone Poetry Prize and earned second Honorable Mention for her chapbook *Flame Above Flame,* which was published through Finishing Line Press' New Women's Voices Chapbook Series. Teneice is cofounder and a poetry editor for Blood Lotus, an online literary journal.

CHANGXIN FANG received an MFA in Creative Writing from University of Utah in 2007. The two poems in this anthology are from her book,

The Garden of Beautiful Transgressions. She received a bachelor's degree in English at Smith College in 2005. She is originally from Shanghai, China, and currently works as a research associate at a renewable energy consulting firm in Maryland.

LYNN FETTEROLF Award winning poet Lynn Fetterolf has been published in *Writers' Digest, Prolog (F&M), Pegasus, Harrisburg Review, Beauty For Ashes, Experimental Forest, Digges' Choice, Steel Point Quarterly, Fledgling Rag, Mad Poets Review, Listening to Water (the Susquehanna Watershed Anthology), Somewhere on George Street* and other publications. She currently has five books in print.

ANNIE FINCH is director of the Stonecoast Low-Residency MFA program. Her most recent book of poetry is *Calendars.* She is translator of Louise Labe's complete poems and has published several books of poetics, most recently *The Body of Poetry: Essays on Women, Form* and *the Poetic Self.* Her Web site is www.anniefinch.com

MAUREEN TOLMAN FLANNERY is a poet, educator, woodcarver, healthcare professional, wife, mother of four and grandmother. Her passions are home-birth, hospice, Waldorf education, trees and words. Her poems have been published in fifty anthologies and over a hundred literary journals. Her books include *Ancestors in the Landscape; A Fine Line; Secret of the Rising Up; Knowing Stones*; and *Remembered into Life.*

STACIA M. FLEEGAL holds an MFA in poetry from Spalding University. Her poems have recently appeared in *Comstock Review, White Pelican Review, 42opus, Earth's Daughters* and *Minnetonka Review,* among others. Finishing Line Press released a chapbook of her poems, titled *A Fling with the Ground,* in fall 2007. She is cofounder of *Blood Lotus,* an online literary journal, a poetry editor for New Sins Press and coordinator of the journals department at the University of Nebraska Press.

ALICE B. FOGEL's latest book is *Be That Empty.* Her poems have appeared in *Best American Poetry, Bedside Guide to No Tell Motel,* and others, and her artwear creations made of reprised goods are featured in *Altered Couture.* Her Web sites are LyricCouture.com and alicebfogel.com.

CB FOLLETT is the author of five books of poems, the most recent of which is *Hold and Release* (2007). *At the Turning of the Light* won the 2001

National Poetry Book Award. Follett is the editor/publisher of *Grr, A Collection of Poems About Bears*, publisher and co-editor of *Runes*, a Review of Poetry, and general dogsbody of Arctos Press. She has several nominations for Pushcart Prizes, a Marin Arts Council Grant for Poetry, other awards and honors and has been widely published.

PRISCILLA FRAKE'S poems appear in *Nimrod*, *Atlanta Review*, *The Sow's Ear Poetry Review*, *The Carolina Quarterly*, *The Midwest Quarterly*, *The Spoon River Poetry Review* and *The New Welsh Review*.. She has lived in New York, New Mexico, California, Texas, West Virginia, China and Scotland. Her chapbook, *Argument Against Winter* was published in the U.K. A former geologist, she now makes jewelry and poems in the Houston area.

JUDY LEE GREEN is an award-winning writer and speaker whose spirit and roots reach deep into the Appalachian Mountains. Tennessee-bred and cornbread-fed, she developed a passion for the written word at an early age when inspired to carry a notebook by Daily Planet girl reporter Lois Lane. Appearing in print hundreds of times, she lives in Murfreesboro, Tennessee, and is compiling a manuscript of creative nonfiction.

PAMELA GROSSMAN lives in Brooklyn, New York. Her poetry has been published in *Lungfull*, *Mudfish*, *Beet*, *The Eliot Review* and other outlets; her journalistic work appears in *The Village Voice*, *Ms.*, *Salon*, *Plenty*, *The Brooklyn Rail* and elsewhere. She promises to be careful when sitting on your couch during certain times of the month.

MELISSA GUILLET's work has appeared in *The Cherry Blossom Review*, *Lalitamba*, *Nth Position*, *Scrivener's Pen*, six Worcester, Massachusetts anthologies and other collections. She is a member of Dr. Brown's Traveling Poetry Troupe, editor at Sacred Fools Press, and teaches Interdisciplinary Arts in East Providence, RI.

ELLEN HAGAN is a writer, actress and educator. Her poetry has been nominated for a Pushcart Prize and can be seen in *Failbetter*, *Check the Rhyme Underwired* and upcoming in *Submerged: Tales from the Basin* and *PLUCK*. She has received grants from the Kemtucky Foundation for Women and the Kentucky Governor's School for the Arts. Ellen holds an MFA in fiction from The New School University, and recently finished her first full-length novel, entitled *BLUSH*.

WILLOW HAMBRICK is a freelance writer and educator from George-town, Kentucky. She holds a BA from Hanover College and an MFA from Spalding University. Her poems have recently appeared in *The Christian Century, The Tobacco Anthology, Voices* and the *Heartland Review*. Her poem *Willow "M"* is from her collection of poems titled *Upholding the Ache*. She is married and has five children.

ALISON HICKS is the author of a novella, *Love: A Story of Images* (2004) and a chapbook of poems, *Falling Dreams* (2006). A two-time recipient of a fellowship from the Pennsylvania Council on the Arts, her work has appeared in a number of journals, including *Pearl, The Ledge, Eclipse* and *Amoskeag*. She leads community-based writing workshops under the name Greater Philadelphia Wordshop Studio.

KAREN HOWLAND howls daily, braving the creative life, teaching weekly women's writing circles, consulting and mothering fiercely Chloe and Arden. Featured on Public Radio, she is an internationally published poet and award-winning singer. Her CDs *Cicada Grace* and *Wild Lullabyes* can be found on MySpace.

MARSHA SMITH JANSON holds an MFA from Warren Wilson College. Her poetry has appeared in journals including *Rattle, Lyric, Jubilat, The Harvard Review* and *Best American Poetry.* Marsha is a member of the Fairview Writers. She has been a recipient of an artist grant from the Massachusetts Cultural Council and lives in Northampton, Massachusetts, with her family.

RUBY KANE has a 23-day cycle, and ovulates on day 10. A freelance writer at work on her first novel, she lives in Seattle with her wife, Ami.

JILL KELLY KOREN is a poet and a full-time mom. She is currently working on a memoir about her grandfather while pursuing her MFA in poetry and creative nonfiction from Spalding University. She lives and works in Madison, Indiana with her husband, Emeka, and their son, Sonny.

REBECCA LAUREN lives on Maryland's eastern shore with her partner, Joe, and their dog, Gus. She teaches English at Eastern University and women's studies and theology at the Oregon Extension Women's Studies May Term. Her writing has been published in *The Southeast Review, The Cincin-*

nati Review and *Spoon River Poetry Review*, among others.

DONNA J. GELAGOTIS LEE's book, *On the Altar of Greece*, winner of the Gival Press Poetry Award, received a 2007 Eric Hoffer Book Award: Notable for Art Category and was nominated for a Los Angeles Times Book Prize. Donna's poems have appeared in *The Bitter Oleander, CALYX: A Journal of Art and Literature by Women, Feminist Studies, The Massachusetts Review, The Midwest Quarterly*, and other journals. Donna's Web site is www.donnajgelagotislee.com

ANNE-MARIE LEVINE lives in New York City. A poet and scholar who began writing while touring as a concert pianist, she's the author of three books of poetry: *Euphorbia, Bus Ride to a Blue Movie* and *Oral History*. Her work also appears in the anthologies *Poetry After 9/11* and *Literature as Meaning*. She's published essays on Gertrude Stein's politics, and on art and trauma, and has received grants from the NYFA, Puffin and Vogelstein Foundations. She performs solo theater pieces based on her poems, and is currently working on a Commonplace Book and a visual arts project called *Box Poems*, being exhibited in New York and California.

ELLARAINE LOCKIE is an award-winning poet, essayist and author of nonfiction books. She has received eleven nominations for Pushcart Prizes in poetry. Her fifth poetry collection has just been released by PWJ Publishing. Ellaraine also teaches a poetry/writing workshop on the creative process for schools, writing groups and libraries.

GLENNA LUSCHEI is the founder and publisher of the poetry journals *Café Solo, Solo* and *Solo Café* (1969–2007) and is the author of many chapbooks, special editions and trade books, the latest being *Total Immersion* published by Presa Press in 2008, and *Libido Dreams* released by Artamo Press in 2007. She was named Poet Laureate of San Luis Obispo City and County for the year 2000. Luschei has also published an artist book of her translation of Sor Juana Inés de la Cruz's *Enigmas*, Solo Press, 2006.

KATHARYN HOWD MACHAN, professor in the writing department and the Women's Studies Program at Ithaca College, is the author of twenty-eight published collections, most recently *The Professor Poems* (Main Street Rag, 2008), *Flags* (Pudding House, 2007) and *Redwing: Voices from 1888* (FootHills, 2005). She directs the Feminist Women's Writing Workshops, Inc.

CAROLINE MALONE teaches composition and literature at South College in Knoxville, Tennessee. She earned the MFA in Writing from Bennington College and has published poetry in *Boulevard, Tangent* and *b.* Her favorite drink is The Cockroach.

ARLENE L. MANDELL, a retired English professor living in Santa Rosa, California, grew up in Brooklyn in the 1940s and '50s. Her poetry, essays and short stories have appeared in several hundred literary publications and eleven anthologies, most recently in *To-Do List,* which reveals her New Year's resolutions when she was fifteen.

LINDA PARSONS MARION is poetry editor for *Now & Then* magazine and author of *Home Fires.* Her poems have appeared in *The Georgia Review, Iowa Review, Shenandoah, Asheville Poetry Review* and *Prairie Schooner,* among others. She has received two literary fellowships from the Tennessee Arts Commission, among other awards. Other works have appeared in *Listen Here: Women Writing in Appalachia* (University Press of Kentucky, 2003), *Her Words: Diverse Voices in Contemporary Appalachian Women's Poetry* (University of Tennessee Press, 2002) and *Sleeping with One Eye Open: Women Writers and the Art of Survival* (University of Georgia Press, 1999). Marion is an editor at the University of Tennessee and lives in Knoxville with her husband, poet Jeff Daniel Marion.

MARTY McCONNELL received her MFA from Sarah Lawrence College, co-founded New York City–based literary nonprofit the louderARTS Project, and is a member of the Piper Jane Project. She has been published in journals including *Rattle, Fourteen Hills* and *Rattapallax,* and anthologies including *Spoken Word Revolution: Redux, Homewrecker: An Adultery Reader* and *Women of the Bowery.*

AMANDA McQUADE neither confirms nor denies anything. Her work has recently appeared, or is forthcoming, in *Aquapolis, Lethe, Pregnant Moon Review* and *Glass.* Every day she learns what it means to be a woman and what it means to be human. Currently, she resides in Los Angeles with her husband, Matt.

AMY MECKLER's poems have appeared in *Atlanta Review, Rattapallax, Margie* and *Lyric,* among other publications. Her first collection, *What All the Sleeping Is For,* won the 2002 Defined Providence Press Poetry Book

Award and was published that year. She works in New York City as a sign language interpreter.

GWENDOLYN A. MITCHELL is a poet and editor. Her poetry has appeared in a number of journals and anthologies including *American Review, Prairie Schooner, Warpland: A Journal of Black Literature and Ideas* and *Essence* Magazine. She received her MFA from Pennsylvania State University. Ms. Mitchell is the author of *House of Women* (Third World Press).

MONICA MODY lives in Delhi, India. Her poetry has appeared in *The Little Magazine* (TLM), *DesiLit Magazine* and *Samyukta—Journal for Women's Studies*. She won the 2006 Toto Funds the Arts Award for Creative Writing which encourages young writers, and spearheaded a poetry in performance series called *"Open Baithak."*

EILEEN MOELLER lives in center city Philadelphia. She has poems in *Feminist Studies, Paterson Literary Review, Caprice, Blue Fifth, Philadelphia Stories, Writing Women, Cries of the Spirit: A Celebration of Women's Spirituality, Claiming the Spirit Within: a Sourcebook of Women's Poetry* and *The Nerve: Writing Women of 1998.*

SONIA PEREIRA MURPHY has had poetry published in many literary journals. She lives in Western Massachusetts with her husband, daughter, and two cats. She is 31-years-old.

CHRISTINA PACOSZ has been writing and publishing prose and poetry for almost half a century and has several books of poetry, the most recent, *Greatest Hits, 1975–2001*(Pudding House, 2002). Her work has appeared recently in *Jane's Stories III, Women Writing Across Boundaries, Pemmican, Umbrella, qarrtsiluni.* She has been a special educator, a Poet-in-the-Schools for several state and city programs, and a North Carolina Visiting Artist. She has been teaching urban youth for the past decade on both sides of the Missouri/Kansas state line where she lives with her husband.

AMY OUZOONIAN is the author of *Your Pill* (Foothills Publishing), and editor of three anthologies of poetry, including *Skyscrapers, Taxis and Tampons* (Fly By Night Press). She lives and writes in Queens, New York and expects to earn an MA in Media Studies and Film from the New School University.

ANDREA POTOS is the author of the poetry collection *Yaya's Cloth*, published by Iris Press (www.irisbooks.com). Her poems are published widely in journals and anthologies, including *Women's Review of Books, Poetry East, North American Review, Atlanta Review, Calyx Journal, Claiming the Sprit Within* (Beacon Press) and *Mothers and Daughters: A Poetry Celebration* (Random House). She lives in Madison, Wisconsin.

SUSAN RICHARDSON has published numerous poems, stories, and articles in various magazines and anthologies, with work upcoming in *The Dos Passos Review, Fiction International* and the anthology *One for the Road*. Her poem "Dawn" recently won runner-up in a Poetry in Motion contest judged by Billy Collins. She is the founder of Winterhawk Press.

LOUISE ROBERTSON lives in central Ohio, where she lives with her family, works at a law school as a webmaster and spends a lot of time on poetry and poetry-related events. She has an MFA from George Mason University and a BA from Oberlin College. See also www.RewritingOvid.com.

MICHELE RUBY, one of the co-editors of this anthology, is a writer, teacher, actor and tap-dancer living in Louisville, Kentucky. Her work, both fiction and poetry, has been published in *Lilith, The Louisville Review, Rosebud, Atlanta Review, Margie* and *Connecticut Review,* among other places. She has an MFA from Spalding University. She is grateful to the wonderful women who have borne this work together, to her husband and daughters for giving her wings, and to her mother and mother-in-law for grounding her.

JANA RUSS teaches writing, non-Western literature and Chinese history at the University of Akron, and is currently pursuing an MFA through NEOMFA, a consortial program of four of Northeast Ohio state universities. Her poems have appeared in *Circle Magazine, The Akros, Riverwind, Penguin Review* and *Poetry Midwest.*

ROBIN A. SAMS is a poet and new mother. She has a BA in English with a concentration in creative writing and in Classical Philology from Hollins University. Robin is a vegan and animal rights activist. She currently resides in British Columbia, Canada.

WILLA SCHNEBERG received the Oregon Book Award In Poetry for her second collection *In The Margins of The World.* Her recent collection is

Storytelling in Cambodia, (Calyx Books, 2006). Poems have appeared in *The Women's Review of Books* and *Bridges: A Jewish Feminist Journal.* She received a grant in poetry from the Money for Women/Barbara Deming Memorial Fund.

ROBIN SILBERGLEID is the author of *Pas de Deux: Prose and Other Poems* (Basilisk Press, 2006). Her work has appeared in journals including *The Truth About the Fact, Folio* and *The Cream City Review,* for which she was nominated for a Pushcart Prize. She is assistant professor of English at Michigan State University.

STEPHANIE SILVIA was born in Brooklyn, New York, where she taught public school after years of directing her own modern dance company in New York City. She received a master's from the University of North Carolina at Greensboro and, also, attended school in Boston and San Francisco. In her early forties, she married a fisherman fifteen years her junior and moved to the Redwood Forest of the northern California coast where they have adopted Lonnie, a poetic and energetic boy-child. Stephanie periodically attends workshops led by Diane di Prima.

SARAH E. HOLIHAN SMITH lives in Charleston, South Carolina, where she teaches at the College of Charleston. She is a graduate of Miami University of Ohio's master's program in poetry, and is also a recent graduate of Spalding University's brief-residency MFA in Writing Program. She is currently working on a memoir.

ANASTACIA (STACEY) TOLBERT is a writer, journalist, workshop facilitator, playwright and Cave Canem Fellow (2007) living in Seattle Washington. She is writer, codirector and coproducer of GOTBREAST? Documentary (2007): A documentary about the views of women regarding breast and body image. When she's not mothering, wife-ing or writing, she obsessively irons her super woman cape, making sure it's ready at all times.

CONNIE WASEM teaches composition and creative writing at Spokane Falls Community College. Her poems have appeared in reviews that include *RHINO, Sycamore Review, 5 AM., Slipstream, The Lucid Stone* and a few anthologies. She lives nestled in the ponderosa pines of Spokane with her preteen daughter and their pets.

AMY WATKINS lives in Orlando, Florida, with her husband, daughter and maniacal mixed-breed dog. She writes poems, paints and pays the bills by proofreading camping guides. Her poems have recently appeared in *Bayou Magazine*, *The Pedestal* and *The Louisville Review*.

DANA S. WILDSMITH is the author of four collections of poetry: *One Good Hand* (Iris Press, 2005), *Our Bodies Remember* (The Sow's Ear Press, 2000), *Annie* (Palanquin Press, 1999), *Alchemy* (The Sow's Ear Press, 1995), and an audio collection, *Choices* (Iris Press). She is widely published in journals and anthologies, including *Listen Here: Women Writing In Appalachia,* (University Press of Kentucky). *One Good Hand* was a SIBA Poetry Book of the Year nominee.

DEMETRICE ANNT'A WORLEY's poetry has appeared in *Permafrost*, *The Spoon River Poetry Review* (where she was a finalist for the 2002 Editor's Prize) and *Clackamas Literary Review* and in anthologies such as *Risk, Courage and Women* (North Texas University Press, 2007) and *Spirit & Flame* (Syracuse University Press, 1997). She teaches writing and African American literature at Bradley University.

MARIANNE WORTHINGTON is the author of *Larger Bodies Than Mine* (Finishing Line Press, 2006), winner of the 2007 Appalachian Book of the Year Award in Poetry. She writes, teaches and lives in Williamsburg, Kentucky.

JANE YOLEN is the author of almost three hundred books, ranging from picture books and baby board books, through middle grade fiction, nonfiction, novels, graphic novels, story collections and poetry collections for children and adults. Six New England colleges and universities have given her honorary doctorates.

Publications from Spinsters Ink

P.O. Box 242
Midway, Florida 32343
Phone: 800-301-6860
www.spinstersink.com

ACROSS TIME by Linda Kay Silva. If you believe in soul mates, if you know you've had a past life, then join Jessie in the first of a series of adventures that takes her *Across Time*.   ISBN 978-1883523-91-6 $14.95

SELECTIVE MEMORY by Jennifer L. Jordan. A Kristin Ashe Mystery. A classical pianist, who is experiencing profound memory loss after a near-fatal accident, hires private investigator Kristin Ashe to reconstruct her life in the months leading up to the crash.
ISBN 978-1-883523-88-6 $14.95

HARD TIMES by Blayne Cooper. Together, Kellie and Lorna navigate through an oppressive, hidden world where lines between right and wrong blur, sexual passion is forbidden but explosive, and love is the biggest risk of all.   ISBN 978-1-883523-90-9 $14.95

THE KIND OF GIRL I AM by Julia Watts. Spanning decades, *The Kind of Girl I Am* humorously depicts an extraordinary woman's experiences of triumph, heartbreak, friendship and forbidden love.
ISBN 978-1-883523-89-3 $14.95

PIPER'S SOMEDAY by Ruth Perkinson. It seemed as though life couldn't get any worse for feisty, young Piper Leigh Cliff and her three-legged dog, Someday.   ISBN 978-1-883523-87-9 $14.95

MERMAID by Michelene Esposito. When May unearths a box in her missing sister's closet she is taken on a journey through her mother's past that leads her not only to Kate but to the choices and compromises, emptiness and fullness, the beauty and jagged pain of love that all women must face.   ISBN 978-1-883523-85-5 $14.95